Y0-BZA-812

Savage Vision

Savage Vision

Cassie Edwards

THORNDIKE
CHIVERS

Henderson County Public Library

This Large Print edition is published by Thorndike Press®, Waterville, Maine USA and by BBC Audiobooks Ltd, Bath, England.

Published in 2006 in the U.S. by arrangement with Leisure Books, a division of Dorchester Publishing Co., Inc.

Published in 2006 in the U.K. by arrangement with Leisure Books.

U.S. Hardcover 0-7862-8265-7 (Romance)
U.K. Hardcover 1-4056-3681-5 (Chivers Large Print)
U.K. Softcover 1-4056-3682-3 (Camden Large Print)

Copyright © 2005 by Cassie Edwards

All rights reserved.

The text of this Large Print edition is unabridged.
Other aspects of the book may vary from the original edition.

Set in 16 pt. Plantin.

Printed in the United States on permanent paper.

British Library Cataloguing-in-Publication Data available

Library of Congress Cataloging-in-Publication Data

Edwards, Cassie.
Savage vision / by Cassie Edwards.
p. cm. — (Thorndike Press large print romance)
ISBN 0-7862-8265-7 (lg. print : hc : alk. paper)
1. Indians — Kings and rulers — Fiction. 2. Indians of North America — Texas — Fiction. 3. Pirates — Fiction. 4. Texas — Fiction. 5. Large type books.
I. Title. II. Thorndike Press large print romance series.
PS3555.D875S334 2005
813′.54—dc22 2005027963

SAVAGE VISION is dedicated to
my dear friends
Jim and Mary Lou Replogle,
a friendship that began between
Mary Lou (Lundeen) and
myself in the 1950s!
Love,
Cassie.

Sing to me of far away places,
of ocean dreams, and different faces.
Sing of mountains, valleys, and the
    eagle flying high.
Sing to me as time passes by.
Sing to me of my ancestors,
    and all these things!
SING TO ME OF DREAMS. . . .
Sing to me of Sister Moon, of the Earth
    my mother,
of the wolf and of the bear, my brother.
Sing of my forefathers, how they fought
    with their hands.
Sing of my people, and the
    "Spirit Dance."
Sing to me of painted ponies running
    free,
of my ancestors, and all these things.
SING TO ME OF DREAMS. . . .
Sing of the winding river, and of the
    whispering wind,
of the hollows, and the plush hills that
    never seem to end.
Sing of the great harvest, and the time

of the black butterflies.
Sing of the hawk soaring through
the skies.
Sing of all these things.
SING TO ME OF DREAMS!

— Sara Key, poet, fan and friend

Chapter One

Texas, 1851

Mossy boulders clad the shore. Fingers of muscadine vine trailed in the water, sheltering wood ducks half hidden under the low branches of weeping willow trees.

Scarlett James, nineteen, stood beside a creek, mesmerized by the exquisite landscape that surrounded her.

She had never known that Texas could be so beautiful. When she had been told by her father that they were moving to Texas so that he could accept a position as sheriff there, she had envisioned hot, dry days, the sun scorching her every time she left the house.

But she had been wrong. In this part of Texas, a few miles from the Gulf of Mexico, the air was sweet with the smells of the sea, and with the wildflowers that grew across the land.

Yes, she was a stranger to Texas and was exploring her surroundings for the first time since she'd settled into the new house with her father. She was glad of the move, for their previous home had held too many memories of her mother.

In this new place on the outskirts of the quaint little town of Coral Creek, she and her father would have a fresh beginning.

Her long flame-colored hair fluttered in the breeze along the slender line of her back as Scarlett fell to her knees.

She was mesmerized by the tiny pinkish-orange pebbles at the bottom of the stream, noting that they were even spread along the embankment between ridges of velvet-soft green moss.

She now saw why the town was called Coral Creek. It was because of the coral rocks at the bottom of this lovely, meandering stream.

Scarlett had chosen this particular place to stop and rest, for the willow trees were lovely as they hung low over the water.

The sun shone through the water onto the lovely rocks, and every now and then she caught the glint of fish in the shallows, gray against the coral color of the pebbles.

She removed her butter-soft gloves and slid them into the left pocket of her split riding skirt, then ran her fingers through the pebbles, gathering some in the palm of her hand.

She watched them filter through her fingers and splash into the water, soon rejoining the others at the bottom.

Scarlett glanced up quickly when a deer suddenly stepped into the water a mere fifteen feet away from where she knelt. It seemed unaware of her presence and she didn't dare make a move, for fear of startling it.

She studied its loveliness, the softness of its brown coat, the long lashes over its big brown eyes. Never had she been as near a wild forest animal as this.

She smiled as the deer trustingly lowered its head and drank from the creek, sunlight glinting from its antlers.

Scarlett's heart throbbed with delight. Never had she seen anything like this in San Francisco, where her father had last worked.

Life in San Francisco had become intolerable after the gold rush. She and her father had fled the city after Scarlett's mother, Penelope, had died on the streets of San Francisco. She had been trampled by drunken prospectors on horseback who were celebrating their success in the gold fields.

Scarlett and her father hoped their lives would be safer in Coral Creek, even though there were Indian villages scattered here and there about the countryside. They had been told by the townsfolk that the Indians in this area were peaceful ones.

Scarlett's thoughts were interrupted and she flinched when the deer's head came up suddenly, its eyes wide and alert. Then the creature bounded through the water to the other side, disappearing beneath the canopy of trees there.

Scarlett quickly realized what had caused the deer to flee. It had heard the sound of horses before Scarlett had. But she was very aware of them now.

She scrambled to her feet, slid her hand inside her right skirt pocket and clasped her fingers around her small pearl-handled pistol just as several Indian warriors on horseback came into sight. They had powerful bows slung over their shoulders, and quivers of arrows at their backs.

Scarlett stood stiffly as she waited for the Indians to get closer, for she knew that she had no chance of fleeing to safety as the deer had done. Her horse was tethered too far away to get to it before the Indians reached her.

As the Indians came into full view, she blushed at how scarcely clothed they were. They wore only breechclouts and moccasins.

All but one of the warriors stopped. This one, whose coal-black hair hung long and loose down his back, and who wore a deadly looking knife sheathed at his right side, rode right up to her before halting.

"We lost the deer because of you," the warrior said, giving Scarlett a hard stare.

"Why . . . because . . . of me?" she stammered, glad at least that he spoke English so fluently. She could not help noticing how handsome he was. He had sculpted features, midnight-black eyes, and it seemed that every inch of him was muscled!

But it was his long, flowing hair that made him truly different from any white man she had ever known. When she had seen Indians in the distance in San Francisco, it had always been their hair that had fascinated her.

As before, she wondered now how it might feel to be in the arms of a man whose hair was so thick, black and long. She had even envisioned how the hair would feel against the flesh of her twined arms, how —

"Had I shot an arrow into the deer, as it stood so close to you, would you not have been afraid?" Chief Hawke said dryly, interrupting Scarlett's thoughts.

Hawke was very aware of how closely

this woman was scrutinizing him. He returned her fascinated stare as he slowly raked his eyes over her. Beneath the rays of the sun, her long hair seemed aflame, its color was so brilliantly red.

And her eyes! They were the color of grass, with long, thick, dark lashes shadowing them.

And then there was her petiteness. He had never seen a white woman up this close, especially one who was so tiny, with such a pretty and delicate face. Yet she hardly seemed afraid that she was in the presence of Indians!

He would have thought that upon first seeing him and his warriors advancing on her, she would have run away, screaming, as he had seen other white women do when they saw red men.

But no. This woman was standing boldly before him, her shoulders squared, her chin high, her one hand —

When he saw the bulge in her pocket where her right hand rested, he recognized the outline of a tiny pistol. He realized that should she want to, she could yank that firearm from her pocket and try to shoot him.

But surely she knew that he could unsheath and throw his knife so quickly that she would not even have the chance to get her finger on her firearm's trigger.

After seeing her, though, and being so close that her loveliness mesmerized him, he knew he could not kill her. He would disarm her instead.

He would take her gun and warn her of the foolishness of trying to kill him with it. No mere woman could ever best a red man, especially one from the Cougar Clan of Caddo Indians.

"Are you saying that you lost the chance to kill the deer because you did not want to frighten me?" Scarlett said, surprised at his gallantry.

She looked past him at the many warriors on horseback who seemed to be waiting for his signal before taking any action. Could this mean that the handsome warrior was a man of more importance than the others?

Could she actually be in the presence of . . . a . . . chief?

She looked quickly at him again and decided that he was in his mid-twenties. Could a warrior of that age be a chief?

She noticed then that he was staring right at the pistol in her pocket. She was sure he'd noticed the shape of her gun.

Not wanting him to feel that he had to

defend himself, she slowly slipped her hand from the pocket and instead, nervously clasped her hands together behind her.

"I believed that seeing several warriors on horseback would be enough to frighten you, so I decided not to do anything that might make you think you were under attack," Hawke explained.

"Thank you for what you did, or should I say . . . for what you did not do," Scarlett said, smiling slowly at the warrior. The longer he sat there on his mighty steed, his hauntingly beautiful dark eyes gazing at her, the more uneasy she felt.

But not for the reason she would have thought if someone had told her that she would come face to face with a handsome warrior today. Her uneasiness was not because she was alone and at the mercy of this warrior and his band.

It was because of the way he made her feel. He mesmerized her, something no man had ever done before.

How could this be?

He was an Indian. A man many would call a savage.

But she saw nothing savage about him, only a gentleness that truly amazed her.

"I will go now," Hawke said. He looked over his shoulder at his warriors, and then gazed at Scarlett again. Something made him reach a hand out toward her. "I am Chief Hawke, a friend. And you are?"

Stunned that he was actually offering a hand of friendship, and realizing that she *was* in the presence of a chief, Scarlett was momentarily speechless.

When she saw his gaze waver, and his hand draw back slightly, Scarlett quickly held her hand out toward him. "I am your friend," she murmured, wishing that her hand would quit trembling. She didn't want him to think that she was afraid. Her trembling was actually caused by his handsomeness and kindness.

"My name is Scarlett," she blurted out.

When their hands made contact, it was as though a bolt of electricity had gone between them.

Very aware of the instant attraction between him and the white woman, and knowing that even friendship between them would be forbidden, Hawke yanked his hand back. In one motion he wheeled his horse around.

Stunned by how quickly the Indian chief had acted, Scarlett gaped openly at him as he joined the others and rode away in the opposite direction.

She watched his long, flowing hair lifting

in the wind as she brought the hand that he had clasped up to her cheek and rested it there. She felt her heart skip a beat when he turned his head and gave her a quick look over his shoulder. Then he fixed his gaze forward again and disappeared from sight around a bend in the stream.

"Did all of this truly happen?" she whispered, her eyes wide as she walked away from the creek and toward her horse. "Or did I imagine it?"

Still feeling the warmth of his hand in hers, and seeing that look in his eyes when he had seemed to have felt the same bolt of electricity that went between them, Scarlett smiled and untied her horse's reins from the low tree limb.

"It was real enough," she whispered.

She mounted her steed, then turned it around and rode in the direction of her home.

"Should I or shouldn't I?" she whispered, as she thought about her father and whether or not she should confide in him what had just happened.

She decided not to, for the incident would alarm him, and he might forbid her to go riding again. He did not have prejudices against Indians, in general, but she knew that he did not trust them either. He had had run-ins with some drunken Indians in San Francisco.

It was at that time that he had warned her against getting near any while shopping in San Francisco.

I cannot see Chief Hawke getting drunk, she thought.

He seemed too noble, too intelligent, to allow his mind to be warped by alcohol, or "firewater," as she knew Indians referred to it.

But her father would not be convinced of that, for he had not met the man. She knew it was best to keep their meeting to herself, and hope that she would see Chief Hawke again soon, preferably without his other warriors!

Chapter Two

Still musing over the events of the day before, Scarlett sat with her father at the breakfast table at their ranch. She had scarcely touched the pancakes set before her by Malvina, the black maid and cook who had been a part of Scarlett's life for as long as she could remember.

Even the rich, delicious-smelling maple syrup on the pancakes could not tempt Scarlett into eating them. She had cut tiny pieces from the pancakes, yet only moved them about the plate with her fork instead of eating them.

"Scarlett, what in tarnation is wrong with you this morning?" her father, Patrick, asked as he set down his cup of steaming hot coffee. "If I didn't know better, I'd think you were acting like a lovesick puppy."

His brownish-golden hair was combed back from his square-jawed face, the freckles on his broad nose prominent against the ruddiness of his flesh. He was dressed in a freshly pressed white shirt, the top button left unbuttoned, and black trousers. A no-nonsense man, he leaned forward and stared directly into Scarlett's face.

"Papa, why on earth would you say such a thing?" she gasped, very self-consciously placing her fork on the plate with her pieces of pancake.

How could her father have guessed that she had a man on her mind?

She blushed as she recalled her preoccupied behavior. Every time she thought about that handsome, scarcely clothed chief, her pulse raced.

"That look on your face, and the way you are toying with your flapjacks, even though they are your favorite breakfast, *that's* why," Patrick said tightly. He raked his long, lean fingers through his hair, then rested his hand on the table before him. "Now, do you want to tell me about it? Or would you rather I drag it outta you like I do those suspects I interrogate at my office?"

"Papa, really," Scarlett said, her eyes pleading. "Can't a person sit and think awhile without being questioned? I was just thinking about my ride on Lightning yesterday and what I found. I now realize where Coral Creek got its name. I came across a creek that had the most beautiful coral rocks at the bottom."

"And that's what caused that dreamy look on your face this morning?" Patrick asked, his eyebrows lifting. "God almighty. I reckon I'd better go and see those rocks myself, if they are that alluring."

He leaned forward. "Is that all that you came across while out horseback riding?" he demanded. "There ain't no cowboy on your tail, is there?"

Scarlett laughed nervously. "No, there is no cowboy," she murmured, then picked up her fork and stabbed several bits and pieces of pancake on it and shoved them into her mouth.

She ate vigorously, truly enjoying the delicious pancakes, and feeling victorious that her father had believed her story. After all, he was one of the most clever interrogators Coral Creek had ever seen.

He was good at what he did.

He was a sheriff who enforced the law with a gentle hand. But when he was riled, there was no stopping his temper.

He hadn't left California until he had seen that those who were responsible for his wife's death were hanged.

One of the first things he had built after his arrival in Coral Creek was a gallows . . .

a sight meant to scare anyone who might even be thinking about breaking the law in his pretty little town.

She felt her father's eyes still studying her, even though she was no longer looking at him. Then she relaxed when she heard him take a lazy sip of coffee and begin eating his pancakes again.

"Yep, this is a mighty pretty place to live," he said, even though his mouth was stuffed full of pancake. "From what I've been told, those coral rocks are scattered all over these hills."

He sighed. "I like this place, especially the way the town itself is tucked up in the hills back from the gulf. Yet we're close enough to the sea if we need it for any reason," he said, still chewing. "I sure enjoy this simpler, quieter life. You can have San Francisco. It's turned into a place I'd describe as hell."

"I'm sorry, Papa," Scarlett said, again resting her fork on her plate.

"Do you miss our home there?" Patrick asked as he, too, rested his fork on his plate. He took a sip of coffee to wash the sweetness down as he gazed across the wide oak table at his daughter.

"I can't help missing our three-storied beautiful home on Nob Hill," Scarlett said, smiling a thank you at Malvina as she cleared the plates from the table. "But I must admit to liking our new ranch house. It's unique. I like the huge stone fireplace in the parlor and the way the sunset lights up the walls of the library each evening. That's my favorite time to choose a book to read in bed before I go to sleep."

"That's fine, Scarlett," Patrick said, nodding. "Mighty fine."

He gazed admiringly at his daughter. It seemed she had grown up into a beautiful young lady overnight, with her fiery red hair and perfect facial features. Her eyes, shaded by thick, dark lashes, were surely alluring to any man who looked into them.

Yes, his daughter was beautiful, and she was used to fine things: a beautiful home, servants, lovely clothes. But she was more a tomboy than she was a lady. Patrick, a man without a son, had indulged her love of adventure, while her mother had tried her hardest to nourish her feminine side. His beloved Penelope had brought out her own precious violin and had given it to Scarlett when their daughter was eight.

He would never forget the look of horror on Scarlett's tiny, sweet face when her mother had laid that violin in her arms and asked Scarlett to learn to play it for her. It had been Penelope's dream to be a concert violinist, but her playing had only been good enough to entertain the members of her family.

Loving her mother so much, Scarlett had learned to play the violin to please her, but, like Penelope, she did not have the talent that her mother had hoped for.

With her mother's blessing only a week before her tragic death, Scarlett had given the violin to a dear friend whose desire was to become a concert violinist.

Instead of bringing such things as violins with her to Coral Creek, Scarlett had begged Patrick to arrange for all her prized steeds to accompany them. Her favorite was the powerfully muscled stallion that had been a gift from her father on her sixteenth birthday, a stallion that had sired many a foal since then.

His name was Lightning because of his special markings — what looked like a streak of white lightning along one side, so vivid against his midnight-black coat.

"What does today hold for you?" Patrick asked when he again saw that same strange look in his daughter's eyes as she gazed out the window, seemingly seeing nothing.

It was a sort of love-struck look that made him uneasy. He could not help thinking that some cowboy had made eyes at her while she had been horseback riding yesterday.

But she was not one to lie, and when he had questioned her, she had denied that anything of the sort had happened.

Then what in tarnation could be causing her strange behavior this morning?

Her father's voice brought Scarlett out of her deep thoughts about the handsome Caddo Indian chief. She hoped that he didn't see the look of guilt in her eyes, or the blush that instantly warmed her cheeks upon again being caught daydreaming.

"What did you say, Papa?" she asked, embarrassed.

"I asked, what does your day hold for you besides daydreamin' about only the good Lord above knows what?" Patrick said, his eyes narrowing as he gazed at his daughter's flushed cheeks. No matter what she said, something was awry with Scarlett this morning, and it surely had something to do with a man!

But he would not delve any further into that subject with her. His daughter was one of a kind, honest to a fault sometimes, and when she was ready to discuss whatever was creating such a blush, then he'd sit and listen.

"Not much," she said, taking the white linen napkin from her lap and placing it on the table. "And you?"

"I'm hirin' a new deputy," Patrick said, following suit. "His name is Sam Baker. He's a fine young man whose parents died a few years ago at the hands of renegades."

The mention of renegades made Scarlett squirm uneasily in her chair, for she was again reminded of Chief Hawke.

Oh, but surely he was anything but a renegade!

He had seemed so kind, so friendly, so noble.

"Papa," Scarlett blurted out. "Have you had any problems with Indians yet? I know there are some who live near enough to Coral Creek to trade there. Are they peaceful? Or are there renegades in the area that I should be wary of while out riding Lightning?"

"I've had some problems with the Caddo Indians," he said nonchalantly, not seeing the look of alarm in his daughter's eyes at the mention of the Caddo tribe.

"What do you mean, Papa?" Scarlett asked, trying to sound merely curious. "What have the Caddo done? I thought you said they were a peaceful tribe."

She again recalled yesterday and how

hunting seemed to be the sole reason for the Caddo warriors' outing. She had caused them to lose a deer, so Chief Hawke had said.

She was thankful that he had not shot at the deer, for it had been very close to her. Had the deer died before her eyes, she would have been sickened.

"The Caddo *are* a peaceful people, that is a fact," Patrick said dryly. "But one or two of them are troublemakers. And I always have to watch for horse stealing. All Indians love a pretty horse, and, daughter, yours are the finest in the area."

He paused, then said, "And I've heard tales of opium traders in the area. Chinese coolies who fled from San Francisco are living hidden somewhere nearby, possibly even in an underground city I've heard about. My main concern is the Indians getting their hands on the opium. Who knows how they'd behave under its influence?"

He nodded, then added, "Yep, it's my first priority to find those coolies and send them packing."

"Papa, I know all about opium dens," Scarlett said, shivering. "If there truly are some of those dens of iniquity established in this area, we might not be any better off than when we lived in San Francisco. Those who partake of opium cause all sorts of trouble, sometimes even murder."

"I must admit to being discouraged to learn that opium seems to have followed us from San Francisco," Patrick said. "I'm discouraged as hell. I've looked in every nook and cranny and haven't found hide or hair of these coolies; nor have I found any signs of an underground city. Perhaps both are just rumors."

"I hope so, Papa," Scarlett murmured. "I know how you wanted our new life to be as perfect as possible. At least the Indians haven't caused you much of a problem."

"Except for one," Patrick said, slowly nodding. "Yep, there is one Indian in particular that's on my watch list. It's Chief Hawke's brother, Fast Deer. On my very first day at the office, the departing sheriff told me about the things to watch for, and who. Fast Deer was at the top of the list, and in the short time we've been here, he has caused me problems more than once. He's a drinker and a gambler, and that's a bad combination."

Then he kneaded his chin thoughtfully. "But now that I'm thinking about it, he hasn't been in Coral Creek for several days," he said. "Perhaps my determination to clean up the saloons and gambling houses has discouraged him enough to keep him at home. I'd like that. Yep, I'd like that."

"You've had to single out this Fast Deer because of the problems he has caused?" Scarlett asked, wondering if she had been wrong about Chief Hawke. Surely if his brother was so disreputable, Chief Hawke could not be all that good, himself.

That idea disappointed her.

"Yep, Fast Deer is someone I'm sure to have to deal with again," Patrick said. "But as for his brother, Chief Hawke, there is no one who does not speak of his kindness. He is known, far and wide, to be a proud and high-minded man. He is a man of good heart. He keeps the peace for his people. I'm certain his brother deeply disappoints him."

Hearing her father speak so highly of Chief Hawke brought a rush of relief to Scarlett's heart, for she did not want to think that Hawke was capable of anything bad. His eyes — ah, those midnight-dark eyes — spoke to her so gently.

And she had thought there was something in his voice that said he was taken with her.

But perhaps it was only her hair that had

intrigued him. Its bright red color was surely something that an Indian would find fascinating after living surrounded by people whose hair was coal black.

In any case, she was relieved to know that Chief Hawke was admired by everyone, and trusted.

"Papa, do you still feel that Coral Creek is as quiet a town as you'd thought now that you know there are coolies, opium, a possible mysterious underground city, and an Indian troublemaker to deal with?" she asked.

"I need a challenge, or why be sheriff?" Patrick said, shrugging nonchalantly. "Nope. I don't regret having chosen this town. I hope to clean up these minor problems and make the townsfolk glad they hired me."

"Papa, I'm taking Lightning out for a long ride today," Scarlett said cautiously, hoping she would not reawaken her father's suspicion. "I want to see more of the countryside."

"I'd rather you didn't, but I know it's wrong of me to treat you like a child. You will soon be leaving your teen years behind when you reach your twentieth birthday," Patrick said. "Just be careful, sweetie."

Patrick was again wondering about what

had brought that blush to his daughter's cheeks more than once this morning. He couldn't let go of the idea that it had to do with a man.

"And, Scarlett, be sure to take your small pistol with you," he quickly added. "You're beautiful. Any man would see you as a prime catch."

His eyes gleamed and a soft smile tugged at the corners of his lips. "And another thing, young lady. You've got a mighty purty head of hair," he teased. "Your scalp could look quite fancy hanging on the end of an Indian's scalp pole."

Scarlett felt the color drain from her face. She gasped as she stared at her father. "Papa, that's not funny," she said, her voice breaking. "That's not at all funny."

Suddenly both of their eyes were drawn to the window when they heard a horse and buggy arriving.

Scarlett looked quickly at her father as he scrambled from his chair, his eyes wide.

"She's here!" he said, his exclamation almost a shout. "Finally! She's here."

Scarlett was stunned by his behavior. She hurried from her chair. "*Who* is here?" she asked as her father came to her and took her by the hands, his eyes dancing. "Papa, whom are you expecting?"

"I didn't tell you earlier because I knew you'd try everything in your power to make me change my mind, and, daughter, my mind can't be changed," he said. In his voice was a strange excitement that Scarlett had not heard for a long time, not since before the death of his precious wife.

"Daughter, I've been terribly lonely since your mother's death," he said thickly. "I can't stand going to bed at night any longer without the warmth of a woman next to me."

Stunned and horrified by what he had just said, Scarlett yanked her hands from his. "No! Papa, please tell me that you've not brought a lady into your life . . . this soon," she said, her voice breaking.

"Yes, I have," Patrick said, looking anxiously toward the window, and taking quick steps away from Scarlett. "Come and meet her, Scarlett."

"Who?" Scarlett said, now following him from the dining room, into the corridor, and to the entry foyer. She was so shocked by what was happening, she hardly felt her feet hit the oak flooring as she stepped outside onto the porch with her father.

She stopped and stared at the horse and buggy that had stopped near the steps that led up to the porch. The driver was a man

Scarlett knew as her father's main deputy; he had two passengers.

Scarlett gazed curiously at a beautiful and petite golden-haired woman dressed in a lovely green silk dress, and wearing a wide-brimmed hat decorated with artificial flowers.

Scarlett noticed something else. The woman's loveliness was somewhat marred by dark circles beneath her blue eyes. She looked as though she might be ill; or perhaps she had had a rough life.

But she was pretty and shapely, just like Scarlett's mother had been.

In fact, except for the hardness about her face, the woman closely resembled Scarlett's mother.

Scarlett's gaze moved over to a small boy with a great mop of golden hair. He was clinging to his mother's gloved hand. He was pale, thin, shaky, and looked very ill. Scarlett guessed he was somewhere between seven and nine years of age.

Scarlett looked over at her father just as he took a step back. She could tell that he was taken aback about something.

"A child?" Patrick blurted out. "You have a child? A child isn't a part of this package. When I sent for a mail-order bride, that's all I wanted . . . not a child."

Scarlett was truly stunned now.

Her father had sent for a mail-order bride?

She had always thought him such a level-headed, intelligent man.

But now?

She thought that perhaps she had never truly known him at all!

The lady hung her head. "I'm sorry," she murmured. "I didn't mean to deceive you."

"That is exactly what you have done, and you can go right back to town and get back on that stagecoach that brought you here," Patrick said, placing his fists on his hips. "I'll gladly pay your way." He slid his eyes down to the child. "And . . . and . . . his."

He gave the driver a stern look. He was Ray Strupp, one of his deputies whom he had asked to meet the stagecoach. "Ray, get her outta here," he said flatly. "Now. Do you hear? Now!"

Ray, a heavyset young man, tipped his wide-brimmed cowboy hat to Patrick. "It's as good as done," he said, but just as he was about to snap the reins against the horse, the lady hurried from the buggy and went up the steps to the porch.

What happened then truly mortified Scarlett. The woman fell to her knees before Scarlett's father. Scarlett covered a gasp of disbelief with her hand when she heard what the lady was saying.

"Please let me stay," she begged, tears streaming from her eyes. "My son is ill. He won't survive another stagecoach ride so soon. Please? Please have mercy?"

Embarrassed for her, Patrick reached down and helped her to her feet.

He gazed at the child, who was still in the buggy, and then at the woman.

"You can stay until the child is well enough to travel again," Patrick said flatly, his eyes flashing angrily at the woman. "But hear me well, Mary Jane, when I say that you cannot stay one minute longer. Once the child is well enough to travel, you must go."

"Thank you, oh, thank you so much," Mary Jane said, reaching for Patrick's hand, then withdrawing her own when she saw him quickly place both of his hands behind him.

Patrick turned to Scarlett, who seemed too shocked by what had transpired to speak. He had never seen such anger and confusion in his daughter's eyes. "Daughter, this is Mary Jane Houser," he said thickly.

He turned back toward Mary Jane. "And your son?" he said, his voice tight. "What is his name?"

"Scottie," Mary Jane said, glancing quickly over her shoulder at the boy, then gazing again into Patrick's green eyes. "Scottie Alan Houser is his full name and he's nine years old."

"And where is Scottie's father?" Patrick asked, feeling pity for the child, who looked so tiny and alone in the buggy. He certainly was small for his age.

Mary Jane hung her head. "He's dead," she murmured, but in her mind she hoped that Patrick never found out the truth. She had no idea who the child's father was. She had never been married. She had been a prostitute when Scottie was conceived.

But she had given up that trade as soon as he was born and had made a living as a dance-hall queen until she had seen a notice on the wall of a bank in San Francisco, an advertisement for a mail-order bride.

"Daughter, as you heard, the child's name is Scottie," Patrick said. "As you can see, he's not in the best of health. He'll be given a chance to get better, and then he and his mother will leave."

He reached a hand to Scarlett's cheek. "Sweetie, I'm sorry about all of this and about the disappointment I have obviously caused you," he said, his voice drawn. "I'll make it up to you."

Scarlett couldn't bear to hear any more. Her father was acting like someone she didn't know. She felt he was being unfaithful to his wife.

Yes, Scarlett's mother was dead, but she hadn't been dead for very long!

It had been six months.

Only . . . six . . . months!

Crying, she ran past her father and the woman who now stood at his side as though she belonged there, and ran with blinding tears to the stable.

She saddled Lightning and rode off, even as Patrick shouted for her to stop.

For the very first time in her life, Scarlett openly and defiantly ignored her father.

"Papa, oh, Papa, what have you done?" she whispered to herself as she felt her heart breaking.

She sank her heels into the flanks of her steed and rode at a fast gallop across a field of wildflowers. She rode on until she couldn't hear her father any longer and didn't have to look upon the face of a woman who had brought turmoil into their family.

"Oh, Papa, how could you?" she cried to the heavens, racing onward without knowing where she was going, or how far.

She just didn't care any longer!

Chapter Three

His straight, jet-black hair flowed down his muscular back as Hawke kicked his gray mustang into a gallop.

His jaw was tight with a mixture of disappointment and anger. He had been searching long hours for his brother Fast Deer, but without success.

It saddened him that his brother's soul had been captured by the love of firewater and cards. Those weaknesses had made his brother a man of *che-kao-koi,* bad heart.

Hawke had been in Coral Creek, checking the few saloons in that small town. All he had found there were frowns from those who openly disliked men with red skin, even Indians like Hawke, who was a man of peace, known for his efforts to keep peace between his people and the white-eyes.

He was proud to say that he was a powerful, beloved leader. He had succeeded in keeping peace and at the same time managed to keep his people's land free of white settlers.

The United States Government had discovered that there were benefits in allowing the peaceful tribes to stay on their land, instead of ordering them to live on reservations.

That word *reservation* brought a bitter taste to Hawke's mouth. He hated even to think about his beloved people being confined in such a way.

But the actions of one man, his brother, were casting doubt in the white people's leader's eyes. Fast Deer had taken the wrong path. If Hawke should fail to turn him back onto the right road, his people could suffer greatly. They could be forced to leave the land they had loved since the beginning of time.

But Hawke had an advantage over most other leaders of the Indian community. Knowing that Hawke would one day follow his father into chieftainship, his mother had urged him to be educated at a mission.

Now he could read and write, enabling no man to easily cheat him. He was a master of both languages — the white man's, and the red man's.

All white-eyes who knew him saw him as a man of iron will and boundless energy.

Although Hawke loved his brother, and he had vowed to his mother, that he would care for her younger son, he was also bound to protect his people. He could not let one man's misguided ways jeopardize the freedom of the rest of his Cougar Clan.

If his brother did not see the error of his ways soon and change for the better, Hawke would have no choice but to banish him from the tribe, as he would any other troublemaker. He could not be blinded by the fact that Fast Deer was his brother; nor could his promise to his mother keep him from doing what he knew was right for their people.

If she were alive today, she would say that enough was enough. All efforts to turn Fast Deer's life around had failed, and now he would have to pay for his wrongful deeds.

Realizing at last that he was not going to find Fast Deer today, Hawke had turned sadly back toward home.

As his horse Misty loped along, he forced his mind elsewhere. Every time he was away from his home, he watched for an elusive white deer and his thoughts turned to the creature now. His father had been hunting this deer for many moons and had gone to his grave without that coveted pelt, for the deer had been too elusive for anyone to find and kill.

If Hawke ever did find the white deer, the pelt would be his father's, but all else would be given to his people for good use. Deer was a prime source of raw materials for the Caddo.

Its brains served to soften leather. Its horns made spoons, cups and ornaments. Its shoulder blades were used to dig and cultivate the soil. Its ligaments were used to string bows; the hoofs to make glue used in tipping the arrows.

The bristles were used to make rope; the wool to make belts, ribbons and other dress ornaments. The skin was used to make saddles, rope, shirts, shoes and coverlets.

Hawke had heard of a recent sighting of the elusive white deer, but the one who told him about the deer had said that it had disappeared suddenly, as though it had wings.

It was Hawke's deepest desire to find this deer so that he could take the pelt to his father's grave and leave it there so he would have it with him for eternity.

He rode onward, then suddenly drew a tight rein when he saw someone in the distance.

It was a woman.

His heart warmed at the sight, for he realized that this was the very same woman he had come face to face with yesterday while he was with his warriors on the hunt.

Today she rode a black steed with white markings on its coat, but he recognized her hair at once. It was the same color as the scarlet coat that he wore on special occasions.

He watched her hair blowing in the breeze now, her chin held proudly high.

He was mesmerized by her. What woman was so brazen as to ride alone, and not only once, but twice?

He saw her as a woman of spirit . . . of courage.

How could he not be intrigued by her?

But he knew he must fight these feelings. She was white. There were very few whites that he trusted, not even pretty ones whose eyes he remembered as being the color of grass!

But he could not help wanting to get a better look, without her seeing him. Yesterday, when they were face to face, eye to eye, he had not been able to study her as he had hungered to do.

Putting aside the many reasons he should avoid her, he rode quickly to a nearby bluff and watched her ride past down below, in the direction of the gulf.

He dismounted, secured Misty's reins, then stretched out on his belly at the edge of the cliff and peered down.

His heart skipped a beat, for he could now very clearly see her face. Her beauty was perfection itself.

Although petite, her body was shapely and alluring in her skirt and blouse. He could not look away.

He wondered why he had never seen her before yesterday.

He remembered what she had called herself.

Scarlett!

But she had not said where she made her home. For certain, he would find out.

And even though it was forbidden for a red man to show any interest in a white woman, this was one time when he would not follow the rules set down by white men. He had never before felt anything for a woman like he felt for this one. He had never married because no woman had caused his heart to pound the way it was pounding now.

Every beat told him he must find out everything he could about this woman.

But first, he had to discover where she lived.

Suddenly his eyes were drawn away from Scarlett. Out at sea he saw a huge ship. Its sails were ripped, and the large vessel seemed to be listing in the waves.

His eyebrows lifted when he saw a black flag with a strange drawing of a skull and bones on it.

He wondered whose ship it might be.

And why did it fly such a strange flag?

Was it going to drop anchor close to this shore?

Surely so. It seemed to be trying to reach the safety of land.

He recalled the hurricane-force winds of not long ago. Could this ship have been damaged by the winds and waves caused by that storm?

He got a bitter taste inside his mouth when he recalled those gale-force winds and what they had taken from him.

His parents!

His father had gone to a neighboring Caddo village that day to trade. He had taken his wife with him by canoe. They had never made it to that village.

The storm had seemed to come out of nowhere. Several homes in his village had been destroyed, but were now rebuilt.

But nothing could be done for his parents.

He was left with only a brother.

Disturbed by these sorrowful remembrances, and deeply disappointed in his brother, Hawke yearned for the comfort of his home.

But he wanted to take one last look at the woman. He would pursue her later and discover where she made her home. He was sure he would see her again, since he had already come across her twice in two days.

When he looked downward, to where she had been on her horse only moments ago, his heart sank. She was no longer there.

He stood quickly and looked into the distance to see if he could spot her again on her steed, but there was no sign of her.

"There is always tomorrow," he whispered to himself.

He took one last look at the ship, then mounted his steed and rode for home.

In his mind's eye, he kept seeing the loveliness of the woman. He could even recall her voice from yesterday. Everything about her seemed soft and pretty . . . and sweet!

But why had he never seen her before yesterday?

That had to mean she was new to the area.

He smiled and nodded his head. "*Huh,* yes, beautiful woman, I will see you again," he said beneath his breath. "I will know much more of you than just your name!"

Chapter Four

The room was dim, smoke-filled, dank and mysterious. The only sound that could be heard was the clink of coins and the shuffle of cards.

Several scruffy-looking men sat around a table, cards in their hands, cigars in their mouths, glasses of whiskey sitting before them on the green felt-covered table as they played poker.

One of those men was noticeably different from the others.

He wasn't white.

He had copper skin, waist-length jet-black hair, and he wore a fringed buckskin shirt, breeches and moccasins. His dark eyes looked guardedly from man to man, his hand trembling as he held cards that were not favorable to him.

He had already lost his horse and saddle today, his bow and quiver of arrows, and his prized Bowie knife.

All that he had left to give up after losing the last hand was his buckskin shirt and breeches, and his moccasins.

He nervously looked over his shoulder.

Through the low-hanging pall of smoke he saw several men and women sitting on the floor on mats along one wall.

For the most part, the women were white, but the men were Chinese, dressed in colorful finery and strange-looking hats.

The eyes of the men and the white ladies were already glassy as they sucked on what Fast Deer now knew were opium pipes.

He had yet to partake in anything like that, but he did love his firewater. He supposed that that love was partially responsible for his having lost every hand of cards up to now.

Swallowing hard, he turned his attention back to the cards in his hand, then smiled crookedly as he slapped them down on the table and began dragging in the pile of coins from the middle of the table.

"Hey, not so quick there, Fast Deer," one of the gamblers grumbled. "You know your cards don't beat mine."

Fast Deer ignored the man. He wanted to get the coins and make a quick escape. He did not want to lose his clothes, although he had to confess that his garments continually changed hands since he was having such a run of bad luck at cards these days. He began picking up the coins, having already put several in his breeches pocket.

"You damn savage idiot," the red-faced gambler shouted as he stood, shoving his chair back so quickly it toppled over on the floor. "You'd better have another look at my cards before you take one more damn coin from the table. Are you too drunk to see that you lost?"

Swallowing hard, Fast Deer felt his hands trembling as he dug into his pocket and retrieved the coins.

"That's more like it," the gambler said, picking up his chair and sitting back down on it. "Hand 'em over, savage." He cackled. "And then your clothes, or you're a dead man."

"I am a dead man anyway," Fast Deer grumbled drunkenly beneath his breath as he shoved the coins across the table to the man. *Huh,* yes, he did feel dead inside because he knew what a disappointment he was to his chieftain brother and his Caddo people.

But he had traveled so far down the wrong road of life, he feared there was no turning back. His only way out would be to take his own life, but he knew better than to do that. Suicide was a forbidden act among his people. Whoever resorted to taking his own life would never join his ancestors in the sky.

Instead, his soul traveled, alone, for all eternity.

He knew how that would feel already because he had already begun that long, never-ending journey . . . the long goodbye!

Feeling despondent and alone, he yanked his shirt over his head.

"Your breeches now, savage," the man growled as he held on to the fringed shirt. "And then your moccasins. I always wanted myself some Injun attire. You've lost them before, but not to me. This time it's my turn."

The man laughed throatily. "I especially want those moccasins. It'll be interesting to see how it feels to walk in the shoes of an Injun."

Fast Deer glared at the man, then sighing, removed his breeches and moccasins and shoved them across the table.

Very aware that he was naked and being gawked at by the gamblers, Fast Deer tried to cover his manhood, then felt a soft hand on his arm.

He turned and found a golden-haired, blue-eyed woman gazing at him, a blanket in her arms.

He saw the glassiness of her eyes, yet she seemed to have enough of her senses left to be kind to a man who had just lost the last of his possessions.

"You can have my blanket," the woman said, her voice slurred. "Come and sit with me. I'll also share my pipe with you."

Always having been afraid that opium might make him even more disoriented than firewater, he hesitated.

But needing the blanket in order to be able to get back to his village without making a laughingstock of himself, and feeling that he couldn't have the blanket unless he agreed to smoke with the woman, Fast Deer nodded. He took the blanket and slung it around his shoulders, relieved to cover his body.

"Come on," the woman said, taking him by the hand. "The pipe is good. You'll enjoy it."

The men at the table guffawed at how easily Fast Deer was lured by the woman. "Yeah, go with the empty-headed broad," one of the men said. "Go with Mary Jane."

The man stopped and lifted an eyebrow as he gazed at the woman. "You're new here," he said. "What'd you say your last name was?"

"I didn't," Mary Jane said, her words

slurred. "And don't ask me again. It's none of your business."

"Goldlilocks, everyone and everything in this joint is my business, 'cause I own it," Gerald Banyon snarled. "So watch how you speak to me, do you hear?"

"Yeah, sure," Mary Jane said, giving him a wicked look over her shoulder, but still not giving him her last name.

He glared at her a moment longer, then resumed playing cards.

But the other men laughed and mocked both her and Fast Deer as Fast Deer sat down with her and leaned his back against the wall.

Mary Jane gave him the pipe and watched him take his first drag from the long stem.

Fast Deer's eyes widened as he realized that this gave him an even more carefree feeling than firewater.

He gazed questioningly over at the woman.

Her nod gave him permission to take another drag from her pipe.

Closing his eyes, he took one drag after another, welcoming the peace it gave him.

His brother! What if his brother saw him now?

Hawke's disappointment would be twofold — opium on top of firewater.

With just enough sense left to make a decision that he knew he must make, Fast Deer hurriedly handed the pipe back to the woman.

"I must *mea,* go," he said, then stopped when she grabbed him by one arm and held him in place.

"You owe me," Mary Jane slurred out.

"I have nothing to pay you for . . . for . . . the smokes," Fast Deer stammered.

He fought to get away from her, but she held his arm as though in a vise.

"*Ob-be-mah-e-way,* get out of my way," he said as he stood up, finally yanking himself free.

But she as quickly and determinedly grabbed his hand and yanked him back down beside her.

"*Hakai,* what . . . what do you want of me?" Fast Deer stammered, his eyes searching hers.

"Make love to me," Mary Jane said, her glassy eyes pleading. "I need loving."

The thought sickened Fast Deer.

Desperate to get out of there, Fast Deer finally managed to yank himself away from her, and this time she allowed it.

His knees wobbled as he stood, but he forced his feet to move, one at a time, away from the woman. She was shouting at him to come back, that he had a debt to pay her.

Stumbling, he finally got out of the building, then made his way through the darkness. On each side of him were shabby, derelict buildings with strange-looking false fronts, the glass broken out of the windows.

But there was no sky.

There were no trees.

There was nothing overhead but a roof of packed dirt and rock as he walked onward through the underground city.

He had been told that this had been a flourishing den of iniquity years ago, where the worst sort of meanness was practiced. But a flood had come and forced everyone out.

After that, the front had been sealed up. The underground city had been totally abandoned, until only recently when a back entrance had been found by several coolies who had fled from San Francisco. Looking for a place to establish their opium dens, they had heard about it from gamblers who were headed there.

The coolies had joined them. All agreed to keep this underground city a secret; it was the perfect place to pursue their illegal activities without the law breathing down their necks.

With the blanket clutched around his shoulders, Fast Deer hurried from the underground city.

But since he had also lost his horse to a gambler today, he was forced to travel on foot.

Although drunk, with the mixture of alcohol and opium in his body, he knew that he could still steal a horse. He had done it many times. He was clever at stealing.

His chieftain brother frowned on such practices, and had scolded Fast Deer, saying that one day when Fast Deer stole a horse, the white lawmen would hunt him down and hang him; but Fast Deer had no choice but to steal another one tonight. He needed to get home. He needed the privacy of his lodge to sleep off the horrors of this day.

He looked skyward. He was glad that darkness was now falling around him. Night would give him the cover he needed not only for stealing, but for traveling half-clothed.

He walked through the woods in the darkness of night until he saw the lights from the windows of a huge ranch house. Beside it he spotted a corral filled with many horses.

He crept stealthily up to the edge of the woods, his eyes surveying everything around him.

When he saw no one anywhere, only lamplight in the many windows of the sprawling ranch house, he decided this was his chance to get himself a horse.

Hurrying to the corral, he chose one of the most muscular steeds, a black one, so that he could blend into the darkness as he rode across open country on the final leg of his journey home.

Skilled at riding without a saddle, he didn't bother to find one as he took the horse from the corral. Clutching the blanket around his neck, he led the horse into the woods.

When he felt that no one at the ranch house could hear the thundering of hoofbeats in the night, he paused. He secured the blanket around himself, tying it at the neck, then mounted the steed and rode out.

After he had been riding just a little while, he saw something white a short distance away. His heart skipped a beat, for he believed that he was looking at a ghost.

But no!

He realized that it wasn't a ghost, but instead the elusive white deer that his brother, and his father before him, had been hunting.

But Fast Deer had no weapon he could use to bring down the deer!

He had to let it go on its way!

He was angry that he must do this, for he could have taken the pelt to his brother. Hawke wanted this deer so badly, surely he would have forgiven Fast Deer for anything.

His heart sinking, he had no choice but to watch the deer bound away into the darkness.

Hanging his head dejectedly, he continued homeward.

Chapter Five

The sound of waves splashing against the sides of the *Eclipse* resounded through the main cabin of the pirate ship.

Beams of moonlight poured through the porthole, reflecting on walls paneled in dark oak and two red leather chairs that sat on opposite sides of a round oak table.

Blue Raven, an aging man who professed to be a pirate, yet who was seen as a lunatic by all who knew him, sat at the table, a map stretched out atop it between him and his best friend, Fat Jaws.

"Me *Eclipse* has been blown way off course," Blue Raven growled as he traced the outline of the Gulf of Mexico on the map with one long fingernail.

The moon's glow cast the shadow of his beaked nose on the far wall of the cabin. His rusty red hair fell down to his shoulders; his thick beard was also red.

Although he was in his late sixties, he was a commanding figure, dressed in a white, loose cambric shirt opened to the waist, where he wore a red sash. A bright gold religious medallion hung around his neck, and loops of gold hung from each of his earlobes.

An elegant brocaded waistcoat rested over black leather breeches, and he wore wide-topped black boots. A brace of pistols were secured at his waist, a cutlass at his right side.

He looked quickly up at Fat Jaws with his flashing, wicked green eyes. "Aye, matie, there'll be no gold for me crew for a while," he said tightly. "The damn gale made certain o' that. It nearly tore me ship apart, it did. It's limpin' like an injured puppy now. All that's missin' is a tail tucked between its legs."

Fat Jaws, dressed all in black, his long, coal-black hair and whiskered face blending in with his attire, tipped a jewel-encrusted mug of rum to his lips and swallowed gulps of the fiery liquid, then slammed the mug down on the table. He belched and wiped his mouth dry with the hairy back of his hand.

"We've time, Blue Raven," he said, his dark eyes flashing. "We've only been delayed for a while. After we repair the ship, we'll be on our way again. Then we'll go and gather us up enough gold to pay for two new ships. One fer you and one fer me. I'll command me own ship then, without ye breathing down me neck."

"And so you want to compete with the likes o' me out there on the wide sea?" Blue Raven said, his eyes twinkling. "Ye know who'll be the winner. I was born to lead, you to follow."

"Aye, that's what you've always said," Fat Jaws said, frowning at Blue Raven. He was tired of being seen as second to Blue Raven, when if truth be known, they had gotten their start together, with only a few coins in their pockets.

After finally getting a ship and then many prizes, somehow it had been Blue Raven who claimed to be the leader of their crew.

Up until now, Fat Jaws had put up with it.

But he was sorely tired of it and wasn't going to take much more.

"Ol' pirate, I guess I'll just have to prove me point now, won't I?" Fat Jaws said, glowering.

"First ye've got to get enough gold to do the provin'," Blue Raven grumbled when he saw that his friend was serious.

"First we've got to get the *Eclipse* repaired," Fat Jaws said. He rose and strode to the porthole, gazing out. "You know that the *Eclipse* has taken on too much water. The ship might not even be salvageable."

"That's where you and I differ, matie," Blue Raven said, rising from his chair. He went and slung an arm around Fat Jaw's shoulder. "All we need is to dock the *Eclipse*, and before long it'll be tight enough to return to the sea. Gold is awaitin' us, Fat Jaws. Never lose sight o' that."

Blue Raven stepped away from Fat Jaws. He gestured toward the door with a hand. "Go and give the orders to the crew to lower the flag," he said as the ship moved on toward a hidden cove, where in a cliff's shadow they could make the necessary repairs.

He had made certain they were not near any town that he could see. He wanted no one snooping around. He wanted to get the ship patched up as quickly as possible and be on his way. No one took much liking to a pirate's ship being this close to land.

"Aye-aye, Cap'n," Fat Jaw mocked, glowering at Blue Raven's commands. He hated being ordered around, but shrugged and went on his way. In time, he'd find a way to best Blue Raven. In time . . . !

Blue Raven grabbed his brass telescope from his desk and left the cabin, hurrying topside.

Standing at the rail, he lifted the telescope to his eyes and slowly scanned the moonlit shore for signs of anyone who might have observed the ship approaching. Anyone noting the black flag with its skull and bones would know the meaning of it.

"Aye, all know this flag belongs to pirates," he whispered to himself as the ship inched closer and closer to where the anchor would soon be dropped. He could not get his ship entirely to the shore, where they could run out a plank, for the water was not deep enough there. His crew would come and go in their longboats as they cut trees for wood to make their repairs.

As his eyes surveyed the land, he thought back to the afternoon, when he had been farther out at sea, looking for a safe harbor where he could take his ship for repairs.

When he had looked through his telescope, he had seen a scarlet-haired woman on a midnight-dark steed, her hair flying in the wind as she rode along the beach. He knew then that was where he would drop anchor.

He hoped to see the lady again. His loins

were aflame even now as he thought of her. Aye, he must have her!

She would be the only person he would allow to see his ship, for she would be brought aboard it and taken with him to San Francisco!

When he handed her a huge bag of gold after he had a successful dig in the hills of California, she would be glad that she had been taken hostage by this red-bearded kin to Bluebeard.

Aye, she would proudly ride the high seas in his *Eclipse* as his queen.

Even though he was aging, he thought himself virile enough still to make a love child with a lady. If it was a boy, they would name him Bluebeard, after the distant relative Blue Raven had idolized for so long.

As the ship eased its way into the cove, Blue Raven paid more attention to what was happening now, instead of what he hoped could happen if he had the chance to find the lady and take her as his prize.

Aye, he was thankful that this water was deep enough to moor the *Eclipse* close to land. They would be able to come and go on their longboats easily.

He gazed at a thicket of trees. There were enough to supply lumber for the necessary repairs to his ship.

He lowered his telescope and turned to look at his men as they rushed around on deck. "Go slow now," he shouted to the man at the wheel. "Get as close to land as possible. We must begin cutting trees quickly. Even at night we must cut 'em. We 'ave to get the repairs made and then get out o' the area before someone sees us!"

Yet there was that one exception. He did hope that the lady would be horseback riding again real soon in this area. He wondered whether she had seen his approaching ship.

A dash of cold fear went through him. "If she did, did she tell someone?" he whispered as he again began slowly scanning the land with his telescope. He did not see anything but the high bluff, the land and the trees.

He smiled when he finally heard the drag of the anchor as it made contact on the rocky bottom far below the surface of the water.

He watched while several longboats were lowered; his men rowed hastily toward land. He knew that they understood the need for haste in repairing the ship so that they could sail back out to sea before being seen by anyone who might report their presence to the nearest authorities.

Although most people mocked him for saying he was a pirate, there were those who felt threatened by him.

"Aye, they'd better fear me," he grumbled to himself as he lowered his telescope and held it at his side.

He watched as the first boat made it to shore and the men scrambled from it, their axes at their sides.

He watched as they found a tree to their liking and began chopping into it with more than one ax.

Fat Jaws came to his side. "I don' like bein' this close to land," he complained. "If anyone was witness to our approach, we can expect trouble."

"It's they who'll have trouble if they try to interfere with us," Blue Raven said, resting a hand on the cutlass at his right side. "Just let 'em try and stop us. There'll be more than a flag wavin' in the breeze when we head back out to sea. I'll have me a head or two if anyone becomes a bother to me."

Fat Jaws placed his fists on his hips. "I'll just feel better when we're back out at sea and on our way again to California," he grumbled.

But Blue Raven scarcely heard what he

was saying. He was peering intently toward land, again recalling the flame-haired lady he had seen only yesterday. He knew it would be dangerous for her if she came this close to where his men were working; most had been without a woman for far too long now.

But if he saw any of his crew approach the lady, that sailor would be the recipient of a ball in his belly. Blue Raven would not hesitate to shoot anyone who'd dare try to take that lady as his.

Chapter Six

The moon was casting its white sheen on a huge, round council house made of poles and thatched with grass. There were no windows. The only moonlight that entered the room came through the open door and the smoke hole overhead; otherwise the fire was the sole source of light.

Hawke sat on a platform at one side of the central fire, so that he could be seen by all of his warriors, who sat on brightly colored reed mats in a semicircle around the fire.

The fire was made from four very long, thick, heavy logs, arranged in the directions of the four principal winds.

There the warriors met to discuss all public necessities and matters of importance. They met when there was a scarcity of rain, or any menace that might cause the destruction of crops.

Tonight the warriors, elders and the shaman were gathered together for their forecasting ceremony. With their faces toward the fire, they prayed to The Great

One On High, *Ayo-caddi-ay-may.*

Eagle Thunder, their shaman, held up an eagle feather which they called *Ygui*. "The eagle whose feather we are using has risen on high to consult with *Ayo-caddi-ay-may* about the weather for the moons to come. It is time to make our new almanac," he said. "After we have approved the almanac, we shall tell all of our people. With the tail of a fox, the astronomer of our Cougar Clan will see future events —"

Eagle Thunder's speech was interrupted by the sound of a horse approaching outside.

Hawke's stomach tightened when he looked toward the open door, knowing that the rider must be his brother, for he was the only man of the village who was not present at this evening's special meeting.

When dogs began barking and snarling, Hawke's eyebrows rose, for if it was his brother, the dogs should not be upset. The village Jubine dogs, with their thin, pointed snouts, were intelligent and cunning.

"I must see who is causing alarm among the dogs," Hawke said, stepping down from the platform.

His jaw tight, he went outside.

He immediately saw that the rider was Fast Deer. The women and children of the village had gathered and were openly gaping at him. He was only half hanging on to a horse that Hawke knew was not his brother's.

And where were his brother's clothes? He wore only a blanket draped around his shoulders.

The way his brother was trying to right himself on the horse, slipping and sliding to one side, was what had alarmed the dogs.

No warrior of this village ever behaved in such an odd manner when arriving on their steeds. They always rode with proud, straight backs, their heads held high.

As embarrassing as it was for Hawke, he had to admit that his brother was anything but noble in bearing, but instead someone whose pride had left him long ago.

In only a breechclout and moccasins, Hawke hurried over to the steed. He knew it must have been stolen by his brother, another cause for embarrassment, since no one stole from the white-eyes' corrals anymore.

He grabbed Fast Deer by the waist and helped him down from the black stallion.

"I cannot seem to think too clearly," Fast Deer said in a slurred fashion. "My brother, I am glad to finally be home."

"You shame me, you shame our departed

parents, you shame our Cougar Clan!" Hawke hissed out as he held on to Fast Deer. He knew his brother would fall if Hawke did not give him this assistance. He winced at the vile smell of his brother's breath. He recognized the stink of alcohol, yet there was something else that he had never smelled before.

"Where have you been?" Hawke asked, his voice tight. "Where did you get this steed? It is not yours, or any of our Cougar Clan's. Where is your own horse?"

He gave Fast Deer a look of disgust as he gazed at the blanket, already guessing what had transpired. His brother had been in similar predicaments more than one other time.

"Your clothes," Hawke said, his voice tight. "Who now wears them since you do not?"

"*Hakai?* You are speaking too fast," Fast Deer said, his voice slurred as he held on to the blanket. "One question at a time, big brother. Please? One . . . question . . . at a time."

"Where have you been?" Hawke said more slowly and distinctly as he led his brother toward his cabin. He could not get him out of the eyes of his people quickly enough. Hawke was glad that out of respect for their chief, most had already disbanded and gone to their homes.

"I cannot say," Fast Deer slurred drunkenly. He raised his free hand to his lips and ran a finger across them. "My lips are sealed."

Fast Deer knew better than to tell his brother where he had been, for all who frequented the underground city had been warned that anyone who revealed the secret of its existence, would die a slow, painful death at the hands of the coolies.

"And will you tell me whose horse this is?" Hawke said, leading Fast Deer on to his cabin and to mats before his brother's firepit, where only cold ashes lay.

"I cannot tell you anything," Fast Deer said, still clinging to the blanket as he sat down on the mats, his head bowed.

"You will tell me everything when you are sober, but now all I wish to know is which ranch you stole the horse from," Hawke said, kneeling down before his brother. He gazed into Fast Deer's bloodshot eyes. "We must return the steed to its rightful owner, and you must admit to them that you stole it."

Fast Deer's eyes filled with panic as he looked up at Hawke. "If I confess to having done that, I will hang," he said thickly. "I stole it from a rich man's corral. There will be no mercy for me. I will be tied up and hanged!"

"Fast Deer, it is obvious to me that you lost everything again today because of your gambling and drinking," Hawke said tightly. "My brother, this must stop, and you must be made to understand how wrong it is to steal. If you are put in jail, it is meant to be. But I will speak in your behalf and blame what you did on firewater."

"You . . . would do this . . . for your brother?" Fast Deer said, searching his brother's dark eyes. "I have embarrassed you again, yet you will fight to save me?"

"*Huh,* I will do this for you, Fast Deer," Hawke said, placing a hand on his brother's shoulder. "I will do this in memory of Mother and Father, but you must promise never to drink or gamble again. And you must, especially, promise never to steal again."

Fast Deer hung his head. "Please do not make me take the horse back," he said, his voice breaking. He gazed into Hawke's eyes again. "If you do not ask this of me, then I *will* promise never to do anything else in my lifetime that will embarrass you, or our people."

"We cannot keep a stolen horse in our

village," Hawke said tightly. "If it is discovered here, all of our Cougar Clan would pay for your crime, not only you. Those who might discover the horse here would think that the Caddo people condone horse stealing."

Hawke gazed slowly at his brother's attire, then placed his hand beneath Fast Deer's chin and lifted it so that again his eyes met Hawke's.

"Brother, I ask you again who wears your clothes now that you do not?" he demanded, trying to hold his anger at bay. "Who rides your horse, and who has your weapons since you have none of them now, yourself?"

"You already know the answer," Fast Deer said. He wiped away his *tosa-amah,* ashamed of his tears. "I lost them all while gambling. Each item you asked about belongs to others now. Everyone but your brother was good at gambling today. I lost everything. Everything!"

Feeling he might not be able to forgive his brother this time, Hawke rose to his feet and stood at the open door. He gazed out at the village for a moment.

Then he turned to Fast Deer again. "*Mea,* go! Get dressed," he flatly ordered. "Then come to me. We will return the horse. And you will be the one who hands the reins over to its owner, no one else, for the guilt is *ein-mah-heepicut;* it is yours!"

Knowing now that his brother was deadly serious, Fast Deer struggled to his feet and went to stand directly before Hawke. "My brother, I saw the white deer that father hunted," he said quickly, trying one last ploy to distract his brother. He hoped Hawke would be more interested in pursuing the deer than punishing his brother.

"Brother, I followed it," he said, the lie slipping easily across his lips. "I now know where it makes its home. I will get dressed. I will lead you there!"

Hawke's eyes narrowed angrily. "You will use a lie to turn my attention from the crimes you are guilty of, because you know that I want that deer so badly?" he growled out. He shook his head, then glared into his brother's eyes again. "You shame me again. These ploys are useless and make you look even more pitiful in the eyes of your chieftain brother!"

He pointed toward Fast Deer's sleeping room. "*Mea,* go!" he shouted. "Get dressed! Then come to the council house. I must go there now, and once again, as I have too many times before, explain the sins of my brother to our brethren. And today you did not interrupt just any meeting of men. You interrupted our forecasting council."

Fast Deer hung his head and stumbled toward his sleeping room as Hawke left angrily and hurried back to the council house.

As he entered, he found everyone still dutifully awaiting him. He knew they had heard what had transpired outside between their chief and his shameful brother.

He hurriedly explained the problem to them. "Warriors, you must go with me and my brother to return the stolen horse," he said. "But only my brother and I will go to the house, leading the stolen horse. You warriors will stay hidden and reveal yourselves to the white-eyes only if you see your chief's life, or my brother's, being threatened."

They all nodded, then went outside and mounted their steeds as Fast Deer came from his lodge.

He went to Hawke, who was leading the stolen horse toward him. Fast Deer's gaze wavered as he grabbed the reins. "I am truly sorry," he mumbled. "I wish that I could erase all the mistakes I made today and have the chance to live this day over again, but in the right way."

"Tomorrow is a new day," Hawke said, placing a gentle hand on his brother's bare shoulder. Fast Deer was now wearing a breechclout and moccasins. "Tomorrow you will be a new man with the ideals of a man of honor, not one of loose morals."

Fast Deer hung his head. He knew that as he stood there, listening to a brother who truly believed in him, he would disappoint that brother again, for the hunger for firewater, and to have cards in his hands, was a fire that burned even now in his belly!

He recalled the wonders of opium, too. He could hardly wait to go and partake of it again.

Huh, he knew that he would dishonor his family's name again, but he could not help himself.

Chapter Seven

The candles in the crystal chandelier above the dining-room table cast their golden light onto a table set for two.

The chandelier was the one thing that Scarlett had asked her father to bring from their family home in San Francisco, even though it did look somewhat out of place in the sprawling ranch house. She had been with her mother when they had purchased it. She would never forget her mother's proud smile as she had watched it installed in their grand dining room, where crystal twinkled like diamonds in a huge oak buffet, and where expensive china gleamed like mother of pearl.

Scarlett stepped into the dining room, where the aroma of baked chicken and dumplings was heavy and wonderful in the air. The dish was a specialty of Malvina's kitchen.

Scarlett started to go to the table, but stopped when her father spoke suddenly behind her as he came from his study. She turned and started to smile, but didn't when the candlelight from the corridor wall sconces revealed a concerned look on his face.

She went to him. "What is it, Papa?" she asked, seeing how tight his jaw was, and that his eyes flashed angrily. "I don't think I need to hear the answer, though. It's Mary Jane, isn't it? Before she came into our lives, you never came to the supper table angry." She sighed. "What did she do?"

"She's been gone all day," he said, his fingers circling into a tight fist at his side. "I have no idea where she is."

"What about Scottie?" Scarlett asked, looking past her father and down the long corridor that led to the bedrooms. "Did you ask him if he knew where his mother went? And . . . is he well enough to come and eat supper with us?"

"That poor child," Patrick said, raking his long, lean fingers through his black hair. "He has no idea where his mother went, or why. And he isn't well at all, not even strong enough to take supper with us in the dining room."

"You brought in a doctor today for Scottie," Scarlett said, going and placing a gentle hand on her father's arm. "What did he say? Did he diagnose Scottie's illness?"

"Doc Mike gave no diagnosis because he doesn't have any idea what is wrong with the child," Patrick said tightly. "He left a couple of bottles of tonic. I pray that it helps the child, and soon. I . . . I . . . want that boy's mother out of my life."

"But what of Scottie?" Scarlett said, dropping her hand to her side. "If he stays with that woman, even if he does show some signs of improving, that child will have no chance in life."

A knock on the door drew them around.

"Now what?" Patrick grumbled. He grabbed up a kerosene lamp that sat on a table in the corridor. "If it's Mary Jane, she'd better be too afraid to walk on into our home after being gone all day, only the good Lord knows where. I have a notion just to ignore her, lock the door and force her to stay outside all night. Let her see how it feels to be abandoned, for that's how she treats her son. She didn't as much as tell him goodbye before leavin' the house. Scottie told me so. Tears fell from his eyes as he confessed that."

"Mercy, mercy," Scarlett said, using the word her mother had always used when she found something or someone beneath contempt.

She followed her father to the door.

When he opened it, they found Jason, their youthful stable hand, standing there, a look of concern on his long, narrow face.

"What is it, Jason?" Patrick asked, raising an eyebrow. "You should've left for your home by now. What's delayin' you?"

"I couldn't leave until I found out what happened to the missing horse," Jason said, looking nervously from Patrick to Scarlett, as Scarlett stepped up to her father's right side and they went out onto the porch.

"What do you mean by 'missing'?" Patrick asked, his jaw tightening again. "What horse? How on earth did it come up missing? Weren't you there today tendin' to the horses? You surely would've seen the horse stray from the property."

"All I know is that one of your most prized horses is gone and I have no idea where," Jason gulped out as he nervously wrung his hands. "Except . . ."

"Except what?" Patrick demanded. "Spit it out, Jason. I don't have all night to stand here jawin' whilst one of my . . . or should I say, my daughter's horses is missin'. Most do belong to her, you know. My interest is only in havin' one to ride to the office each day, nothing more."

Before Jason had the chance to speak

again, Patrick glared past him at the stable. "Mary Jane must've taken it," he said tightly. "If she did and she sells it for money, I'll be out for more'n her hide."

Scarlett stood there, speechless over what she had just heard — that someone had as good as stolen one of her horses!

And to think that Mary Jane had the nerve . . . ?

No. Scarlett wouldn't think the worst until she was certain. That woman had already caused enough strain in the family. Oh, surely she wouldn't be brazen enough to steal one of Scarlett's horses!

"No, the woman didn't take the horse," Jason said solemnly. "I saw it a short while ago, and the woman has been gone most of the day. So someone must have sneaked up and stolen it while I was away doing something else. But . . ."

"But?" Patrick almost shouted.

"That woman . . . that Mary Jane . . . *did* take a less valuable horse when she left," Jason blurted out. "I discovered it gone at almost the same time I found the black stallion missing." He looked toward the floor. "I knew you were asking about the lady's whereabouts earlier. I should've told you I saw her leave, but by then I already knew about the other missing horse and was afraid to tell you. I feared for my job."

"Then there are two missing horses?" Scarlett gasped out.

Suddenly they were all aware of the sound of hoofbeats. The moon's glow soon revealed two Indians on horseback, with another horse trailing along behind them on a rope.

"Why, there's *one* of the missing horses," Jason cried, his eyes wide as the two Indians came closer and closer, the lamplight now falling on their faces, revealing who they were.

Scarlett could hardly believe her eyes when she quickly recognized one of the two Indians.

Oh, how could she ever forget anyone as handsome as this Indian?

And he wasn't just any Indian. He was a chief!

He was Chief Hawke, of the neighboring Caddo tribe.

The first time she had seen him, he had stolen her breath away. This second time she was no less affected by him.

She awaited his arrival at the house, wondering why he should be there.

Then she knew.

She recognized the horse trailing behind Chief Hawke and the other warrior.

It was her very own stallion, the one that Jason had reported missing.

Hawke's spine stiffened when he saw people on the porch of the huge ranch house. He was close enough now to see the faces, and his heart skipped a beat when he saw that one of them was the flame-haired woman he had come upon during the deer hunt.

How could he ever forget her? Her face was one of perfection, as was her body!

And even under the dim lights of moon and lamp, he could still see the flame color of her hair.

He could even now recall how it had blown in the wind, long and thick, as she rode her horse earlier that day.

He hated having to reveal to her that his brother was a horse thief. He hoped the news would not make her think less of Hawke, himself.

Surely he would not be blamed for the actions of a brother who had gone astray one time too often.

"Chief Hawke," Patrick said, then glowered at the Indian who rode beside him. "And look who else is here — none other than Fast Deer. Scarlett, Fast Deer is the troublemaker I told you about. He's Chief Hawke's brother. That redskin Fast Deer has become a thorn in my side and it pierces deeper tonight, it seems. That's your horse, Scarlett, trailing behind the Indians. I'm certain Fast Deer stole it, not Chief Hawke."

"Yes, that's my horse, alright," Scarlett murmured. She could hardly concentrate on anything but the handsome Indian chief, whose eyes had never left her as he rode closer and closer. She knew that he recognized her, as well.

She wondered why he was staring at her in such a way. Could it be because he was as taken by her as she was by him? No man had ever created such feelings inside her as this Indian was arousing. She felt a strange sweet fluttering in the pit of her stomach. Her knees even seemed rubbery, as though they might buckle at any moment.

She forced her emotions under control as the two Indians drew a tight rein close to the porch.

Hawke moved his eyes away from the fascinating woman and instead met the gaze of the man he now recognized as the sheriff of Coral Creek.

It angered Hawke all over again that his brother had been so foolish. That one act of thievery could cause a strain between his Caddo people and the new sheriff that might never be healed.

But he *must* make certain that a friendship with this sheriff was made and kept, not only for the sake of his people but for his own needs as well. Hawke had never become infatuated with a woman the way he was with this flame-haired beauty. Up until now, he had guarded his feelings well.

Hawke dismounted. He walked up to the steps and held out a hand of friendship.

"I come tonight, as chief of the Cougar Clan, to make right something my brother has done today," he said thickly. "He wrongly took one of your horses. He brings it back tonight with apologies."

Scarlett was struck by this man's genuine goodness and how he had humbled himself tonight to come to them after his brother had committed such a crime as horse stealing. That was an offense that usually led the thief straight to the hangman's noose.

She grimaced at the thought of the gallows her father had had erected only one day after his arrival in Coral Creek. He was a man of determination. He felt the need to show the town's citizens that he took his appointed job very seriously.

But these men who had come tonight weren't citizens of Coral Creek, they were Indians.

She glanced quickly at her father, who seemed as dumbstruck as she over what was happening.

She saw his eyes dart to Fast Deer with pure contempt in their depths, but his expression changed when he looked back at the Caddo chief.

She held her breath as her father walked down the steps and stood before Hawke. "Chief Hawke, I accept your apology," he said thickly. "I have never met anyone who knows you who has not spoken of your honesty and kindness."

Then he slid his gaze toward Fast Deer again. "But I must admit to you that no one has such kind words for your brother," he said, his voice drawn.

"He is a man whom even I, his brother, do not understand," Hawke said, turning to look at Fast Deer, who had yet to dismount. Instead, his head was lowered and he seemed ready to pass out as his body swayed in the saddle.

Hawke knew that his brother was still quite disgustingly drunk.

He looked at Patrick again. "My brother's mind was gone from him today," he said sadly. "He enjoys firewater too much. His belly is filled with it tonight. He was not thinking clearly when he chose to steal a horse."

"I know that your brother enjoys drinking and gambling too much," Patrick said, nodding. "But I did not hear that he is a horse thief."

"My brother is many things when he fills his belly with firewater," Hawke said. "He is a horse thief tonight, but he has brought the steed back to you. I hope that you will accept it along with an apology. I swear that my brother will never do anything like this again."

"You do know that most horse thieves are hanged for their crimes, don't you?" Patrick said, placing his fists on his hips. "I have the power to order your brother's hanging since I am Coral Creek's sheriff."

"*Huh,* I understand that you are sheriff, and the powers that go with that title," Hawke said tightly, afraid that he might have stepped into a hornets' nest. "I do know this, and if you must sentence him, I will accept it. But I would be sad at heart, not only over my brother's death, but because honesty tonight was ignored."

Patrick kneaded his chin.

Scarlett's heart raced as she awaited her father's response. She knew how much he hated horse thieves.

She gazed from Chief Hawke to his

brother, and then looked at her father. She was relieved when she saw that her father seemed ready to forgive.

"Yes, honesty is always admired, and tonight it will be rewarded," Patrick said. "But I warn you that there cannot be a second time. If Fast Deer steals from us again, or anyone else, he will die with a noose around his neck."

"I thank you for your generosity and forgiveness tonight," Hawke said.

He went to Fast Deer, determined that his brother would apologize. "It is time for you to return the stolen horse to its rightful owner," he said. "Dismount, brother. Do what you must. It is necessary."

Seeming not to comprehend what was being said, Fast Deer still sat in his saddle, slowly swaying back and forth.

"Now, little brother," Hawke said firmly. "*Namiso,* hurry. Dismount now. *Mea,* go. Take the horse to its rightful owner now!"

"That person is my daughter," Patrick said, turning and gesturing toward Scarlett. "Come, daughter. Your horse is being returned to you."

Scarlett still could hardly control her rapid heartbeat and prayed that her feet would carry her from the porch.

She could not drag her gaze away from

Hawke. He was a striking man of great beauty and commanding appearance. She dared not look down, for he wore only a brief breechclout!

She was not only impressed by his looks, but also by the fact that he was obviously a very honest man. She saw courage in his actions tonight, for anyone who stole horses was liable to be hanged.

"Scarlett?" Patrick said, reaching a hand out for her. "Come on, Scarlett."

Feeling foolish, Scarlett shook herself out of her reverie and hurried down the steps just as Fast Deer finally brought the horse to her and handed her the reins.

"I am sorry," Fast Deer stammered, his eyes glassy. "I will never do such a thing again. I . . . I . . . offer you my apology. It is sincere."

"I can tell that it is. Your apology is accepted," Scarlett murmured as she took the stallion's reins. "Thank you for returning my horse. It is truly appreciated."

"Thank you for your kindness," Fast Deer said, smiling drunkenly at Scarlett. Then he turned and mounted his horse, but only after a struggle to get into the saddle.

Before Hawke mounted his own steed, he took one more look at Scarlett.

His heart skipped a beat when their eyes met and held. He saw something in the woman's eyes that told him she would be more than just a passing acquaintance.

He wanted this woman!

He truly believed that she wanted him.

Patrick saw the exchange, and the looks of appreciation in both his daughter's and the Indian's eyes. He stepped between them, blocking their view of one another.

"Do not tempt fate here," he said tightly, his arms folded across his chest. "Chief Hawke, you had better leave while you can. Never look at my daughter again in such a way, or it will be you who will hang!"

Hawke didn't like being threatened. He stared at Patrick, then wheeled his horse around and rode away with his brother at his side.

Scarlett was stunned by what her father had said. She was humiliated by it, as well as angry. Chief Hawke had done nothing to deserve such a tongue-lashing. Yes, he had gazed into Scarlett's eyes with appreciation, as she had gazed into his. But that was all.

For now, she thought to herself, for she knew that she would come face to face with Hawke again, no matter what her father said, or thought, about it!

She started to walk back inside the house but was stopped when her father grabbed her by the wrist. "Forget that chief," he said in a cold, flat voice — a voice of authority that Scarlett did not like. It was as though he were talking to one of his jail inmates!

Well, she was far from that. She was his daughter, a woman who took orders from no one.

She started to ask him if he truly meant to be so harsh, for she was not used to being talked to like that by her father, a man she adored.

But she didn't get the chance. She turned quickly when Mary Jane came riding up the path on a horse in the other direction from that which Hawke and his brother had just taken. She was on the other horse that had been taken from the stable.

Scarlett winced when she saw that Mary Jane was as unsteady in the saddle as Fast Deer had been. A moment later, she fell to the ground.

Patrick rushed to her. He leaned over her. He could smell something unfamiliar about her, but there was one thing he was certain about. She was drunk!

He gazed up at Scarlett. "This woman is

obviously looped," he said tightly. "But the smell on her breath is different from alcohol. I just can't recognize what it is."

He lifted Mary Jane in his arms and carried her past Scarlett. "The wench," he grumbled. "I can't wait until the day I'll never have to bother with her again. I'm afraid this is just the beginning of the trouble she's going to bring into our lives. I hope Scottie gets well quickly, or else . . ."

Scarlett didn't follow him when he went inside the house with Mary Jane still in his arms. She chose to stay outside for a moment longer.

She looked in the direction that Hawke and his brother had disappeared.

No.

She would not heed her father's warnings. She must see this handsome chief again. She must!

She was mesmerized by him.

She had never been affected by any man like this before. She had to understand why.

Chapter Eight

Needing to get away from the tension at the ranch, now that Mary Jane was a part of the household, Scarlett set out the following morning on Lightning. Before long, she found herself once again near the gulf.

She passed through a stand of timber some hundred yards in width, forded a creek that also had the beautiful coral pebbles at the bottom, then rode up a steep embankment so that she could rest atop a bluff before venturing onward.

She was hoping to find the Caddo village, but she had no idea where it was.

She had not asked.

She knew that would be the last place her father would want her to be.

And now that she was near the gulf, she had something else on her mind. She recalled having seen a ship not far from shore when she was out riding yesterday.

She wondered if she might see it again today.

She wondered if it had made it safely to shore. She recalled that its sails had been ripped and torn, and that the ship had wallowed in the water instead of gliding quickly through it.

She had been fascinated to see a black flag with a white painting of a skull and bones on it flying high on the ship, reminding her of tales she had read about pirates.

It was exciting, yet scary, to think that perhaps there were still pirates out there somewhere, plundering and taking prizes back to their ships.

As she reached the edge of the bluff, she drew rein. She gasped when she saw just below her, hidden in a cove, the very ship she had just been wondering about.

She knew that it was the same because she had noticed the name painted on its side: *Eclipse*.

Its sails were lowered. The strange skull-and-bones flag was nowhere in sight.

She saw men rowing back and forth between ship and shore in longboats, and others cutting trees and taking logs to the ship.

Too interested in what was going on down below to travel onward, Scarlett dismounted and stepped closer to the edge of the bluff. She stared at the men who were chopping down trees below her.

She gasped when she saw that they were dressed in what she thought of as pirate garb: wide-topped black boots, brightly colored breeches and flowing, loose white cambric shirts. They wore short sabers, or manchettes, held within leather scabbards at the right side and pistols at the left.

They were all scruffy, dirty, and unshaven, with greasy-looking hair clinging around their shoulders.

"Surely they *are* pirates," she whispered to herself. "Right out of a storybook!"

Suddenly she heard a noise behind her.

Afraid that it might be one of the men from the ship who'd seen her climb to the bluff, she drew her tiny pistol from her right pocket and swung around to face whoever might be there.

But in her fear, she moved clumsily and tripped. Her finger slipped on the trigger, accidentally firing the pistol.

Her eyes widened and her heart skipped a nervous beat when she saw a red-bearded man dressed in an elegant brocaded waistcoat and black leather breeches. He grabbed at his right leg as blood streamed through his fingers.

"Damn ye, ye shot me!" Blue Raven shouted. "Why, lassie? I meant ye no 'arm."

She was stunned not only by what she had done, but also by being in the company of someone who was the very image of the pirates she had seen in picture books. His red hair fell long past his shoulders, his beaked nose seemed to push through his thick red beard, and he wore the same sort of weapons as the men below. Scarlett stood frozen to the ground.

The men! she thought, knowing they must have heard the report of her gun. Soon she would be accosted by more than one man . . . more than one pirate!

And she was right. Before she had the chance to explain herself, several of the men she had seen felling trees came running, some with manchettes drawn, others with pistols.

"Drop yer firearm," Blue Raven said, glowering at Scarlett. "Drop it now or die!"

Trembling, her eyes wide and wild, Scarlett did as he demanded, then watched as the men drew closer to the pirate who seemed in charge. One of them fell to his knees and inspected the wound she had accidentally inflicted.

"Grab 'er, men," Blue Raven growled out. "She shot me! Take 'er to the ship. Throw 'er in the brig. Chain 'er to the wall. She looks like she might be from a rich family. She'll be worth a lot of money if I choose to use 'er for ransom."

"Ransom?" Scarlett gulped out.

Horrified and scared, but not too scared to fight the men as they approached, she clawed them with her fingernails and kicked at them, but all to no avail. She was finally grabbed and hauled down the hillside, where she was thrown into one of the longboats.

After her wrists were tied behind her, and the rope was tied to the side of the boat, she was rowed to the ship by two of the men. There, she soon found herself shackled to the wall in a barred cell.

Her heart pounding, Scarlett gazed around her. The place was filthy. It reeked of rot and mildew . . . and rats.

Scarlett screamed when a rat scurried across the floor, then disappeared beneath a pile of chains and debris.

Then Scarlett's heart seemed to stop inside her chest when the injured pirate limped into the room, his wounded leg already wrapped. She trembled as the man came close to her.

"Ye'll get yer due, ye will," he snarled in her face. "Don't ye know that ye are in the presence of the great pirate Blue Raven, kin to the famed Bluebeard?"

He gazed into her eyes for a moment longer, then stepped away and raked his gaze slowly over her, smiling mischievously. "Ye are a perfect specimen of a woman, ye are," he said, kneading his red beard. "Ye'll be missed by someone, that's for certain."

Laughing menacingly, he limped from the cell, hung the ring of keys on a peg on the wall, then returned and spoke into her face once again. "I'm leavin' ye alone for now, but not for long," he said, his eyes again traveling slowly over her. "Lovely wench ye are. Aye, a lovely, red-headed wench.

"Ye are a perfect match for this old pirate, ye are," he said, smiling crookedly. "It would be a waste to use ye for ransom. I just might keep ye for meself!"

"You are a loony bird . . . crazy, especially if you think I'll ever let you lay a hand on me," Scarlett said, then laughed at him. "Never. Do you hear? Never!"

Blue Raven glared at her. "No one calls Blue Raven loony and lives to tell it," he snarled out. "Except perhaps ye, pretty wench. I have plans for ye, I do."

He took a step away from her. "No one is to touch 'er," he shouted to the men who had followed him to her cell. "She's mine, do ye hear? I want 'er fresh and clean!"

He looked her slowly up and down again. "Aye, ye look like a woman who's untouched as yet," he said, again in a snarl. "That's good. That's the way I likes me women."

He limped away, groaning with the effort that it took to move his injured leg. Scarlett was left all alone in that terrible place as the other men followed the older pirate up the steep steps.

Scarlett looked around desperately for a way to escape.

Lord, no one knew that she was there.

She was doomed.

Yet there might be a chance.

Her pulse racing, she gazed at the open cell door, and then at the keys that hung nearby on a peg on the wall. Escape was just a few footsteps away if only she could get free of her bonds.

Yet as she tried to work her wrists free, all she succeeded in doing was making her skin raw.

After years of being adventurous, surely this was the worst fix she'd ever been in.

If that man who called himself a pirate intended to rape her, what could she do about it?

She no longer had her pistol.

If he did come for her and take her to his cabin, she would take advantage of that one chance to escape. She could play along with him, make him think that she was interested in making love with him, and then when he let his guard down, she would do more than shoot him in the leg this time! She would grab one of his weapons and . . .

The thought of actually killing someone made Scarlett feel suddenly sick to her stomach.

"I doubt that I could," she whispered, tears spilling from her eyes.

But if she didn't, how else could she ever be free of this crazed man's clutches?

"I must, I must . . ." she kept whispering to herself as she watched rats playing on the floor not far from where her feet rested on the rotted-looking wood.

When she heard a sudden hammering, she grew cold inside. The ship had no doubt anchored close to land because it needed repairs. Once they were made, the ship would return to the high seas! If she was still aboard it, her life would never be the same again.

Dying inside, she dropped her head and cried.

Chapter Nine

Hawke was numb as he stood on a bluff where he had a full view of the ship moored a short distance from the shore down below. He had been riding alone, searching again for his brother, who had once more lied to him.

When Hawke had awakened, he had discovered that Fast Deer had left the village even though he had promised not to leave without telling Hawke where he was going.

This would be the last time his brother let him down.

Huh, when Hawke found Fast Deer, he would make his brother stand before the entire council and then he would banish him.

Considering all of the trouble that Fast Deer was brewing, Hawke knew his warriors would approve of the banishment. In fact, Hawke expected them to strongly encourage it.

But at this moment his brother was not the most important thing on Hawke's mind.

As he was riding from Coral Creek, where he had gone looking for Fast Deer, gunfire had drawn him to this bluff. He had stood upon it, shocked to see what had just happened below him.

He had seen the flame-haired woman, Scarlett, rowed to the ship in a smaller boat. He had watched her being roughly manhandled, and from the way her wrists were tied, he knew that she was taken to the ship as a prisoner.

"I cannot allow her to be harmed," he whispered to himself, his fingers doubled into tight fists at his sides.

He could not deny to himself that she was a part of him now.

She . . . was . . . his destiny!

When he had first seen her standing beside the creek, he had sensed that he'd been drawn there to that spot at that particular time by destiny.

No matter who her father was, the woman was on this earth to marry a proud and powerful Caddo chief — Chief Hawke!

"I must help her," Hawke whispered to himself, watching the activity of the men on the ship, and on the shore.

He could only surmise that the ship was in the process of being repaired.

Knowing that the ship would not depart until the repairs were completed, and also knowing that he was only one man against many, Hawke had no choice but to leave.

He had to return home for help.

He and his warriors must arrive at the ship in force in order to save the woman who was now a part of Hawke's heart.

He turned to Misty and quickly mounted, then rode down from the bluff and set off at a hard gallop toward home.

When he arrived, he called a council and explained what he was asking of his warriors.

This mission had nothing to do with his people, but everything to do with the safety of his woman.

"The woman's life is in mortal danger," Hawke told his warriors. "If we do not arrive quickly enough to free her, she could be taken far out to sea and never seen again."

"Perhaps her father and those who follow him should attack the ship, not we Caddo warriors," one of the warriors suggested. "It is *his* duty, not ours."

"When we see someone helpless and in danger, it is always our duty to attempt a rescue," Hawke argued back. "And let me say this only one time to all of you, my warriors. This is not just any ordinary white woman. She is someone who has a special destiny, and that is to be this chief's woman."

He heard the gasps of disbelief and saw disapproval in his warriors' eyes. He realized the risk he'd taken in admitting such a thing to them, for even if they saved Scarlett, what would it gain him but humiliation in the eyes of his people if she refused to accept him?

Hawke knew that he had no choice but to chance that, for he could not let her be taken away.

If she turned her back on him, so be it. Hawke would live down the embarrassment and disappointment.

All he could think about now was saving her.

"I understand why you are puzzled," Hawke said tightly. "Even I am somewhat puzzled by my feelings. But all I know is that I want this woman at my side as my wife. *Huh,* her skin is white. But she had no control over whose womb she came from, or the color of the skin of her mother and father. I do not see color when I see her. Nor should you."

He looked past his warriors, outside to where the sun had already set. The moon was now creeping up, snow white against the black backdrop of the sky. He knew that the rescue would be best accomplished while the sun's bright eye was sleeping.

He wanted to blend into the night as he and his men approached the ship. He hoped that most of the sailors would be asleep.

"Time is wasting," Hawke said as he walked toward the door. "*Mea,* go. Ready your steeds. Come with me to where the ship rests in waters close to Caddo land. We will leave our horses tethered when we arrive there. We will swim to the vessel."

"Your brother?" one of the other warriors asked, stopping Hawke in mid-step. "What of him? Did you not find him?"

Hawke turned and looked at his warriors, who were standing and ready to follow him outside. "No, and my brother comes second now to the woman," he said, his tone stern.

He looked from man to man, the fire's glow on their faces revealing their disbelief at what they had just heard.

Hawke understood.

They had never seen their chief put a woman ahead of anyone, especially his brother.

But they also understood that he had surely run out of patience with his brother and he would not let Fast Deer's transgressions get in the way of saving the white woman.

Once he was in his saddle and riding away from the village, his men following, Hawke smiled as he recalled Scarlett's father's threats. He wondered if the white man would still speak so harshly to the man who saved his daughter's life.

"It does not matter what he thinks or does, for once I save Scarlett, she *will* be mine!" he whispered to himself, seeing her beautiful face in his mind's eye.

But then that image was supplanted by a vision of the way he had last seen her, with her wrists tied, and being treated roughly by the white men as they rowed her away.

His jaw tightened. "I must save her, and pity anyone who tries to stop me!" he said, this time loudly enough for those who were near him to hear.

He avoided their eyes, riding determinedly onward, his long, thick black hair blowing behind him in the night air.

Chapter Ten

Worn out from a harrowing day at the office, during which he had discovered that his newly appointed deputy was a loser, Patrick walked dejectedly into his home. He had just hired the young man and now had the unpleasant chore of firing him.

And then he would have to start the process of finding someone to replace him.

The bright spot of each evening was his daughter. Although there had been a strain between him and Scarlett of late, since he had brought Mary Jane into their home, he knew that she would soon get over it. Besides, Mary Jane would be gone as soon as Scottie was well enough to travel.

And then be hanged about women! Patrick would never have another one.

He'd learned his lesson the hard way. No one could ever replace his precious Penelope.

Walking down the long corridor to the dining room, where Scarlett would more than likely be awaiting his arrival and concerned about him since he was late coming home this evening, he tried to force a smile to his face. No, he had never brought his troubles home, not when his wife was alive, and not now, when it was only himself and Scarlett.

But he had to remind himself all over again that they no longer had the house to themselves. There *was* that woman and her child.

Patrick would not relax again in his own home until that woman was gone. He cursed the very moment he had decided to advertise for a mail-order bride.

But it would be over soon.

Thank God, Scottie was already showing some signs of improvement. The child was eating better, and he was no longer as listless as before.

The child couldn't get well soon enough to suit Patrick. He just wouldn't be able to tolerate Mary Jane's antics for much longer.

He didn't like having her under the same roof as his family. She could steal him blind, then kill him and Scarlett as they slept!

That thought sent a chill down his spine.

The candles burning in the sconces along the wall lit his way as he hurried into the dining room.

Patrick stopped and stared at the empty table, where no food awaited his arrival. Nor was his daughter seated there.

He then looked quickly at Malvina as she came into the room through the swinging door that led from the kitchen. She was dressed in her usual black attire with its white collar, and her gray hair was arranged in a tight bun atop her head. Wrinkles crisscrossed her heavy jowls, the darkness of her flesh having faded somewhat with age.

His eyebrows rose when he saw that she wasn't bringing food to the table.

Instead, she had stopped just inside the room and stood there now wringing her hands, her eyes filled with fearful concern.

"What's going on here?" Patrick asked as he walked further into the room.

He placed his hands on the back of a chair at the table.

He gazed at the chair where Scarlett usually sat, then questioned Malvina again with his eyes.

"Our Scarlett ain't come back from her ride yet," Malvina said, her voice drawn. "It's way too late, ain't it, Mastah Patrick, for her to still be out there on her horse?"

"Are you saying that Scarlett hasn't been home all day?" Patrick asked, his heart pounding at the prospect of what might have happened to Scarlett.

"No, and nor has that woman Mary Jane," Malvina said, her cheeks becoming flushed with agitation. "Both left at about the same time, Mary Jane just shortly after Scarlett, on one of Scarlett's horses. What do you think, Mastah Patrick? Mightn't they be somewheres together? I've taken care of that child Scottie. He's already eaten and is in bed fo' the night."

Patrick snorted at the thought of his daughter being anywhere with Mary Jane. Scarlett despised the loose woman too much to have anything to do with her.

Then he grew somber again at the knowledge that Scarlett might be in danger.

"What do I think?" he said, running his fingers through his hair. "Damned if I can figure any of this out."

He went to the window and gazed out at the moonlit night, and then toward the stables.

Jason had left already, as soon as Patrick arrived and handed the youngster his horse's reins.

So Patrick couldn't go and ask him about Scarlett. He couldn't care less where Mary Jane was. He hoped that she had chosen to ride on past Coral Creek with plans of never returning.

Yet, on second thought, what if she had done that, leaving him with the responsibility of her ailing child?

"I've got to go and find Scarlett," Patrick blurted out. His daughter came first. He would deal with Mary Jane and Scottie later.

He turned and ran from the room, not stopping until he got to the stables and was on his steed and heading back into Coral Creek. He would go from establishment to establishment, door to door, until he had a huge posse formed.

He had one place in mind to go searching with that posse!

To that damn Caddo chief's village.

He would never forget how Hawke had looked at Scarlett. Patrick had been able to tell that the man was smitten with Scarlett.

What if the chief had found her riding on her horse and had lured her to his village? Patrick felt sure she would have followed him, as a moth is lured into the flames of a fire.

He glared into the moonlit night as he reached a hand to one of his holstered pistols.

Yep, he might have a man for hanging tonight. If that savage had even touched his Scarlett, he would pay.

The lights of the saloons and the one gambling hall in town were twinkling just ahead of him. He urged his horse on, then turned him down the main street of Coral Creek.

When he entered the first saloon, everyone turned to face him as he took up a position in front of the long bar. "I'm in need of several men for a posse," he shouted. "My daughter's missing. Who among you is willin' to go to the Caddo village to see if she's been taken there? I believe Chief Hawke has had a hand in my daughter's disappearance!"

There were gasps in the room at this accusation. No one would have thought that the likable Caddo chief would stoop to such a dark deed as that.

Yet in the heat of the moment, most who sat at the gambling tables and the bar rose quickly and volunteered.

After Patrick had visited every establishment in town, a huge posse rode out of town, heavily armed.

"If you took her, you'll be sorry," Patrick vowed beneath his breath, while seeing the hangman's noose at the back of his jail in his mind's eye.

His eyes took on a menacing glitter.

Chapter Eleven

Dressed immaculately in an elegant brocaded coat and red breeches, his red hair combed back from his face, his beard free of tangles, Blue Raven sat at his dining table awaiting Scarlett's arrival.

His wound was bound up with a fresh, clean bandage, but he was pale and weak from loss of blood.

Eager to be with Scarlett again, and this time alone, Blue Raven had sent for her. He would have supper with her, then have her confined someplace other than the filthy cell.

He couldn't stand the thought of her being in the company of rats any longer.

But he wasn't strong enough yet to bed her. The prospect of that pleasure would hasten his recovery.

Aye, he had decided to keep her, not use her for ransom.

She would be his kitten . . . his queen . . . forever.

"She'll be me wife," he said, his face flushed with the excitement of being alone with her tonight, sharing food and talk with her.

He had been without the company of a lady for too long, and this one was especially beautiful. Surely she was intelligent, too, he thought. The intellectual side of him ached to have a decent conversation with someone who had at least a measure of intelligence.

He nodded as he thought further about his plans for her: She would sail the high seas with him.

Fortunately, his ship wasn't in as bad shape as he had first thought. The repairs were all but done.

His *Eclipse* would head out for the high seas tomorrow.

"I'll take me lady to me island," he said, stroking his beard.

Yes, he'd take her to Pirates' Point. There he had his own castle filled with beautiful trinkets that he had taken from ships — his bounty.

But Scarlett was his best prize of all!

He looked quickly at the door as it opened.

He smiled cunningly as he watched Scarlett fight the two sailors as they dragged her into Blue Raven's cabin.

She kicked at them. She managed to get

one hand free. She clawed one sailor's face until he captured her wrist again.

Blue Raven continued to watch, his eyes gleaming, as she was forced onto a red velvet chair and secured there with her left wrist bound to the arm.

Scarlett glared at Blue Raven. She noticed that he had cleaned himself up. He had on fresh clothes, his hair was neatly combed, and his beard was no longer a tangled mess.

But it was the gleam in his eyes that drew most of her attention. She was afraid of what his plans might be for her later tonight.

Her eyes went to the feast that was spread atop a long oak table. She saw piles of meat on huge platters, bowls of vegetables and sliced fruits.

But the things that held her attention were two jewel-encrusted gold goblets set before her and the man who professed himself to be a pirate. Surely the goblets were worth a great deal of money; she wondered where he had got them.

But everything in the cabin was grand. The walls were lined with red leather, and maroon velvet drapes hung on each side of the small porthole. The cabin was large enough for a good-sized bed, and it was covered with a velvet coverlet that matched the drapes; huge mounds of pillows were thrown across it.

Her cheeks grew hot with a blush, and fear entered her heart. Was he going to feed her, then . . . then . . . seduce her?

She was once more aware of just how helpless she was.

This man, this lunatic, could do anything to her . . . with her . . . and no one would ever know, for she doubted that he would ever release her.

She was a true captive, the captive of a madman!

"Good evenin', me lady," Blue Raven said as he sat across the table from her. He gazed at one of his sailors. "Pour 'er some port. Then pour me some, as well."

He leaned across the table and gazed directly into Scarlett's eyes. "Me best port for the most beautiful lady in the world," he said, his eyes twinkling.

"I don't want your port, or anything from you but my freedom," Scarlett said, her eyes narrowing angrily. "My father surely has a posse out looking for my abductor by now. When he sees this ship, he'll realize it's you."

"Me ship is hidden well enough in this cove," Blue Raven said, waving the two sailors from the room. "Ye only found it by chance."

"My father will search everywhere for me," Scarlett said, her chin rising proudly. "My father is the sheriff of Coral Creek. He's known for hanging those who are guilty of such crimes as abduction."

"Yer father is a sheriff, eh?" Blue Raven said, leaning back against his chair. "Is that s'posed to frighten this old pirate?" He laughed sarcastically. "Nothin' scares me . . . nothin'," he said haughtily.

He took a drink of wine, then set his goblet back down on the table. "Drink up, me lady," he said, reaching over and shoving her goblet closer to her. "Ye'll relax more and accept yer fate much better."

"I don't want your wine," Scarlett said from between clenched teeth, but took up the goblet anyway.

But she hadn't lifted it to drink from it. Instead, she threw the wine into the old pirate's face.

This elicited a growl from him as he reached for a napkin and wiped his face clean.

Then he leaned across the table toward her again, a scowl on his face, as some wine dripped from his beard. "Ye've assaulted me twice now," he growled out. "First with a gun, and now with me finest port. If you try a third time, I'll slit yer throat and toss ye overboard out at sea where sharks'll feast on yer flesh."

Realizing that he was surely capable of carrying off such a threat, Scarlett shrank back in her chair and clamped her lips tightly together.

"We can talk some more, or eat and then talk, whatever is to yer likin', fair one," he said, his voice softening as he leaned back in his chair. He placed his ring-filled fingers together before him. "What is it to be? Food or talk?"

"I want neither," Scarlett said, lying about the food, for she was starved. "I . . . I . . . just want my freedom."

"Ye're a fool, ye are," Blue Raven said, grabbing his goblet and taking another deep swallow of the wine.

Then he set it down on the table again. "Well, seems I'll do some talkin' to acquaint ye with me, and then we'll eat," he said, nodding.

Knowing that she had no choice but to do as he wished, Scarlett sighed heavily and listened.

"When ye're me wife, I promise ye many trinkets to please ye," he said, smiling at her. "I've many a pretty thing for ye. I made me money first by being a merchant seaman. Even then me and me crew plundered the cargoes of many a ship as we roamed the seas.

"It was then that I knew me destiny was to follow in the footsteps of me famous pirate relation Bluebeard," he said, chuckling. "And I've done fine at it, too. But no pirate ever has enough gold. Me and me crew were on our way to the gold fields of California. There I planned to add to me wealth. But me ship was forced to come to land by a crippling gale. We've all but finished the repairs now, so I plan to leave tomorrow. But now that I have ye to consider, I will point me ship back toward me island, not the gold fields, for ye are prize enough for this ol' pirate."

"You'll not get anywhere with me," Scarlett said sourly. "My father will find me before you set sail. You'll wish you never laid eyes on me."

"Me cannons will hold back anyone who tries to take ye from me," Blue Raven growled. "So just prepare yerself for bein' me bride. Ye have no choice but to accept the life I plan to hand ye."

He nodded toward the food. "Eat now, and then ye will be taken to a cabin instead of the brig," he said thickly. "Eat up now. Me bones and me wound ache. Sleep is what I crave, not lovin'."

When she still didn't pick up her fork to eat, he slammed a fist down on the table, causing the dishes to leap up, then fall back down on the table. "Eat," he shouted. "When I give orders, they are obeyed."

Suddenly truly afraid of him, Scarlett began eating, all the while keeping a nervous eye on him.

"Aye, me whole family were famous pirates," he said, nodding, his temper cooled. "I plan to be as famous as Bluebeard. Not even yer bullet could stop me." He chuckled throatily. "I have nine lives like a cat, don't ye know?"

His crazed laughter made Scarlett wince, and she dropped her fork.

But when he quickly sobered and glared at her again, she quickly picked the fork up and continued eating.

She was glad of one thing. She was glad that he felt too weak to seduce her.

He suddenly yawned. He looked toward the door. "Come in here, ye blokes!" he shouted, and two men hurried into the cabin. "I need to go to bed. Take 'er to the cabin that's been prepared for 'er. See that she's comfortable."

He leaned forward and glared at the men as one of them loosened the rope binding her to the chair. "She's mine," he snarled. "Don't ye forget that."

Scarlett was led from the cabin and taken to one right next to Blue Raven's. She was surprised by how lovely it was, with its own huge bed covered by a quilted comforter, and a dresser that held pretty perfume bottles and other toiletries.

She was so glad when the rope was removed from her wrist.

Before she could thank the two sailors, they were gone, and her heart sank when she heard them lock her in from the outside.

Trembling, she went to the porthole. To her despair, it was far too small to crawl through, even if she were able to break the glass.

She had no choice but to go to bed, for she was exhausted. But she doubted she could actually fall asleep. Every sound alarmed her. She was so afraid that Blue Raven would change his mind and come and. . . .

She shuddered at the thought of being in bed with such a scoundrel as he!

Chapter Twelve

Patrick placed a hand on one of his holstered pistols while holding his horse's reins with the other as he rode with the posse into the Caddo Indian village.

His spine stiffened when several of the Caddo people's strange-looking Jubine dogs snarled and barked. Some leapt toward him and his posse, yet none of them actually made contact with the horses or men. The dogs fell back just in time as though they sensed they would be shot if they got closer.

With the aid of the brilliant light of the moon, and the huge outdoor fire that burned in the center of the village, Patrick could see mothers rushing to children and pulling them into their homes. Only the elderly men remained, sitting on mats close to the fire, the bowls of their colorful, feather-decorated, long-stemmed pipes resting on their knees.

Those old men's eyes watched each and every movement of the horses and the white men riding them as they came further into the village. Patrick rode toward the huge, dome-shaped council house that sat some distance from the fire. Patrick had not been in the village before, but he had been in others and recognized a council house when he saw one.

As he continued to make his way there, he noticed some warriors standing at the doors of their lodges, long-barreled rifles in hand, their eyes glittering with suspicion.

These warriors left their lodges and began walking toward Patrick and his posse of men, soon stepping in their way and halting their progress.

Patrick and the others drew rein, Patrick pulling slightly ahead to show the warriors who was in charge of the posse.

He saw no Indian that he recognized, for most stayed mainly within their village. They only came into Coral Creek to trade at the post, which sat at the far end of the main street of Coral Creek.

Since none had ever caused any trouble, Patrick had not yet met them.

It was at this moment that he wished he had. He would like to have at least one warrior whom he could talk to, man to man, especially now because he didn't see Chief Hawke among them.

It was apparent that he was gone. As

chief, he would have been the first to make himself known to the posse.

"What do you want here?" White Horse asked as he stepped closer to Patrick, whom he recognized as the sheriff. He had seen him standing at the door of his office in Coral Creek, with the badge on his shirt.

Thus far, there had been no reason for White Horse to be introduced to him.

Not until now.

And White Horse wanted no introductions. He just wanted to know the reason why this man had brought so many white men into the village and why they were so heavily armed. He wanted them to leave soon, for White Horse knew the children must be terrified.

"We are here for only one reason," Patrick said, his eyes holding White Horse's. "I'm looking for my daughter. Her name is Scarlett, but I'm sure you already know that."

He looked past White Horse and scanned each individual lodge. Then he gazed down at the warrior again.

"And why would you think your daughter is here?" White Horse asked, his pulse suddenly racing at the mention of that woman's name. She was the reason his chief was not in the village.

But he would not allow this lawman to know that, or know where his chief was, or why. Although White Horse was one of those who questioned whether his chief should become involved with the woman, he would not voice this doubt aloud, especially to white men . . . especially to the woman's lawman father!

His chief had made a decision. White Horse and everyone else supported him in it. Chief Hawke had taken with him only enough warriors to rescue the woman.

The rest remained to protect the village and their families.

Patrick dismounted after sliding his rifle into the gun boot at the side of his saddle. He knew that if he was ever to find his daughter, he had to deal with these Indians as peacefully as possible.

"Why?" he echoed, standing beside his horse. "Because your chief paid extra attention to my Scarlett when he came to my ranch last night, that's why."

He frowned at White Horse. "And now my daughter is missing," he said between clenched teeth.

"Have you come to my village with accusations against my chief?" White Horse said, his hand tightening around his rifle.

"All I want is to see whether my daughter is here or not," Patrick said. Out of the corner of his eye he noticed more warriors coming slowly out of the doors of their lodges.

He suddenly felt trapped.

He gave a quick look over his shoulder at the posse, gave the men a wink, which had been agreed upon as a signal to raise their firearms, then quickly yanked his own rifle from the gun boot.

As his men held the warriors at bay, Patrick pointed his rifle at White Horse's belly. He was glad that his men had been quicker than White Horse's, for none of the Indians had had the chance to raise their firearms before they found rifles aimed at them.

"Drop your rifle," Patrick flatly ordered, seeing the seething anger in White Horse's midnight-dark eyes. "Tell the other warriors to also drop theirs. I don't want any trouble here. All I want is to see if my daughter is in your village."

"She is not, and you risk much by aiming your firearms at we Caddo warriors," White Horse growled. "You are on land of the Caddo now, not the white man."

"I know exactly where I am, and why,"

Patrick said flatly. "Now drop your guns and tell the others to drop theirs. Pronto."

Patrick leaned his face closer to White Horse's. "Your name?" he asked bluntly.

White Horse glared into Patrick's eyes, then knew he had no choice but to drop his rifle. Nonetheless, he would not give this white lawman the satisfaction of knowing his name.

"My brethren, disarm yourselves," White Horse shouted to his warriors. As Hawke's cousin, he was second in command at the village.

"That's more like it," Patrick said, squaring his shoulders and leaning away from the warrior who refused to give him his name.

"If you bring more than threats into this village, you will pay later," White Horse said, his arms folded across his bare chest.

"Like I said, all I want is my daughter," Patrick repeated, again looking past the warrior and at each of the lodges.

Then he gazed into the warrior's eyes once more. "Where is your chief?" he asked tightly.

White Horse's lips clamped together tightly, for he was not about to respond to that question. His chief's life was in danger if this lawman knew of his connection with his daughter, even though Hawke was risking his own life to save the woman.

It was up to Chief Hawke to explain to this white man why he cared enough to save his daughter.

Patrick's face grew flushed when the warrior did not respond.

"If you won't cooperate, then I have no choice but to check all of your lodges to see if my daughter has been brought here as a captive," Patrick said, nodding over his shoulder to the men of his posse.

They had made plans while traveling to the village. Four men had been chosen to search the lodges if that were to become necessary.

Those four men dismounted, and with their rifles clutched in their hands, they went from one lodge to another, ignoring the wails of the children who were frightened by the intrusion.

"Be sure to search the council house. Check whether there is any place inside it that could be used for hiding someone," Patrick shouted at the men.

He stood his ground and kept a close eye on the warrior who stood before him.

When one of the searchers came out of the council house and shook his head, silently telling Patrick that no one was in there, Patrick's heart plunged, for it was becoming obvious that Scarlett wasn't in the village.

Then another thought came to him, and it made his heart skip a beat. Perhaps the chief had ambushed Scarlett and was holding her hostage in a hiding place elsewhere.

"I should apologize for having come here like this, interrupting your evening with accusations, but I cannot apologize just yet, not until I know your chief isn't holding Scarlett somewhere else," Patrick said tightly.

"He is not with the woman," White Horse said, hating the lie, for he was not a man of deceit, but knowing he had to protect his chief in whatever way he could.

And just perhaps his chief, at this moment, was not with the woman, at least not yet, so it would not be a lie.

"Where is he?" Patrick asked, searching the warrior's eyes to see if he was lying.

"He and others are on their way to a place where there are many deer," White Horse said, making up a story as it came to him. "Early in the morning is the best time to hunt. My chief awaits dawn and then will hunt and bring home a prime catch."

When he saw that the white man did not

totally believe his lie, White Horse continued to expand upon it.

"Have you heard of the white deer in this area?" he said quickly, seeing a sudden keen interest enter the lawman's eyes.

"No, I haven't," Patrick said, unknowingly lowering his rifle. "Is there such a deer in the area?"

"*Huh,* there is," White Horse said, finding it easy now to make conversation with this white man. "My chief, who is my first cousin, hungers to have the deer. One day Chief Hawke will bring home the prized pelt."

"I would like to see it when he does," Patrick said, suddenly realizing that he was conversing easily with this Indian, and beginning to believe that Chief Hawke had had nothing to do with his daughter's disappearance.

"You are not a hunter?" White Horse asked.

"No . . . well, yes, maybe I am, but not for animals," Patrick said, slowly smiling. "My interest only lies in hunting down humans who need to be caught and jailed."

"It is good that you do not wish to hunt the white deer yourself, for I would feel as though I betrayed my chief by drawing your interest to the white deer," White Horse said.

"No, no need to worry about having betrayed your chief about the deer," Patrick said. He looked over his shoulder at the posse. "Men, I'm convinced that Scarlett is not here. Let's head out. We'll search elsewhere."

He looked at the warrior again. He extended a hand. "Sorry about tonight," he said sincerely. "But when it comes to my daughter, I'd go to hell and back to find her."

White Horse hesitated, then shook Patrick's hand. "I, too, have a daughter," he said quietly. "If she were missing, I would also do what I must to find her."

"Thank you," Patrick said. Then he shoved his rifle into the gun boot again and swung himself into his saddle.

The Caddo women and children slowly came from their lodges as Patrick rode from the village with the posse.

When they were quite a distance from the village, Patrick drew rein and turned to gaze at his men. "I truly don't know where else to search," he said, his voice breaking. "Do any of you have any ideas?"

"I hate to say this, but perhaps some drifter came along and saw Scarlett. Perhaps he grabbed her up and forced her to go with him," Ray Strupp said tightly.

Patrick paled. "Lord a' mighty," he gasped. "Why didn't she listen to me about being careful? Lord, Lord."

He raised his chin and gazed at the men again. "We'll search some more, and then if we still don't find Scarlett, we'll disband until morning," he said. "If we don't find her tonight, perhaps we will tomorrow. I've done a lot of tracking in my day. When it's daylight, I'll try my luck at it again."

Suddenly they were aware of a horse approaching in the dark.

"Draw your guns," Patrick said, only loud enough for the men to hear. "We just might have come across the culprit who took my daughter."

The horse came closer and closer, and then Patrick's heart sank when he saw what horse it was, and that its saddle was empty.

"It's Scarlett's," Patrick choked out. "It's . . . it's . . . Lightning!"

He rode up to the horse and grabbed its reins, then dismounted. He walked slowly around the horse. He studied it for any signs of blood, and when he saw none, ran his hands down the horse's neck.

"If only you could talk," he said softly.

Lightning whinnied, then nuzzled Patrick's hand as he held it out to him.

"Yes, if only you could talk," Patrick mumbled, slowly shaking his head back and forth.

Chapter Thirteen

The moon was hidden by clouds as Hawke and his warriors arrived at the bluff that overlooked the cove where the ship was moored.

Hawke's spine stiffened when he saw the activity just below him, on shore. Several white men were loading equipment into boats.

From what he could tell, the men were putting in everything that he had seen them using to cut down the trees. Did this mean that the ship would soon leave?

If so, Scarlett would leave with it, for he doubted that the red-bearded man had brought her back to land. He had abducted her.

Hawke quickly dismounted, as did his warriors. They secured their horses.

He grabbed his rifle from its gun boot as his men circled around him.

"*Kee-mah,* come. We must move in haste," he said, only loud enough for them to hear. "From what I have seen, it appears that the ship is preparing for departure. We cannot allow that. The woman is surely still on board, as the red-bearded man's captive."

"Chief, what do you want us to do?" Bent Arrow asked, his jaw tight. "Tell us. It will be done."

Hawke turned and walked to the edge of the bluff. He peered downward. The men that he had seen loading the smaller boats were still there, but they would not be for long.

He turned back to his men. "We must hurry down from the bluff and quickly disable all of the white men on shore. If necessary, use your knives to kill them. Then we shall swim to the ship and overcome the men we find there, all but one, who will lead me to Scarlett," he said. He gazed at the rifles in each of their hands.

"We cannot take these weapons with us, for we will not be able to swim with them," he said tightly. "Secure your rifles on your steeds. You must depend on the knives sheathed at your sides."

"How will we knock the white men out if not with the blunt end of our rifles?" Bent Arrow asked.

"We will each choose a good-sized stone as soon as we reach the embankment," he said, already sliding his rifle into his gun boot. His men quickly followed his lead.

Then they all gathered around Hawke again, their right hands resting on the knives sheathed at their sides.

"We must hurry," he said. "We must save the woman, and then return to our steeds and take her quickly away from this place."

His warriors nodded.

They all made their way down from the bluff, then moved cautiously and stealthily along the rocky shore.

Making certain not to be seen or heard by the white men, the warriors each chose a stone, and working as though they were of one body, one mind and one strength, they quickly subdued the pirates.

"Secure your knives and swim with me to the ship," Hawke said, his eyes following the movement on the top deck.

Luckily, the moon was still hidden behind clouds, making it hard for the white men to see anything on shore. They would never see those who would be making their way toward their ship.

"Why do we not use the boats to get to the large ship?" one of the warriors asked.

"When we arrived at the ship, we would be seen at once," Hawke said bluntly. "We would be targets. We would be killed."

That warrior nodded and stepped away

from Hawke, as Bent Arrow stepped up in his place. "Tell us what we must do, and there will be no one else questioning your judgment," he said, glaring over his shoulder at the one who had questioned Hawke's plan.

"Do you see the chain that reaches from the water up to the ship?" Hawke said. "From what I know about ships, that chain holds what is called an anchor at the end. That anchor keeps the ship in place. We will swim to that chain, then climb up it to the ship. Then we must carefully overpower any men we come upon, one by one, until they are all taken care of. But we will leave one unharmed. He will be the one who will lead us to the woman."

The men nodded, then dragged the unconscious white men behind some brush, so that no one from the ship would see them.

Soon all of the warriors were swimming toward the ship, thanking *Ayo-caddi-ay-may* for the clouds that still hung over the moon.

When they reached the chain, they grabbed their knives from their sheaths, placed them between their teeth, then one by one climbed the chain until all were on deck.

Once there, they went in separate directions. Each warrior disabled any white man he came across with a blow to the head.

Only one white man was left conscious. Hawke held him immobile in front of him, a gag secured across his mouth, his arms tied behind him.

Hawke's eyes darted from place to place, to make certain no white man except the one that stood with him had been left free.

Hawke watched his men assemble in a close circle around him, their eyes on their chief as the clouds scattered, revealing the moon, with twinkling stars all around it.

They all looked proud of what they had thus far achieved, smiling at their chief.

Hawke returned the smiles, then with his free hand yanked the white man around and gazed threateningly into his frightened eyes. "Take me to the woman," he growled out.

With one hand Hawke held on to the man; with the other he yanked his own deadly sharp knife from its sheath. He held the knife close to the man's throat, causing his breath to come in short rasps.

"Show me where the scarlet-haired woman is being held," Hawke demanded. "And listen well, white man. Should you try in any way to warn the captain of this ship of what is transpiring, my knife kills silently and swiftly."

Still gagged, the man could only nod.

"That is good," Hawke said. "You are wise to listen to this Caddo chief, or else . . ."

The moon was now so bright that it turned the night almost to day as the man led Hawke to the cabin on the top deck. Glancing toward shore, Hawke saw something gleaming in the light of the moon.

His heart skipped several beats when he realized it was the white deer standing on the embankment, seemingly staring out to sea.

Hawke had hunted it for so long, and now here it was, so near and yet so unattainable.

It looked proud and noble standing there, as though it knew Hawke would have to let it remain free for now. The only way he could catch it would be to abandon Scarlett altogether.

For a moment Hawke hesitated, longing to finally have the deer's pelt for his father.

Should he give up his plan to save the woman in order to go and capture the deer?

It did not take long for him to make a decision. No. He could not sacrifice Scarlett. He must save her and hope that the opportunity to find the deer would come again.

He watched the deer turn and bound away into the darkness as though the animal had read Hawke's mind, and knew he had chosen the woman.

Oh, how his heart ached to follow!

But he centered his attention once again on his mission.

The woman!

Huh, at all costs, even losing the white deer, he must save Scarlett.

The white man led him to a cabin, stopped and stepped aside.

Hawke gazed at the man. "Is the woman in this cabin?" he asked. The man nodded.

Hawke released the man's wrist. "Open it," he flatly ordered. "Now!"

The sailor did as he was told, using a key that hung just outside the cabin.

Soon the door was open and the man led Hawke into the room, where candle glow revealed Scarlett asleep on a huge bed on the other side of the cabin. She was completely unaware of what was going on around her.

Hawke's heart warmed at the sight of her. He was relieved to see that she did not seem harmed in any way.

He now knew he had made the right decision about coming to save her. At this moment in time, nothing more could be as evident as how he felt about her.

Odd as it might seem to others, he knew that he had fallen in love with this woman as soon as his eyes had looked upon her loveliness. He must have her.

But it would not be in the capacity of captive.

After her release, he would do what all men had done from the beginning of time, to woo their women. He would make her fall in love with him!

And she would, if she hadn't already. He thought he had begun to see signs of love in her behavior.

Hurriedly, yet quietly, Hawke found a rope and tied the sailor in a chair, his gag still in place to assure his further silence.

Then Hawke went to the bed and stood over Scarlett. The moon spilled in through the round porthole and onto her face. Just seeing Scarlett made his heart pound with a strange sort of passion that he had never felt before . . . not before *her.*

When he saw her thick, dark eyelashes fluttering, proving that she was awakening, he knew what he must do. He could not chance her screaming. It would alert anyone on the ship that had not been disabled.

As gently as he could, he clasped a hand

over Scarlett's mouth.

Scarlett awakened fully. Fear filled her; then her eyes widened when she saw by the moon's soft glow that it was the Caddo chief, Hawke, who was standing over her.

She peered up into Hawke's eyes for a moment, questioning him with them, then looked quickly to the right when she heard someone trying to speak. A sailor was tied to a chair, his eyes wide above the gag over his mouth as he peered back at her with a look she could not identify. It was a mixture of all sorts of emotions.

But her own emotions were very identifiable to her. She knew that she should be afraid, for this Indian chief was a stranger to her, yet she could not feel any fear while near him.

Just as before, when he had come upon her near the stream, she was not afraid. She was mesmerized by him. She knew without a doubt that he had come aboard this ship for only one purpose.

To rescue her!

"I am here to save you," Hawke said, still holding his hand over her mouth. He was happy that she had not struggled or tried to push his hand away.

That was proof of the trust she showed him, and it touched his heart.

"I want to take you away from this ship, to land and safety," Hawke said, seeing how her eyes softened and how she nodded slightly.

"You understand," Hawke said, slowly lifting his hand away from her mouth. "That is good. You could have taken me as another enemy, wanting you for all the wrong reasons."

Her lips now free, Scarlett licked them, then smiled at Hawke.

"Thank you," she said. "I will go with you eagerly. Oh, Chief Hawke, thank you . . . thank you so much."

"I will tell you later how I knew you were on the ship," Hawke said, lifting her into his arms and carrying her toward the door. "We must be quiet. As far as I know, the ship's captain is still in his cabin and unaware of what is happening."

He stopped and gazed down at the sailor, whose eyes were fearful as he gazed back at Hawke.

"If you tell what happened here tonight, or who did it, you will die quickly when I come looking for you," Hawke warned the man. "As it is, all of the others were silenced before they had a chance to see who attacked them. They were approached from behind. So you are the only one who knows. If anyone comes to make trouble at my village, you will be hunted down. You will die."

The man's eyes widened even more fearfully. He eagerly nodded, his head moving rapidly up and down.

"Good," Hawke said. "You seem to understand."

The man nodded in confirmation again.

"Where *are* the other sailors?" Scarlett asked, clinging to Hawke's neck as he left the cabin with her in his arms and hurried across the top deck, where she now saw his warriors waiting for them.

"They are not dead, but knocked unconscious. But they may awaken soon," Hawke said, stopping when they reached the rail. He placed her on her feet. "You can swim?"

"Yes, I am a skilled swimmer," Scarlett said, looking over her shoulder at the warriors who stood quietly gazing at her.

She had to wonder what they thought of their chief's interest in a woman who had white skin and red hair. Her face flushed at what they must be thinking. Surely they could tell that she and Hawke had feelings for one another.

She knew now that the two of them had been brought together for a reason. She believed in fate.

"We must leave now," Hawke said, looking from man to man. "Dive. Swim. We will come together again on the bluff where we left our steeds."

One by one the men dove into the water, followed by Scarlett and Hawke, who dove in side by side.

When they reached the shore, Scarlett hesitated while the other warriors began climbing the incline to the bluff.

"My horse," she gasped. "When I was abducted, my horse was left behind. I don't know what happened to him." Tears came to her eyes. "Lightning was my favorite. For so long."

"I am sorry about your horse, but this is not the time to worry about it. *Kee-mah,* come. We must hurry. I will take you safely home on my steed."

He took her by the hand and led her toward the bluff. She followed willingly.

"You are so kind," Scarlett said, lifting the hem of her skirt as she climbed the steep incline. "I am very grateful to you for rescuing me. What can I ever do to repay you?"

They were halfway to the top when Scarlett paused to gaze up at Hawke as he answered.

"The only payment I want is some time alone with you," Hawke said, looking down into her grass-green eyes.

"In . . . what . . . way?" Scarlett asked guardedly.

Hawke immediately understood what she might be thinking. "I just want to talk with you," he quickly said. "I want to know you . . . truly know you."

"Tonight?" she asked, searching his eyes.

"Tonight would be good," Hawke said, his eyes searching hers in turn.

"I should go home and let my father know that I am alright," Scarlett murmured.

Before answering, he took her by the hand and urged her upward with him.

He was afraid that the pirates might have awakened. He was even more afraid that the ship's captain might go and check on Scarlett and find her gone. Hawke wanted to be long gone before that happened.

"I doubt that your father is home," Hawke said finally. "When he discovered you gone, I'm sure he went right away to search for you. I have heard that when a sheriff needs assistance, he forms a posse. Do you not think that posse might even now be looking for you?"

"Yes, and that posse might find its way to your village," Scarlett said, glad to finally reach the summit of the bluff. She was winded.

"Your father has no reason to go to my village to look for you. I have never caused him any problems," Hawke said, leading her to his horse. He bent and removed the stone that held the reins in place. "And I do not like to think of taking you to your home if your father is not there. The pirates might come looking for you. Their search could lead right to your home. Come with me to my village for a while. Give your father time to return. Then I will take you home and feel it is safe to leave you there."

"What you are saying makes sense," Scarlett said, nodding a silent thank you to Hawke as he lifted her to his saddle, then mounted in front of her. "So, yes, I would love to go with you to your village, but just for a little while. I do not wish to cause my father unnecessary heartache."

She did so badly want time alone with Hawke. She twined her arms around his waist as they rode off on his steed, his warriors following closely behind them.

Yes, she was fascinated by Hawke. He aroused feelings within her that she had never known before while in the presence of any man.

She knew that it would be so easy to fall in love with him. Perhaps she had already.

She felt as though she were living a dream as the horse began to gallop, causing Hawke's long, black, sleek hair to flutter against her face.

She relished this moment when she could smell his hair, when she could feel his muscled body as her arms clung tightly to him. She felt as though she belonged with him.

She leaned closer to him and laid her cheek against his bare back.

Ah, yes, this was what dreams were made of, but she hoped this wasn't a dream, for she wanted it to last long beyond just one night.

Chapter Fourteen

Fat Jaws awakened with a throbbing head. Groaning, he reached up and found a lump on the back of his head the size of a goose's egg. He realized that he was lying on the floor of the top deck, and he wasn't alone. Scattered here and there were others who were stretched out on the wooden planks, unconscious.

"What the 'ell?" he grumbled as he scrambled to his feet, stopping for a moment to steady himself when he felt light-headed.

He inhaled a deep, nervous breath. Then his eyes widened.

"Blue Raven!" he gasped out, finally finding the strength to rush toward Blue Raven's cabin.

All around him the other sailors who had been temporarily knocked out were groaning as they too, awakened. He couldn't understand how everyone had been disabled without any of them crying out to warn the others.

He wondered if somewhere in the darkness one or more of the sailors might be dead. Were those who had caused this catastrophe still on the ship, waiting to finish the job they had started?

And what of Blue Raven? Fat Jaws thought sarcastically to himself. Fat Jaws had roamed the high seas with Blue Raven for many years now, enjoying gathering up prizes to take to their castle.

Aye, they did own it jointly, but Blue Raven seemed to have forgotten that somewhere along the line. Lately he'd been claiming it all as his. When he talked about the ship, he called it "me ship," not "ours."

And then there was the way Blue Raven had brought that wench on their ship. He had not even consulted Fat Jaws about that decision.

Recently, Fat Jaws had hesitated to argue with Blue Raven, for he knew the old pirate was not far from being a lunatic. He was dangerous in more ways than one.

Aye, more often than not now, Blue Raven was a stranger to Fat Jaws. He did things that sent chills up and down Fat Jaws' spine.

Aye, Fat Jaws realized that if he ever got caught double-crossing the pirate, Blue Raven would not hesitate to kill him.

Even now, Fat Jaws hoped that Blue

Raven wouldn't accuse him of negligence because of what had happened on this ship tonight.

He looked toward the cabin where the woman had been taken for the night. His heart sank when he saw the door to that cabin ajar; she was gone.

She was the cause of their latest misfortune. Someone had come and stolen the woman away!

His heart raced, for he knew that that news would send Blue Raven into a fury. He had truly been mesmerized by that red-headed wench.

"What 'appened?" one of the sailors asked Fat Jaws just as he reached Blue Raven's door. "Me head's still swimmin'. Who did this, Fat Jaws? Where are they? I'll plunge me knife into each and every one's 'eart, I will."

Fat Jaws ignored him. Instead he hurried inside the cabin and found Blue Raven soundly sleeping, his snores rumbling across the room.

Hating to awaken Blue Raven but knowing that he must, Fat Jaws placed a hand on his bare shoulder. A huge, bold blue tattoo in the shape of a naked woman glowed on Blue Raven's arm where the moonlight fell through the porthole onto it. When Blue Raven stirred and moved his arm, the breasts on the tattoo seemed to move.

Blue Raven sat quickly up on his bed, his eyes wide as he first saw Fat Jaws standing over him, and then the outline of one of his sailors at the open door.

"Why are ye here disturbin' me sleep?" Blue Raven asked, groaning as he slipped from the bed, his wounded leg throbbing.

The wooden floor was cold to his bare feet as he stood tall over Fat Jaws, who was squat and fat, his jaws always looking like they were filled with nuts, like a squirrel.

Blue Raven flailed a hand in the air as he looked back at the sailor at the door. He realized now that several others stood behind him, some groaning and moaning.

Then Blue Raven gazed at Fat Jaws again. He saw that he was rubbing the back of his head as if in pain.

"Well? Has a cat gotcher tongue, or what?" he shouted. He placed his hands on Fat Jaws' shoulders. "What's 'appened?"

Then he paled as he thought of Scarlett. "Is it the lady?" he asked, his voice rising with each word.

When Fat Jaws nodded, Blue Raven let out a roar and limped past him, shoving his sailors aside as he hurried from the cabin.

His feet could not take him fast enough to the cabin beside his. He stopped and stared in disbelief when he saw that the door was ajar.

His heart pounding, he limped inside the cabin and found what he had feared the most. Scarlett was no longer on his ship. Instead, one of his crewmen was bound and gagged in a chair.

The best prize he had ever taken was gone!

When the freed sailor could give him no information about who had attacked him, Blue Raven whirled around and limped back out on deck. His arms folded across the tight, red ringlets on his bare chest, he gazed from man to man. Each seemed to be in pain, some rubbing lumps on their heads, others groaning aloud.

"And so yer captain can't even sleep without the rest of ye lettin' me ship go to the dogs!" Blue Raven shouted, his eyes blazing angrily. "Tell me what 'appened? Who was allowed to come aboard me ship and take me lady away?"

Fat Jaws stepped up to his side. "No one saw anything or anyone," he said thickly. "It all 'appened so fast. It was as though ghosts came aboard this ship and disabled all of us, then whisked the lady away."

"Are ye sayin' that none of ye saw who did this?" Blue Raven shouted again. "Are ye sayin' ye are all worthless? I'd be better off captaining mindless creatures from loony bins than depending on the likes of ye men!"

He laughed sarcastically and flailed a hand in the air. "Men?" he said, laughing sarcastically. "None of ye are men. Ye are women!"

He gave Fat Jaws a hard look, his eyes narrowing. "Even ye?" he said. "Where were ye when this 'appened? Ye are the most skilled pirate of all next to me and ye let this 'appen?"

"Like I said, it was as though ghosts did this, not humans," Fat Jaws said defensively.

He felt that Blue Raven was making him look foolish in the eyes of the other men.

He took a step toward Blue Raven. "If even ye had been on deck yerself, ye would've been laid low by a blow to yer head, as we all were," he said tightly. "As it was, ye were in the comfort of yer bed."

Suddenly they heard shouts from the water down below.

Everyone rushed to the rail and gazed down. Approaching in their boats were the sailors who had gone ashore to gather the equipment they had used for cutting timber.

It was obvious that they, too, had been attacked.

"Ye blokes!" Blue Raven shouted down at them. "Ye let someone board me ship and take me lady!"

"They came out of nowhere," one of the sailors responded. "It was as though they weren't real —"

"Enough of that hogwash!" Blue Raven shouted, raising a fist in the air. "Excuses! Excuses! Ghosts indeed! Can't anyone admit to havin' let this old pirate down to-night? The lady is gone! Gone!"

Those in the longboats gasped at the realization that they had been attacked be-cause of the woman.

In short order the men clambered aboard, and the boats were soon hoisted up.

"I guess it's up to me to go and find 'er," Blue Raven growled. He turned to go back to his cabin to get dressed, but one of his men nudged him in the side, nodding to-ward land.

Blue Raven looked at him sourly, then glanced toward shore, and suddenly felt his heart skip a beat.

"Curses, foiled again," he growled as he stared at a group of men on horseback ranged along the shore, the barrels of their firearms glinting in the moonlight.

He knew a posse when he saw one and realized that someone besides himself was concerned about the woman's whereabouts.

Those men were surely looking for her, too!

"The anchor!" he shouted as he turned to his men. "Lift that anchor and unfurl those sails and get the wind into 'em! The *Eclipse* is able enough! Head 'er back out to the high seas! Now!"

"But what about the woman?" Fat Jaws asked as he sidled closer to Blue Raven, following him toward his cabin.

"This old pirate can't chance those men discoverin' me role in abductin' the scarlet-haired lady," Blue Raven said. He flashed Fat Jaws an angry scowl. "I won't let a hangman's noose stop me fun at sea."

"But what about the woman?" Fat Jaws repeated as he entered Blue Raven's cabin with him. "Ye were quite smitten with 'er. Can ye truly forget about 'er this quickly?"

"She's outta me sight, but not me mind," Blue Raven said. He gave Fat Jaws a quick, smug smile. "Do ye truly believe I'm about to forget 'er? I'll be returnin' for the lady another time. Whoever took 'er from me will pay the price!"

He hurriedly dressed, then went back out onto the deck with Fat Jaws.

They stood together at the rail as the wind filled the sails and the ship moved quickly away from shore.

"Aye, I'll be back for me lady," Blue Raven said, seeing Scarlett again in his mind's eye as she rode that midnight-black horse, her scarlet hair fluttering in the breeze behind her.

He would never forget those moments when he had shared port with her, and talk. His eyes twinkled when he also recalled her spirit, how she had the courage to empty her glass of port onto his face.

He again felt the sting of the wound in his leg, but he held no grudge against her for having caused it. It was a token of sorts from her that he would carry with him until he had her again, this time in his bed.

He watched the men on horseback ride away. They had obviously realized they could not pursue him.

Blue Raven clutched the rail and chuckled beneath his breath.

Chapter Fifteen

Hoping that she wasn't wrong to go to Hawke's village with him instead of directly home, Scarlett clung to Hawke's waist as they entered his village.

Beneath the moonlight, she immediately noticed that the village had been built in the shadows of a destroyed mission. She was surprised to see that the dwellings were cabins instead of tepees.

Hawke's warriors disbanded, each going his own way, while Hawke continued onward toward his own home.

As they went through the village, Scarlett noticed there were gardens behind the lodges.

She also saw what she thought must be doghouses, which sat together behind the cabins. At this late hour, the dogs and the people were in their homes, with only an occasional bark from one of the dogs.

The village sat amid a grove of mesquite trees, bound by open woods of oak, hickory and plum trees.

Nearby was a river, the moon's glow

revealing a bluish clay on its banks, instead of the coral rocks that she saw in most other bodies of water near Coral Creek.

As they rode onward, she saw that the village was made up of twelve to fifteen cabins. One cabin was much larger than the others, located behind a domed structure which she surmised was their council house.

She guessed that the larger cabin must belong to the chief, and she was right. Hawke drew rein in front of the cabin, quickly dismounting.

He turned to Scarlett and reached up for her.

She didn't hesitate to slide from the horse and into his arms. It was as though she had done this countless times, as though she knew him intimately.

She longed for that to be true. The more she was with him, and every time she gazed into his midnight-dark eyes, she knew that she felt something for him. She knew her father would want her to fight those feelings, yet she did not want to. This Caddo chief was stealing her heart.

And he was so gentle, especially now as he eased her to the ground. Her feet did not even feel as though they made contact with the earth, but she found herself standing before Hawke, his arms still at her waist, his eyes still locked with hers.

"Thank you for rescuing me," she blurted out, needing to say something to break the spell between them. "Had you not come . . ."

Then her eyes widened. "How did you know I was there?" she asked.

"I happened by when you were being rowed to the ship," Hawke said. "I was alone. I had to take the chance of returning to my village for help. We came as quickly as we could to rescue you."

"Had you not, I would have been taken far out to sea, for they were going to leave at dawn," Scarlett said, swallowing hard.

So thankful that this Caddo chief had cared enough to risk rescuing her, she flung herself into his arms.

"Thank you," she softly cried. "Thank you."

With her in his arms like that, their bodies touching, Hawke felt emotions that were new to him.

He had not loved before.

And then his heart skipped a beat. Perhaps Scarlett was behaving this way toward him only out of gratitude. Perhaps she did not feel the same wonder in their being together, as he!

If not, he would look the fool in his people's eyes. Even now, anyone who happened to look Hawke's way would see the woman clinging to him.

Yet he could not ask her to step away. He wanted her there for as long as she wanted to stay. If she was only showing gratitude, tonight would perhaps be the only time he would ever hold her.

"Come inside my lodge," Hawke said, gently easing her away from him.

He had only one thing on his mind, and that was to learn the truth about how she felt about him.

"I can't stay long," Scarlett said as she followed him into his cabin, where a low fire burned in the grate, and a kerosene lamp on a table sent a soft glow through the cabin.

"I know," Hawke said thickly. "I will take you to your home soon."

"My father must be worried sick," Scarlett said, her voice breaking. "He does care so much for me."

"Who could not, especially a father?" Hawke said, gesturing with a hand toward the brilliantly colored mats that lay before the fireplace.

"Thank you," Scarlett said as he led her down onto one of the mats, then sat on one beside her after placing a log on the fire.

She recalled now having seen wood piled along the outside wall.

He got up again and went to the fire, arranging the logs with a poker and stirring up sparks that glowed orange against the back of the fireplace.

Scarlett looked slowly around her at the way he lived.

There were many more reed mats of different colors positioned around the room on the wooden floor. There were also large baskets made of strong reeds, some with corn, some with beans inside them.

Elsewhere she saw a row of very large earthen pots. There was a large platform above the door, upon which lay ears of corn. She also saw wooden chests, hampers, and baskets of all kinds, in which were nuts and acorns.

If she leaned out far enough, she could see into another room where a lamp was also lit. There she saw a bed, three or four feet up from the floor, which was covered with brightly colored blankets.

She couldn't tell whether or not a woman lived in the cabin, but thought that one might, since everything was so homey.

When Hawke sat back down on the mat

beside her, she wished to ask if he had a wife, but she did not want to ask such a personal question.

Perhaps she had been wrong to come to Hawke's home with him. Having second thoughts about her actions, she jumped to her feet. "I should go home," she murmured, her cheeks flushing at the thought of having accepted his invitation in the first place.

How must she look in the eyes of this powerful chief?

Brazen?

Oh, she hoped not!

"You have been here for only a little while," Hawke said, sensing her sudden discomfort in being there, alone, with him. "Why would you want to leave so quickly?"

"My father . . ." she said, her voice trailing off as he stood and gazed into her eyes, causing her knees to almost buckle beneath her.

"Stay for a while longer and then I will take you home," Hawke said, reaching a hand to her cheek and gently touching it. "Once you leave, you might not be able to come again."

Almost melting beneath the touch of his hand, her heart pounding in her chest,

Scarlett knew that she should flee, yet . . . yet . . . she just couldn't.

Not yet, anyhow!

She knew that what he said might be true, so she must take from this one visit all she could. She desperately wanted to understand her overwhelming attraction to this man.

"Alright, but just for a little while," Scarlett murmured, sorry when he took his hand away, yet knowing it was wrong for him to leave it there longer, especially if he had a wife.

She looked past him and again saw the bed in the other room. She felt a ray of hope when she realized that no one was in that bed.

And if he did have a wife, wouldn't she have made herself known by now? Surely he wouldn't have brought her into his home like this if he already had a woman.

She sat down beside him again, pulling her skirt closer around her as she folded her legs beneath her.

"I noticed that your village has been built beside the ruins of a mission," she said, searching for anything to say to get a conversation going. "Why is that?"

"Even though it was a good distance from our village back then, the mission was important to me when I was a child," Hawke said, remembering himself as that child, so eager to learn the things that whites knew. He had realized even then that for a red man to survive among white settlers on his land, he had to have the same knowledge as whites. He had been right. No white man could outwit him.

"My mother took me there as often as possible so that I could become educated in the ways of the white people," he explained. "I learned to read and write, and I am a master now of more than one language."

"Who taught you?" Scarlett asked.

"Priests," Hawke said, nodding his head. "But there was one priest who became special to me."

"He was the one who taught you the most?" Scarlett asked softly.

"No. He was special for a different reason. He was the lone survivor after renegades destroyed the mission and everyone else who lived there," Hawke said thickly. "I was grown then and already a learned man, a man who was ready to walk in the moccasins of my father as chief. I went and found the one remaining priest, who was blind. I brought him home with me to my village. The priest urged my father to build where the mission had been, for it was holy ground, and fertile land. To appease the old man who had lost so much, my father agreed. So then, until Priest Joseph died, he was near the graves of those he loved. He died a happy man. He lies among his loved ones even now behind the ruins."

"That's such a sad yet lovely story," Scarlett murmured. "Your father? Where is he? Since you are chief, does that mean that your father . . ."

"*Huh,* it means that my father is no longer of this earth," Hawke said, his voice strained. "Nor is my mother. They died during a storm at sea as they were traveling in a canoe. It was then that I became chief of my Caddo people."

"I'm sorry about your parents," Scarlett said, then looked guardedly at him. "Do you . . . have . . . a wife?"

"No, I have not spoken vows with any woman," Hawke said, glad that she had asked. It was a sign that she was interested in him.

"Nor have I with any man," Scarlett murmured, feeling a blush grow hot on her cheeks to have been so open with him.

"Tell me about your family," Hawke said, his eyes searching hers. "I know of your father. What of your mother? Are there any brothers or sisters?"

"My mother died a terribly tragic death on the streets of San Francisco," Scarlett said, her voice breaking. She lowered her eyes. "I don't like to talk about it."

"Then do not," Hawke said softly. "Speak of other things."

"I have no brothers or sisters," she said, again gazing into his eyes. "My father is all that I have."

"Then you are all that he has?" Hawke asked quietly, still gazing intently into her eyes.

"Yes, until recently when someone came to our ranch, a woman who thought she was going to marry my father," Scarlett said tightly. "And she brought a son with her, a child who is not very well. If not for the boy, my father would have sent the woman away as soon as he made acquaintance with her."

"Why did she think your father would marry her if he did not send for her or want her?" Hawke asked, raising an eyebrow.

"I hate to say it, but my father actually sent for her without having ever seen or known her, without having been told there was a child involved," Scarlett said, sighing heavily.

"Why would he send for someone he did

not know?" Hawke asked.

"She was a mail-order bride," Scarlett said, her jaw tightening. "My father actually sent for a mail-order bride." She swallowed hard. "I still can't believe he did such a thing. Now he has both the woman and child to worry about until the boy is well enough to travel again. When he is, they will be sent away. My father doesn't want to marry the likes of her after all."

"The child is ill?" Hawke asked.

"Yes, he's quite weak and pale," Scarlett murmured. "Doc Mike came and checked him over but can't decide what's wrong with him. The doctor says the child's illness is a mystery to him, so he can't do much for him."

"Bring the child to my village," Hawke urged. "My shaman, Eagle Thunder, will do what he can for him. He often works miracles."

"It will take a miracle to cure this child, I think," Scarlett said softly. She leaned closer to Hawke and looked him straight in the eyes. "Are you serious? Do you think your shaman can help the child?"

"Eagle Thunder tries his hardest with children, for they are the future, are they not?" Hawke said. He smiled. "Bring him tomorrow?"

"Yes, I will," Scarlett said, but she wondered if her father would allow it. Once he knew of her escapade tonight, that she had gone to the Indian village before going home, he might watch her every move from now on to keep her from what he would call "foolishness."

Well, she would just remind him that she was no longer a child; that she had her own mind. If she wanted to associate with the Caddo people, especially their chief, she would! He would have to tie her up to keep her away from Hawke.

"I have someone who is ill, too," Hawke said, his voice drawn.

"You do?" Scarlett asked.

"My brother," Hawke said solemnly. "You know of him. Fast Deer, the one who stole your horse. He is a lost soul . . . lost to drink and gambling. He has disappeared again. This time I fear that I may never see him again."

He reached a hand out toward her and then ran his fingers through her long, scarlet hair. "Your name," he said softly, "it is the same as the color of your hair. It is beautiful. You are beautiful."

"I have never met a man like you . . . so good-hearted, so caring and gentle . . . so handsome," she blurted out, blushing anew that she had actually told him she thought he was handsome.

Then they both gazed quietly into one another's eyes as Hawke lowered his hands to her cheeks, framing them between his fingers. He continued looking into her eyes as he slowly drew her face closer to his, their lips coming together in a soft, sweet kiss.

The touch of his mouth did strange yet beautiful things to Scarlett. She had never felt anything as sweet and blissful as this kiss. His arms swept around her waist and drew her against him.

But then she made herself remember where she was, and that she was alone and vulnerable. She eased her lips from his.

Their eyes met and held again.

"I . . . I . . . truly must go," she mumbled awkwardly, her cheeks hot with a blush. "Surely my father is home by now. I don't want to worry him needlessly. He is a good man."

She paused, then added, "I am all that he has."

"Did my kiss offend you?" Hawke asked as she scooted even farther from him.

"No, never," Scarlett said, slowly rising to her feet. He rose, as well.

"Will you bring the child tomorrow?" he

asked, finding it hard not to reach out for her again. He ached to hold her and kiss her over and over again.

"Yes, I will bring him," she murmured, knowing that she should leave the cabin now, but unable to. It seemed that her feet were frozen to the floor. Her heart was beating so rapidly, it was as though she could feel it clear down to the tips of her toes.

"I . . ." Hawke began. Then, unable to help himself, he reached for her and again swept her against him, his lips pressed hard into hers as they kissed passionately.

"I . . . shouldn't . . ." Scarlett managed to whisper against his lips.

"Yes . . . you . . . should. . . ." Hawke whispered back, again kissing her hard, deep and strong.

Her insides melted.

She twined her arms around his neck and forgot everything but being with him, kissing him, being held by him!

Suddenly there was someone speaking outside Hawke's door.

"Hawke, it is I, White Horse," White Horse said. "I need to tell you something. Now, Hawke."

Hawke and Scarlett broke away from one another, yet still gazed in an entranced fashion into each other's eyes.

"Hawke?" White Horse prodded.

"I must see what he wants," Hawke said, slowly running a hand down her cheek. "You are so beautiful. Your kisses are like sweet pollen."

Scarlett smiled sweetly at him, then watched him go to the door and open it.

When she heard what White Horse was saying about her father having come to the village earlier with a posse, and how he had searched all of the cabins, her heart sank.

When Hawke came back into the cabin, his eyes met hers. "We must go," he said. "Now. I will explain why as we travel toward your home."

"I already know," Scarlett said softly. "I heard."

They embraced again, then hurried from the cabin and got on Hawke's horse together, Scarlett again behind him in the saddle, clinging to his waist.

Again she thought about her own horse, her wonderful Lightning, and hoped that he had found his way home. She would hate losing Lightning because of a crazed man who thought he was a well-known pirate, when in truth he was a lunatic.

She was oh, so glad that she was no longer the pirate's captive.

As though it were natural to do so, as though she had done this countless times before, Scarlett placed her cheek on Hawke's bare back, knowing that if it were not for him, she would still be at the mercy of that madman Blue Raven!

Chapter Sixteen

Dispirited, filled with anguish over his failure to find Scarlett, Patrick walked into his house, then stopped abruptly when he found Mary Jane passed out on the floor just inside the door, her son sitting beside her.

"What now?" Patrick groaned, staring from mother to son. But he was not at all surprised to see Mary Jane in such a condition. She had been gone from the ranch more than she was there, and when she returned, it was with the foul smell of alcohol and something unknown to Patrick on her breath.

He was glad for one thing. The child seemed somewhat stronger tonight. The boy knelt now, tears flowing down his cheeks, his eyes looking pleadingly up at Patrick.

"It will be alright, son," Patrick said thickly.

He knelt and placed a reassuring hand on the child's bony shoulder, noting that the pajamas he had purchased for the boy were too large for the tiny, bony frame.

"Is Mother dying?" Scottie sobbed out as Patrick helped him up from the floor. "I heard her come home. When she didn't come to the bedroom right away, I was afraid. I . . . I . . . came and found her here."

"Where's Malvina?" Patrick asked, gazing down the long corridor toward Malvina's bedroom. He saw that the door was closed and no lamplight flowed from beneath it. The cook must be asleep and unaware of what was going on.

"I haven't seen her since she brought supper to me," Scottie said, wiping tears from his eyes with the backs of his hands as he stood shakily at Patrick's side.

"I'm taking you back to your bed and then I'll see to your mother," Patrick said, sweeping Scottie into his arms and carrying him to his bedroom. When he laid the child in the bed, the one that he shared with his mother, Patrick patted him gently on the head. "I'll go for your mother now. I believe all she needs is some shut-eye and then she'll be as good as new in the morning."

"She's usually gone in the mornings before I wake up," Scottie said, again wiping tears from his eyes with his hands.

"I know, son," Patrick said tightly. "I know, and there isn't much I can do about it. She's a woman who listens to no one, not even my threats to send her away before you are well if she doesn't shape up."

"Oh, please don't send us away," Scottie begged, desperately grabbing Patrick's hand as he drew a quilt up to the boy's waist. "I . . . I . . . like it here. I like you and Scarlett. And I like Malvina, too. She's so kind to me."

"She's kind to everyone," Patrick said, smiling at the child. "There isn't one mean bone in her body."

"But there is in Mama," Scottie said, tears filling his eyes again. "I hoped she'd change when she came out here and married you. But she won't. She never will."

"I'll go and see to her now," Patrick said, again patting Scottie on the head. "Don't you fret, young man. I promise not to send your mother, or you, away until you are stronger and can fend better for yourself."

"Thank you," Scottie said, his eyes slowly closing.

As Patrick walked toward the door, he turned and gazed over his shoulder at Scottie, and saw that the child was already asleep.

The child was far from well enough to

travel. The slightest bit of activity still exhausted him.

"That wench," Patrick whispered beneath his breath as he left the room. He went and knelt beside Mary Jane.

"Where have you been so late?" he demanded. "Why can't you care enough for your child to try to change?"

Mary Jane stirred as Patrick sat there, trying to decide what to do. He truly needed to get rid of this woman, yet he had feelings for the child and just could not send him away to be at the mercy of this woman once again.

Mary Jane licked her lips as she opened her eyes and found Patrick kneeling there. "Where . . . am . . . I?" she said, her words slurred.

Then she sat quickly up and stared into Patrick's accusing eyes. "I passed out," she said, slowly edging away from him. "And you . . . you . . . are looking at me as if you'd like to wring my neck."

"Yes, you got that right," Patrick said, his voice filled with disgust. "Mary Jane, where have you been? I'm tired of fooling around with you. Where did you go today to get this drunk?"

He sniffed. "And what is that other God-awful stench I smell on your breath?" he said, raising an eyebrow. "I know liquor when I smell it, and this stench on your breath isn't something that came from a whiskey bottle. I've smelled it before. Tell me what it is."

"I'm too tired to think," Mary Jane said. "Please, oh, please quit questioning me. Please help me to my bed. I'll sleep it off, then talk with you tomorrow morning."

"Sure you will," Patrick said, laughing sarcastically. "You're always gone before I even see the light of day in my bedroom window. Where on earth do you go?"

"Please quit questioning me," Mary Jane begged. She held her head with her hands. "My head's throbbing something terrible."

"Yes, I'm sure it is," Patrick mumbled.

He struggled to get her to her feet. When he finally managed to help her up and she fell back to the floor, he knew he had no choice but to carry her to bed.

Grumbling obscenities beneath his breath, Patrick lifted her into his arms.

When she twined an arm around his neck, he shuddered, yet left her arm there, for he had only a few feet to go. Then he would be rid of her until their next confrontation.

"You know that you deserve no kindness at all from me, don't you?" Patrick said as he carried her down the dimly lighted corridor, where the candles had almost burned down to their wicks in the wall sconces.

"Don't preach at me," Mary Jane said in an ugly tone. "You know you can't do nothin' about what I do, not while Scottie is so sick. You know he isn't fit to travel yet. So let me be, Patrick. I'm not doing anything that hurts you. I leave early each day and come home late. Isn't that what you want? To have me out of your sight?"

"I want you out of my sight, alright," he growled. "I want you gone!"

He swallowed hard. "But always, there is Scottie to consider," he admitted. "I won't do anything to harm that child. I'm keepin' my word. I won't force you out of my home until the child is much better, at least well enough to travel by stagecoach to God knows where you will go next to trick and betray some innocent man."

"I'll be just as glad to get away from you as you will to be rid of me," Mary Jane said, looking quickly at Scottie when Patrick all but threw her down on the bed beside her son. "Poor baby."

Patrick scarcely heard what she was saying. His attention was drawn to something that had fallen from Mary Jane's pocket, landing on the floor as he placed her on the bed.

He reached down and retrieved it. He studied the object as Mary Jane went suddenly quiet, her eyes guardedly watching him. What he held was small and golden. When he turned it from side to side, he discovered that it looked like the sort of container that some people used to carry medicine. It was surely a pill box.

"Don't —" Mary Jane gulped out as Patrick opened it.

He didn't see her stretch out and pull the cover over her head, her breathing suddenly coming in short, frightened gasps.

"What the . . . ?" Patrick mumbled, his eyebrows lifting when inside he found a small, golden object in the shape of a cobra, as well as a gold nugget.

But what interested him most was the white powder that the other things were resting in.

His spine stiffened when he placed a fingertip into the powder and brought it to his lips.

"Opium," he gasped out as he looked quickly toward Mary Jane.

Yes, he knew the drug very well. He had fought those who used it in San Francisco, especially in Chinatown, where coolies smoked opium in strange-looking pipes.

He'd detested the drug then, and he hated it even more now, if it had arrived in the genteel town of Coral Creek to corrupt its people.

He closed the container and set it on the table beside the bed.

"Uncover yourself, Mary Jane," he said tightly. "Tell me where you got this."

"A . . . a . . . gift from a man," she gulped out, still holding the quilt over her head. "I just got it today. I . . . I . . . didn't know something was inside it."

"You are lying," Patrick said, doubling a hand into a tight fist at his side.

"No . . . I . . . I'm not," Mary Jane cried. "Why would I? Please let me alone. I'm so tired."

Having had enough of her lies, Patrick angrily yanked the quilt away from Mary Jane. She was cowering and shivering with fear, her eyes wide as she gazed up at Patrick.

Scottie awakened with a start and gazed from Patrick to his mother, and then to Patrick again.

"What's wrong?" Scottie gulped out, seeing how frightened his mother was, and how angry Patrick looked.

"Child, as usual, I've got an issue with

your mother, that's all," Patrick said thickly, hating that the child was awake and a witness again to his mother's lunacy.

"Mama?" Scottie whimpered, gazing at her.

"Patrick, why make such a fuss over everything? I truly got this as a gift from a man who seemed interested in courting me, and since *you* aren't, I saw nothing wrong in accepting his attention . . . and his gift," Mary Jane said softly, still ignoring her son, who looked ready to cry. "Can I help it if men are drawn to me? Can I?"

Needing to get away from her — her lies, her stench, and the feelings he had for her innocent child — Patrick gave Mary Jane a pitying stare. He turned and left the room, closing the door behind him.

As he went to his own room, he thought again about what he had found in the pill box. He found he couldn't focus on yet another problem, not when he was so worried about his daughter.

Completely disheartened, he flung himself onto his bed and cried for the first time since his wife's death.

Suddenly he heard a soft voice beside the bed.

"Why are you crying?" Scottie asked. "Is

it because of what my mama did?"

Stunned that Scottie had actually made it to his room, Patrick could only marvel that Scottie should show such concern for him. He gazed into the boy's eyes and saw loneliness and despair in them.

"Why am I crying?" Patrick said, hurrying from the bed.

He lifted Scottie into his arms and carried him to a rocking chair, the one that his wife had kept ever since she had used it to rock Scarlett when she was a child.

Tonight another child was going to be rocked.

Patrick couldn't help cuddling Scottie on his lap. He slowly rocked him, his heart melting when the child snuggled even closer to him.

"I was worried about Scarlett, but I'm not crying any longer, Scottie. Everything is going to be alright," Patrick said reassuringly. "*You* will be alright. Child, I'll see to it."

He heard Scottie sob and then become quiet as he fell asleep snuggled in Patrick's arms.

"Child, child," Patrick whispered, his eyes going quickly to the window. "And Scarlett, oh, daughter, where are you?"

Chapter Seventeen

The moon spilled its white sheen down onto Scarlett's face as she gazed into Hawke's eyes. He had just brought her home. He was standing at the edge of the yard with her. She had felt that it might be too dangerous for him to go closer since her father would not know just yet why she was with him.

Hawke took her hands in his. "You will come tomorrow, will you not?" he asked, searching her eyes. "You will bring the child? My shaman, Eagle Thunder, is known to work miracles. It does not matter the color of the skin of those he prays over."

"Yes, I will bring Scottie to you," Scarlett murmured. "But first I must convince my father that that is the thing to do."

"If he is anything like his daughter, he is a man who is reasonable about things," Hawke said, smiling at her. "He will see the good in what I offer."

"My father is kind and reasonable except

when he is given cause to be otherwise," Scarlett said. "He is a man who believes in justice. As you know from the way Father behaved when your brother brought my horse back, even those who cross him are first given a chance to explain their misdeeds."

She gazed at the hitching rail in front of the house and saw that her father's favorite horse was there, which surely meant that he had arrived home only a short while ago. She knew she should not tarry much longer. If he was pacing the floor, worried almost mindless about her, she should not delay in letting him know that she was alright.

"I really must go now," she said, feeling Hawke's hands tightening around hers.

She still couldn't believe what had transpired tonight between herself and the Caddo chief. He had not only rescued her, but also drawn her into his arms and kissed her.

She would never forget that moment . . . that kiss . . . that embrace! She knew now without a doubt that she was lost, heart and soul, to this man, forever.

She knew this was why she had been attracted to him so quickly. It was a love that had been destined from the beginning of time.

Hawke gazed into her eyes for a moment longer, then swept her into his arms and kissed her, his heart pounding so hard from the passion he was feeling, he wondered if she could feel his rapid heartbeat through her clothes.

He hated releasing her to her own world, when he now knew that he wanted her to be a part of his.

But he knew, too, that this love affair might take time, for she was of a different world and of a different color.

Also, she had a father who might not wish to let go of her, and not only because the man who wanted her was Indian. Her father was a lonely man . . . a man without a wife, and a father who adored his daughter.

But Hawke would find a way to see that her father accepted the union between his daughter and this chief who cared so much for her.

Finally Hawke had found the woman he wanted to be his wife, and if it became necessary, he would fight for her.

Scarlett's knees were weak from the passion his kiss was evoking within her. She could not help reaching her arms around his neck and returning the kiss. She even found herself pressing her body against his.

Yes, she knew there could be a special love between a man and a woman. She had seen it with her mother and father.

But she had never thought much about love, or men. She had been happy in her own little world, loving horses and riding them.

She just enjoyed being alive.

But now?

She had never felt any more alive than at this moment, and it was because a noble, handsome Caddo chief was holding her and kissing her.

Now that she knew the wonders of passion, she felt that nothing could ever be any more wonderful.

Once again, she remembered her father. She had to reassure him that she was alive and well.

She drew gently away from Hawke and gazed into his eyes. "I must really go, *now,*" she said softly. "It isn't fair to make my father wait any longer. I . . . I . . . feel guilty for having made him wait this long, but I truly wanted to go with you to your village, at least for a while. I am so grateful to you."

"Gratitude is not why you kissed me in such a way," Hawke said, placing a gentle hand on her cheek. "There was more in your kiss than that."

She smiled sweetly at him. "Yes . . . yes, there was," she murmured. She hated to, but she reached up and took his hand from her face. "I truly, truly must go."

"Until tomorrow?" Hawke said huskily, everything within him awakened to feelings he had long denied himself.

"Yes, until tomorrow," Scarlett said, her breath stolen away when he once again swept her into his arms and kissed her, but this time only briefly.

He stepped away from her.

Her pulse racing, she watched him mount his steed and ride away, soon lost to her sight in the darkness.

Then she turned and gazed at the house, where lamplight still burned in her father's bedroom and the entry foyer.

She broke into a run and did not stop until she came to her father's open bedroom door. There she froze, gazing disbelievingly at what she saw.

"Scottie?" she whispered, her eyes widening when she saw the child asleep in her father's lap in the rocking chair her father had said he could never part with.

She vividly recalled being rocked in that chair by her mother. She, too, had sat there as her mother read her children's books.

That her father would take the boy into his arms was one thing to marvel over. But for him to take him on his lap and sit in the rocker was still more astonishing.

Yes, her heart was warmed by the sight. Scottie was snuggled against her father and Patrick had fallen asleep, too.

Her guilt at delaying her return home was swept away by this sight. Her father had found another person to think about, to help.

She was certain this child had never been held and rocked as he had been tonight.

She hated to wake either of them, yet knew that she must. She couldn't just go to bed without telling her father that she was home. She knelt down beside the rocker and placed a gentle hand on her father's shoulder. Slightly, ever so gently, she shook it. "Papa?" she said softly so as not to startle him or Scottie. "Papa, I'm home."

Her father's eyes opened quickly, and when he saw her kneeling there beside him, instant tears flooded his eyes. "Scarlett?" he said, his voice trembling.

"Yes, Papa, I'm home, and I'm alright," she said. Without disturbing the child's sleep, she took one of her father's hands in hers. "Papa, it was horrible, but I am truly alright."

"What happened?" Patrick asked, his fingers twining through hers, his eyes quickly going over her, and soon seeing that she was unharmed. His gaze met hers now. "Where have you been? With whom?"

"I'll start from the beginning," Scarlett said, her eyes moving quickly to Scottie when the child sighed, but didn't awaken, only snuggled even closer to her father's chest.

"I was taken captive by a man who claimed to be a pirate, who called himself Blue Raven," Scarlett said, eliciting a shocked gasp from her father. "I was taken on his ship. He had brought it close to shore to make repairs. I was on the bluff looking at the ship when suddenly he was there behind me. But before I turned to see who it was, I grabbed my pistol from my pocket, and then . . . then . . . I accidentally shot him in the leg."

"A pirate? And you actually shot him?" Patrick gasped, recalling the ship that had fled his posse out to sea. "Go on. Tell me the rest."

"Several of his men came when they heard the gunshot. Some helped Blue Raven from the bluff, while others, at his command, grabbed me and took me to a longboat and rowed me out to the ship," she murmured. Then her eyes grew sad. "And, Lightning — I was forced to leave him behind when I was taken on board the ship."

"He is safe in the stable as we speak," her father quickly reassured her. "When I found him wandering without you in the saddle, I knew that you had come across some sort of trouble. I had formed a posse when you didn't come home at night. Lord, Scarlett, we searched everywhere. We even went to the Caddo village and searched their homes, but when we didn't find you there, we left and continued searching."

She paled. "Papa —" she began, but he interrupted her and continued his story.

"The Caddo people were held at gunpoint while my men searched their homes," Patrick said. "Their chief wasn't there. I had actually thought that he might be responsible for your disappearance. I had seen how he looked at you. Do you remember how I warned him about looking at you in such a way?"

"Papa," she blurted out. "Chief Hawke is the one who *saved* me. He saw me being taken to the ship. He went home and gathered together a number of his warriors. They swam out to the ship, disabled the sailors, then found me and set me free. It is because of him that I am alright."

"The Caddo chief . . . ?" Patrick gasped, paling.

"Yes," Scarlett murmured. "He came on board the ship and rescued me. He is the only reason I am here, Papa. The only reason."

"That's why he wasn't at the village when we were?" Patrick said, his voice drawn. "He and his warriors were surely on their way even then to rescue you. I expect White Horse was afraid that if he told me, I might take it the wrong way."

"I imagine," Scarlett murmured. "And so you see, don't you, how wrong you are about the Caddo? They are a fine people, especially their chief."

Before they could say anything else, Scottie woke up. He rubbed his eyes with his fists, gazing at Scarlett, then up at Patrick. "She's home," he said, sudden excitement in his eyes. "She's safe!"

"Yes, son. Thank God, Scarlett's safe," Patrick said, running his fingers through Scottie's thick shock of golden hair.

"Thanks to Hawke, I'm safe and at home with you both," Scarlett said, smiling from the child to her father. And had she heard right? Had her father actually called Scottie . . . son?

And then she suddenly remembered what else she must tell her father. But she didn't want to discuss this subject in the presence of Scottie. She had to get her father to approve of her taking Scottie to the shaman. Once she had her father's approval, she would tell the child where she was taking him.

"What do you mean?" Scottie asked, straightening away from Patrick's chest. "Who is Hawke?"

"He is a powerful and kind Caddo chief," Scarlett said, gently taking one of Scottie's hands in hers. "He rescued me from a terrible pirate."

"A pirate?" Scottie said, his eyes widening with keen interest. "There are such things as pirates? Truly? They don't just exist in books?"

"Well, now, I'm not so sure I should have called this man a pirate," Scarlett said softly. "He's loony, a man who professes to being kin to that famed, terrible pirate Bluebeard."

"He is kin to Bluebeard?" Scottie asked, more interested by the minute.

"Anyone can profess to being kin to anyone, but that doesn't magically make it so," Scarlett said. "And who would want to be related to Bluebeard anyway, unless they were crazy, which this man obviously is."

"Will you tell me all about it?" Scottie asked, a building excitement in his voice. "Will you tell me about the ship? Did it have a black flag with a skull and bones painted on it like I saw in picture books when I attended school?"

That he had been able to attend school at all, and had had some contact with other children of his own age made Scarlett happy. She did care for Scottie, and knew that her father did as well.

But there remained the problem of his mother. When his mother left, Scottie would be forced to go with her.

"Not tonight," Scarlett murmured. "It's time for you to go to bed."

"I don't like sleeping with my mother," Scottie said, visibly shuddering. "She doesn't smell good. I . . . I . . . don't even like for her to touch me."

Scarlett and her father exchanged quick, pitying glances. Then she watched her father stand with Scottie in his arms and walk toward the door.

She followed him out into the corridor and waited for him to return after putting Scottie in bed.

When he did, they went to the study and

lit a lamp there, then sat down and talked at length.

She explained everything in more detail to him, omitting only the fact that she had gone to the Caddo village instead of straight home. She would never let him know that she had taken a side trip to spend time with Hawke.

"I told Hawke about Scottie and how he can't seem to get well," she finally said. "Papa, he encouraged me to bring Scottie to his village so that his shaman, Eagle Thunder, can take a look at him. He truly believes that his shaman might be able to help him."

"A shaman? Eagle Thunder?" Patrick asked. "Scarlett, they believe in superstitious hogwash. No. I don't think you should take Scottie there. Anyway, after what I did tonight, I doubt that the Caddo would even let you near the village."

She still couldn't tell him that she had already been there. But she knew that she would always be welcomed by Hawke and his people.

And now, so would Scottie.

She would not be dissuaded!

"Their chief has the last word, and if he has asked me to bring Scottie, then no one will question that decision," Scarlett said.

"Papa, please give me your permission. I would like to see if the shaman can do something for the child. No one else has been able to."

Patrick kneaded his chin. "It is a fact that once Scottie is better, I can get Mary Jane out of my hair," Patrick said, then nodded and dropped his hands to his sides. "Yes. Take him. What can it hurt? And if there is even the smallest chance that something might come of this, it's worth givin' it a try."

He sighed. "Maybe if you do this, it might help mend the animosity those people are surely feeling for me," he said. "Yes, go. Hopefully, they will forget my stupidity."

She was so excited, she could hardly contain herself. She knew that it would be very strange if she flung herself into his arms to thank him. He would then know that this plan was far more important to her than it should be.

"You won't be sorry," was all she said, in a voice that was very controlled. "I'll go to-morrow."

"For now, I think it's time to go to bed," Patrick suggested, reaching a hand out for Scarlett. "Come on, daughter. I'll walk you to your room."

He put his arm around her waist, and she leaned against him as they walked down the long corridor. At this moment, Scarlett was more content than she had been since before her mother had died.

Now she had something to look forward to. No, not something, some*one!*

Chapter Eighteen

Scottie had willingly agreed to go to the Caddo village when Scarlett told him that there was someone there who might make him feel better and stronger.

Now she sat in a bedroom of Hawke's cabin, where Scottie lay awaiting the shaman's arrival. Scarlett smiled to herself when she thought of the other reason Scottie had agreed to travel to the village. All white children were intrigued by Indians, and Scottie was no different.

She saw how his eyes were watching the opened bedroom door, awaiting the arrival of the shaman.

"My people's shaman, Eagle Thunder, will be here soon," Hawke said, noticing the way the child was watching the door.

"Does he look like you?" Scottie asked as he turned his eyes quickly to Hawke. "Or will he have paint on his face as I have seen in picture books?"

His question was quickly answered, but not by Hawke. Eagle Thunder entered the room in all his fancy finery. He was a short, squat man with a pinched look on his wrinkled face. His gray hair was so long it dragged on the floor as he walked.

His floor-length buckskin robe was ornamented with big rolls of feathers. He wore a necklace made from the skins of coral-colored snakes, which were very showy.

On his head was a crown of skins and feathers, and he carried a buckskin bag in one hand and fanned himself with a fan made from eagle feathers with the other.

He made quite a sight and Scarlett saw that Scottie was duly impressed. His eyes were wider than she had ever seen them before, and his mouth was agape.

She knew that his reaction was not from fear, but utter fascination.

She gazed again at Eagle Thunder and the necklace made from the skins of coral snakes, shuddering when she thought of how poisonous those snakes were. She wondered how this old man had managed to catch them without being given a lethal bite.

"Your help is needed," Eagle Thunder said to Hawke as he set his bag down and laid the fan at the foot of the bed. "I explained earlier about what you can do for me to further this healing process."

Scarlett found his kind, smooth voice

pleasing. He gave her a friendly nod, then once again gazed at Hawke as the chief rose to his feet and walked to the door.

"The coals in your fireplace are ideal for my needs," Eagle Thunder said, pulling up a chair beside the bed.

Scarlett was stunned when Hawke returned to the room with a ceramic basin of hot coals, which Eagle Thunder immediately placed beneath the bed on which Scottie lay.

Then as Hawke came and sat down beside her again on mats on the floor, Scarlett leaned closer to him. "Why did you do that?" she whispered. "Isn't it dangerous to put those coals beneath the bed? Won't they catch the bed on fire?"

"The coals are needed to make the child sweat out his illness," Hawke whispered back. "And, no. The bed will not catch fire. Scottie is safe."

Although Scarlett wanted to believe that, and trust in everything Hawke said or did, she could not help doubting her decision to bring the child here.

Yet she saw that Scottie wasn't afraid. Instead, he seemed more intrigued by the minute as he lay there so trustingly, continuing to watch everything the shaman did with his innocent blue eyes.

But Scarlett? She scarcely breathed as she turned her attention back to the performance of the shaman. She suddenly recalled how her father had called this kind of medicine superstitious hogwash, but even he had agreed to let her bring Scottie here. She now wondered if her father might be right as the shaman took a vial of something covered with foam from his large bag and drank from it.

"Eagle Thunder drinks a mixture of brewed herbs," Hawke whispered to Scarlett.

"Why?" Scarlett whispered back, still keeping her eyes on the shaman.

"The drink is stimulating and will help his performance as shaman," Hawke said as he leaned closer to her. "Do not doubt anything my people's shaman does. It is all for good. What he does is guided by *Ayo-caddi-ay-may,* our people's God. So do not fear it. Marvel over it instead, for you will soon see how much better Scottie will be as a result of Eagle Thunder's skills."

After placing the vial back in the bag, Eagle Thunder reached over to Scottie and slid the child's shirt over his head. Scottie trustingly allowed the shaman to do whatever he pleased.

Scarlett could only surmise that the child's willingness was a result of Scottie's desire to be as well as other children. He did not budge even as the shaman began a new activity.

Scarlett leaned forward to get a better look as Eagle Thunder tapped his long, lean fingers along Scottie's thin frame while singing and chanting.

Eagle Thunder did this for a while, then took a whistle from his bag. It was a polished stick with slits along the top, cut in the shape of a rattlesnake's rattlers. He then took a container of some sort of cream from his bag.

"The cream is made of medicinal herbs," Hawke quietly explained to Scarlett.

"I hope the child's delicate skin can tolerate whatever herb it is," Scarlett whispered back.

"The child trusts my shaman: so should you," Hawke said in a gentle tone, drawing Scarlett's eyes quickly to him.

"It's not that I don't trust him," Scarlett explained, being careful to speak only loud enough for Hawke to hear. "It's just that this is all so new to me."

"It is also new to the child, and look at him," Hawke said, gesturing with a hand toward Scottie. "See how he lies so trustingly quiet as my shaman works his magic on him?"

Scarlett turned her eyes back to Scottie and Eagle Thunder. She was truly amazed at the trust the child showed toward someone he had never known . . . someone who wore strange-looking clothes and behaved quite peculiarly.

Scarlett inhaled a quick breath, declaring silently to herself that she must be as trusting as that child, for she did not want to disappoint Hawke.

No. She never wanted to disappoint Hawke. She loved him. She now knew with every fiber of her being that she loved this wonderful, gentle and caring Caddo chief.

She found herself feeling more comfortable with the situation and continued to watch Eagle Thunder as he set the cream aside and began playing a strange-sounding tune on the whistle. He stopped at intervals to apply the cream to Scottie's chest, rubbing it in circles, until it all but disappeared from sight, leaving only a slight greasy residue.

Eagle Thunder continued this treatment, playing his whistle for a while, then applying more cream, then playing again.

Scarlett's breath caught in her throat when she saw that Scottie suddenly began to sweat profusely. She knew it was not only from the hot coals beneath the bed, but also from the herbal cream that had been applied to his chest.

She did not question Hawke, for she was afraid that if she showed doubt or mistrust in the shaman one more time, Hawke might look at her in a different light. He might think she was not someone worthy of his love, and, Lord, she never wanted him to stop loving her!

Suddenly Eagle Thunder placed all of his things back in the bag, stood and gave Scottie a soft smile. Then he turned and gave Scarlett and Hawke a nod, and left.

"That's it?" Scarlett asked, rising to her feet and going to stand over Scottie.

"He has worked his magic," Hawke said, rising, too, and going to the bed. "Small brave, how do you feel?"

Scottie's eyes widened at being addressed as a brave. "I'm hot," he murmured, wiping sweat from his brow with the back of a hand. "But I do feel better."

"In what way?" Scarlett asked, pulling his shirt back over his head as he sat up on the bed.

"I just do," Scottie said, softly shrugging. "Let me show you."

He crept from the bed.

When his feet touched the floor, he did not weave back and forth with weakness as he usually did. This time he stood straight, tall and still, as both Scarlett and Hawke watched him.

He took one step, and when his legs were steady, took another and another.

He turned and laughed gleefully. "I am stronger," he said, his eyes filled with proud surprise.

Scarlett bent to her knees and swept him into her arms. "I'm so glad," she murmured. She then leaned back from him and gently pushed his damp, golden hair off his face. "In time, you will be completely well."

"*Huh,* yes, in time," Hawke said, nodding.

He bent to his haunches and reached beneath the bed to remove the tray of coals. They were no longer glowing orange, or even the slightest bit hot.

He took the coals back to the fireplace in the outer room and shook them into the hearth. Then he smiled at Scarlett and Scottie as she walked with the child into the room.

"I must really get him back to my house," Scarlett murmured, placing a hand on Scottie's shoulder. "I'm so eager to show Malvina how much better he is. Father will be so happy when he returns home from work." She sighed. "I hope that Mary Jane is there so we can also show her how well her son is, but I doubt it. She disappears on us every day."

"Mother told me she won't leave the ranch house today," Scottie said, gazing wide-eyed up at Scarlett. "It's not because she doesn't want to. Your father gave her an order not to. He told her that he doesn't want any more of her shenanigans."

"Yes, I know," Scarlett murmured. "But your mother doesn't always do as she is told."

Scottie hung his head. "I know," he said, then looked quickly up at her again. "Scarlett, if I am well now, I'll be made to leave with my mother. Your father will make us leave."

He suddenly turned and flung himself against her, hugging her. "I don't want to go," he said, sobbing. "I've never been as happy as I've been with you and your father. And Malvina. She is so good to me!"

Scarlett knelt down and gathered him into her arms. "I'll see what I can do to keep you from having to leave," she murmured, even though she knew she shouldn't have said anything. She didn't want to get his hopes up, when in the end, her father might order the child to leave with his mother.

Yet in her mind's eye, she saw what she

had found last night when she had returned home. She had found the child on her father's lap in the rocking chair.

She knew then that her father had formed a special attachment to Scottie, and Scottie to him. Perhaps that bond would cause her father to send Mary Jane away, but keep Scottie.

She knew that Mary Jane would gladly part with her son. He was just a nuisance in her life.

"I hope I can stay," Scottie sobbed, clinging to her.

Scarlett suddenly felt the warmth of a hand through her blouse, on her shoulder. She turned her eyes up to Hawke.

"I hope your father will listen to reason about the child," Hawke said thickly. "Like my brother, the child's mother is a lost soul. If the young brave stays with her, his future is bleak. He will be as lost as his mother."

"I know," Scarlett said, gazing into Scottie's eyes as she turned back to him. "I know."

"My hope that your father will do the right thing goes with you as you return home," Hawke said as Scarlett moved to her feet. She felt Scottie's hand cling to hers as he stood close at her side.

"Thank you," Scarlett said, searching Hawke's eyes. "You are so gentle-hearted and kind. I . . . I . . . have never met a man like you, except for my father, whose heart is also large with caring."

"Scarlett, after you take Scottie home, can you return to my village?" Hawke asked as he walked her and Scottie out of the house to the horse and buggy. He lifted Scottie onto the seat as Scarlett climbed up on the driver's side. "My people are having two special celebrations today — the First Corn Ceremony and the Calumet Ceremony."

"Can I come, too?" Scottie asked, his eyes wide as he looked first at Scarlett and then Hawke.

"We'll see," Scarlett said, smiling down at him. "We'll see just how strong you are after we arrive back home."

"But will you come?" Hawke persisted, drawing Scarlett's eyes back to him. "I would like for you to know everything about my people. Today's celebrations will teach you much."

"You want me to learn . . . ?" Scarlett asked, her pulse racing. "Everything?"

"Everything," Hawke said, walking around to her side and taking one of her hands. "Will you come?"

"Yes, I shall return soon," Scarlett said. "Nothing could keep me from it."

He smiled at her and placed a finger to her lips. He slowly brushed it across them, then stepped back to allow her to leave.

Scarlett was glowing inside from that touch on her lips. She smiled down at Hawke, then turned her face forward and drove through the village.

Everyone made way for her, stopping and staring. She wondered if Hawke's people were interested in her because their chief was paying so much attention to her? Or was it because they resented this special treatment?

How could they forget what her father had done?

"I do hope I can come back to the village with you," Scottie said, breaking into Scarlett's thoughts. "Will you please talk my mother into it?"

Scarlett gave him a sideways glance, for it didn't seem right to have to ask that woman's permission. She showed no affection whatsoever toward the boy.

She guessed, though, that Mary Jane would not even be there to ask. She would be gone again, doing whatever ugly thing she did every day. She was not the sort to listen to orders, especially from a man she had learned to despise — Scarlett's father.

"Yes, I'll talk to her," Scarlett said anyhow, nodding. "And I'll be glad to take you back with me to the village, but only if I see that you are truly strong enough."

Scottie smiled. "I am," he said, lifting his chin proudly. "Eagle Thunder made me strong."

Scarlett smiled at him, for she truly felt that this child's life had begun anew today. She had never seen hope in his eyes, nor heard it in his voice, before.

She firmed her jaw. She was determined to see that this child's future would not be under the guidance of such a woman as Mary Jane. Somehow she would see that Scottie's life would not be ruined by a mother who cared only for herself.

"Things will be alright," she said, drawing Scottie's eyes quickly to her. "I shall see to it, Scottie."

The smile these words produced made Scarlett determined to see that her promise would be kept.

Chapter Nineteen

A hawk flew by outside, keening its shrill cry, and Scarlett looked up momentarily. Then she focused again on where she was. She could hardly believe that she was actually sitting beside Hawke on a square wooden bench slightly elevated from the earthen floor, upon which were laid red reed mats. She and Hawke were in a huge council house, facing the other members of his Cougar Clan.

Ah, how handsome Hawke was today! He wore a scarlet coat, which he said was saved for special occasions. He also wore fringed buckskin breeches and matching moccasins.

His hair was twisted in one long braid down his back, and he had on a headband ornamented with tiny shells, and a necklace to match.

His copper face and dark eyes shone with contentment and pride. This was a man of peace and goodness, who made those he was with feel the same deep inside their hearts.

Scarlett was so proud to be his special guest. She wore one of her most beautiful dresses — a pale green silk creation with white embroidery work of flowers on the long and full skirt. Her hair was long and loose, adorned with a sprig of lily of the valley she had found in the forest.

She felt beautiful and hoped he saw her that way. She believed he did, because he looked at her so often with what seemed to be deep appreciation in his midnight-dark eyes.

Quite a bit of space separated her and Hawke from his people. A fire burned in the middle of the earthen floor, the smoke escaping through a hole in the ceiling above her.

She smiled when she searched the crowd and found Scottie. He had been allowed to attend the First Corn Ceremony. She found him sitting among the children at the far right, his eyes wide and excited as the young braves talked with him.

She had passed by them a short while ago as she entered the council house with Hawke, and she had heard the questions the children asked Scottie about his life among whites.

Scarlett had heard his first response, and her eyes had widened when she realized that he was making up answers to the questions. He was describing a life very different from his own, probably what he wished his life could be.

It made Scarlett sad to know that lies were the only way he could make himself seem equal to those who sat with him. If he told the truth about how he had been forced to live with his horrible mother, the children would be stunned to know that a mother could treat her son in such a way. It was obvious that the Indian mothers adored their children, boys and girls alike.

She looked elsewhere, at the women who were bringing food into the huge lodge. They were placing it on a platform near the fire.

Hawke had told her about some of the food that would be served. There would be balls, like hard taffy, made of a thick paste of parched, roasted corn and sunflower seeds.

There would be corn that had been cooked in the ashes of the women's homes, boiled first, then mixed with Brazil beans, and wrapped in corn husks.

Sunflower and watermelon seeds, mixed with corn, were used to make fine tamales, while another kind of seed, like cabbage seed, were ground with the corn and seasoned walnuts to make another tasty dish.

She had noticed, upon first entering the huge lodge, other benches where she saw huge peaches, slices of watermelon and pumpkin, as well as plums, grapes and an assortment of shelled nuts.

Earlier Hawke had told her that his people gathered huge quantities of thick-shelled nuts and acorns to last the whole year.

But the main reason for the gathering of the people today was to celebrate the beginning of their corn harvest. Some women had gathered a great number of ears, boiled them and put them into a hamper which had been placed upon a ceremonial stool a short distance from the central fire, awaiting the arrival of their shaman.

"Scarlett?"

Hawke's voice brought Scarlett's eyes quickly to him.

"Scarlett, today is a good day. It is a day that proves my people's crops are doing well. The ground of the gardens is tilled daily by wooden hoes made of seasoned walnut, but today we celebrate only our corn. There are two kinds of corn," he said, his voice low so that no one else could hear. "One kind matures a month and a half after having been planted, the other in three months." He nodded toward the hamper that sat on the ceremonial stool. "The corn inside the hamper has been cooked in different ways. Part of it has been toasted, and some has been ground to make *atole*."

Scarlett started to ask what *atole* was, but stopped when Eagle Thunder entered, causing a hush throughout the crowd. Their eyes followed him as he sat down on a small scaffolding raised about four feet off the floor a short distance from where Scarlett and Hawke sat.

As Eagle Thunder sat down, a blanket fell away from his shoulders, revealing that he wore a brief breechclout. His hair was drawn back from his face and woven into a long, thick braid that fell down his bare back.

Suddenly Eagle Thunder raised his eyes and hands heavenward and prayed for a moment. When he was done, a woman went to him and gave him some food from the hamper.

Eagle Thunder nodded a silent thank you to the woman, waited until she was again seated among the others, then threw part of the offering into the flames of the fire, and ate the rest.

"Hear me well, my people," Eagle Thunder said in a solemn voice, his eyes looking slowly around him. "If any more of our corn crop is cut before the prayers are made at harvest time, the guilty one will be bitten by a snake."

Scarlett heard gasps of fear from the children, and she, herself, was stunned by what he had said.

She looked quickly at Scottie and saw that he was gazing at the shaman. It was a look without fear, for Scottie knew this man had made him well enough to attend the festivities today. It was a look of utter adoration, and Scarlett knew that Eagle Thunder had made a devoted friend for life out of the boy.

A woman rose from the crowd and went to the food. She arranged a sampling of what was there on a pretty little platter of black wood in the shape of a duck. This she brought to her chief, while another woman brought two earthenware mugs and handed one to Scarlett, the other to Hawke.

Scarlett said a soft thank you; then her gaze moved slowly to a far wall where she had earlier noticed figures of birds made of wood. There were also images of dragons, serpents and toads painted on another wall. It seemed that the black food platters had been made purposely to match those figures.

She hoped that one day she would understand all of these things, for she wanted to know everything that had to do with the Caddo, because she wanted to know everything that had to do with Hawke.

Scarlett looked questioningly into her cup, then up at Hawke.

He saw her hesitation to drink from it. He smiled at her as he spoke. "The drink is made of brewed wild olives," he said. "Do not fear its taste. It is pleasant."

Smiling back at him, Scarlett took a sip of the drink, her eyes widening at the pleasant taste.

"It is good?" Hawke asked, searching her eyes.

"Very," Scarlett murmured.

"The food is good, as well," Hawke said, handing her the pretty platter that had been brought to him, which was to be shared with her. "Taste. You will enjoy it all. The Caddo women are good food makers."

She had recognized most of the food. There was hominy, which she knew was also called sagamite. She also saw bread, beans, pumpkins and various meats. She tried each delicacy, and found she enjoyed most of them. Glancing over at Scottie, who was still sitting among the children, she noticed he was eating even more eagerly than she.

It gave her a peaceful feeling to see the boy eat so heartily. Until today, he had scarcely touched what was placed on his plate.

She knew that he had been given a new lease on life, not only by her father's love, but also by Malvina's kind sweetness, and Scarlett's own attention to him.

Bringing him to Eagle Thunder had been the final step in the healing process. It was obvious Scottie was at peace with himself.

Scarlett had to find a way to make certain that he stayed with her and her father. If he went with his mother when she was ordered from the house, he would be doomed to a life of degradation. She would hate to see the newfound hope erased from his eyes.

As Scarlett continued to eat, she looked around at the women and young girls and how they were dressed. Some wore the finest deerskins, with ruffles decorated by little white ornaments.

Others wore very black deerskins, with

bracelets and necklaces that she had been told were worn only on feast days.

Some of the younger women wore dresses with fringe that had many little white nuts sewn on them, and necklaces of glass beads.

After everyone had eaten and the plates were taken away, Scarlett's eyes turned to the open door, where a group of old men, followed by some young men and women, walked into the lodge, singing.

A young brave who led the procession carried a calumet pipe, ornamented with various kinds of feathers.

He stepped up to Hawke and stopped, then handed him the pipe.

Hawke stood holding the pipe as another young brave came and spread grass around Hawke's feet, while still another lad brought clear water and a buckskin cloth in an earthen bowl. The lad wrung out the cloth, then washed Hawke's face with it as Scarlett watched, almost spellbound by what was happening.

Eagle Thunder came forth and stood before Hawke as he reseated himself beside Scarlett. Eagle Thunder proceeded to place two forked sticks in the earthen floor in front of Hawke, on which he then laid a crosspiece, all painted red. He spread over this armature a tanned buffaloskin, and then a deerskin that had been dressed white.

Eagle Thunder stepped away as Hawke leaned toward the covered crosspiece and gently laid the calumet pipe upon these skins.

Several women stood up and went to a circle that had been made of green canes stuck in the ground a short distance from where their chief sat, his back straight, his arms folded across his bare chest, watching.

The women danced to the music of hollowed-out gourds filled with little stones, and drums made from hollow logs, upon which were tightly stretched skins. There were also flutes carved of crane bone.

Surprising Scarlett, some older women used a drum made out of an old kettle that was partly filled with water and covered with a piece of wet rawhide.

She looked elsewhere and saw hollow logs, covered with green branches whose ends were buried in the earthen floor. Eight women sat at intervals with sticks in each hand, playing this sort of makeshift drum to the accompaniment of calabashes which several old men played.

Several other women danced in a circle

as men joined them, facing the women, moving only their feet.

All music and dancing stopped as a young brave stepped forth toward the central fire. He threw a handful of tobacco into the flames, then little pieces of roasted meat. He also threw dried corn from last year's crop into the flames, which proceeded to pop. The white popcorn spewed out all over the floor.

Then Eagle Thunder came forth again, a painted feather now at the back of his head, tied into his hair. He took up the calumet pipe, filled it with tobacco, lit it and presented it to Chief Hawke.

Just prior to entering the huge council house, Hawke had quickly explained to Scarlett some of today's rituals. He had told her that his people's tobacco, grown in small patches away from the vegetable gardens, was never allowed to get perfectly ripe.

She remembered his saying that, because she noticed that the smell of this tobacco was so different from any tobacco she had ever smelled before. It wasn't unpleasant — just different.

Hawke continued to smoke the pipe, then passed it around to his warriors. Eagle Thunder was the last to partake of it, and it was he who placed the calumet back in its deerskin case.

Eagle Thunder handed the calumet pipe and case to Hawke. "Carry this with you as always before when you meet with those who need to be convinced that we are a people of peace," he said. "All who know anything of the Caddo know that this pipe is a calumet of peace."

"I shall do this," Hawke said as he took the case and rested it on his lap. He bowed his head, then raised it again and gazed into Eagle Thunder's old eyes. "Thank you, Eagle Thunder. Thank you."

Eagle Thunder nodded, then walked away.

Scarlett watched as the shaman went and knelt beside the group of children, choosing to rest a hand on Scottie's shoulder.

Scarlett didn't see any resentment in the other children's eyes over this friendly gesture toward a white child by their shaman. They were too intent on gazing into the old man's eyes as he said something to each of them, then took longer to say something to Scottie.

Scarlett's eyes widened in wonder as Scottie leapt to his feet and ran to grab one of her hands. She could feel his hand quiver as he gazed anxiously into her eyes.

"Eagle Thunder has asked me to come to his lodge," he said, speaking so quickly the words tumbled over each other. "He wants to talk with me alone. He wants to teach me things. He says he sees much potential in me."

Scottie's eyebrows rose. "What does 'potential' mean?" he asked, looking anxiously from Scarlett to Hawke.

"Potential means many things, but when this word is spoken by a powerful shaman, it means only one thing," Hawke said. "It means that my shaman sees you as someone who can learn many things. Go to him. Listen well to what Eagle Thunder says. You will come away from his lodge feeling stronger and more confident."

Hawke had realized from this child's shyness and behavior that Scottie had never had a good life. No one had shown interest in him in any way, except for what he had been shown by Scarlett and those who lived with her.

Huh, surely his shaman had singled the young brave out purposely to help build his confidence in himself. Hawke only hoped the Caddo children would not resent this special attention from their shaman to a child of another skin color.

But they had all been taught not to feel jealousy for one another, or resentment, or envy. They had been raised by caring mothers and fathers, with their chief and shaman a big part of their lives from the moment they had taken the first breath of life. They rarely had cause to feel jealousy, envy or resentment. These things never came into the life of someone who had been given the love one needed to thrive in this world.

"Can I go with him into his home?" Scottie asked, looking anxiously over his shoulder where Eagle Thunder waited for him.

Hawke looked over at Scarlett, then smiled when she reached out for Scottie and drew him into her arms as she gave the permission he so eagerly sought.

"Go and enjoy yourself," Scarlett murmured, hugging Scottie one last time before he turned and ran as fast as his thin, long legs would take him back to Eagle Thunder.

She was deeply touched when she saw Eagle Thunder take the time to hug each of the other children individually, saying something to each, before going on to his lodge with Scottie.

She watched as the children resumed sitting with each other, smiling and laughing as they talked among themselves, obviously having already forgotten that their shaman had chosen someone besides themselves to take to his lodge.

"Each child has had time alone with Eagle Thunder," Hawke said, smiling at Scarlett as she turned to look at him. "They see this as Scottie's time."

"I would think they would resent his even being here, much less being taken into their shaman's home," Scarlett said, searching his eyes.

"They have been taught how to share, how to give," Hawke said quietly.

"But they are only children," Scarlett said, glancing back at these children who were now giggling and playing some sort of game like tag.

"They might be children, but they have the hearts and minds of adults," Hawke said, nodding. "They are taught early in life those things that make them ready for adulthood long before they reach that age when they leave all games behind them."

"I think it's wonderful," Scarlett said, watching now as everyone began leaving the council house, until only Scarlett and Hawke remained.

"You are wonderful," Hawke said,

drawing Scarlett's eyes quickly back to him. He reached a hand to her hair and ran his fingers through her long, red tresses. "I cannot take my eyes from your hair. Its beauty is so much like your inner self."

"Truly?" Scarlett murmured.

"You are beautiful like the rare butterfly known only to a few," Hawke said, his fingers now tracing the outline of her face.

"Which . . . rare . . . butterfly?" Scarlett asked, her pulse racing as he traced her lips with a fingertip.

"It has no name, at least not one that I am aware of, but its beauty speaks so that it does not need a name," Hawke said thickly. "It is something that takes one's breath away as it flits amid wildflowers, its distinctive silvery-gray and blue wings making it unique."

"Why, that sounds like a butterfly that my Aunt Emma wrote to me about from New England," Scarlett gasped, amazed.

"It has a name?" Hawke asked, raising an eyebrow. "Do you believe that we are speaking of the same kind of butterfly?"

"I only know that when my aunt described this rare butterfly to me, she used the same words as you," Scarlett murmured.

"Its name is?" Hawke asked, looking into her green eyes. His heart raced as they again captivated him.

"It is called the Karner Blue because of its color," Scarlett said.

"My Aunt Emma always called butterflies 'flying flowers,' " she went on, picturing her Aunt Emma now in her mind's eye. She had passed away one year prior to the death of Scarlett's mother, who was her Aunt Emma's sister.

"You sound as though you were quite fond of your Aunt Emma," Hawke said softly.

At that moment Eagle Thunder appeared at the door without Scottie.

The shaman came into the lodge, this time wearing a long robe, his hair loose and flowing down his back. He stepped up to Hawke. "My chief, the child has fallen asleep," he said softly. He looked at Scarlett. "Should I awaken him so that you can return home? Or will you be here long enough for him to rest before you leave?"

"He is surely worn out from the day's excitement," Scarlett said. She looked at Hawke. "What do you think? Should I awaken him and take him home? Or let him rest?"

Hawke didn't take long to respond, for

he knew what he wanted. He wanted more time alone with Scarlett, and not in this lodge where anyone could happen along at any time, but in his own cabin. There he hoped to taste of her lips again, where there would be no audience to his true, deep love for her.

"Let him rest," Hawke said, rising to his feet. He reached for Scarlett's hand, which she gave to him as she rose up beside him.

"Yes, let him rest," Scarlett murmured. "When I get ready to leave, I will come for him."

Eagle Thunder nodded, then left the lodge.

Hawke swept his arms around Scarlett's waist and drew her close to him. His midnight-dark eyes bored into hers, and then he kissed her so passionately, she almost swooned in his arms.

"Let us go to my lodge now," he whispered huskily against her lips.

"Yes, yes," Scarlett whispered back against his lips, her heart pounding so hard, surely it would leap from inside her chest if it raced any faster.

She had heard the huskiness of Hawke's voice, even though he had spoken in a whisper.

Something told her that there might be

more than kisses when they got alone, where no one would dare disturb their chief.

A part of her warned not to allow herself to be carried away by any man, but another part of her argued that this was not just any ordinary man. This was the man she had fallen in love with, and would love forever.

How could she not do as her heart and soul urged her to do?

Feeling as though she were walking on clouds, Scarlett went with Hawke to his lodge, very aware that he made certain the latch was locked behind them.

When he turned to her, his eyes said everything that she was feeling.

Without further thought about whether this might be right or wrong, she flung herself into his arms.

When he stepped slightly away from her, her lips still hot with his kiss, and questioned her with his eyes, she knew this was the true moment of decision.

Her response was to lay her cheek against his chest. He then carried her to his bedroom, where he gently laid her on his bed.

Everything happened so quickly then, she felt as though she were in a whirlwind of passion. Moments later she found herself without clothes, and Hawke's hands searched her naked body for those places that made a woman's knees become weak.

Then he drew away from her and gazed deep into her eyes. "Are you certain . . . ?" he asked, searching her face. "Is this what you want?"

"It is my first time with a man," she murmured.

When he left the bed and turned his back to Scarlett, her lips parted with wonder. . . .

Chapter Twenty

Suddenly feeling very aware of her nakedness since Hawke had left the bed, Scarlett scrambled for a blanket at the foot of the bed and swept it quickly around her shoulders.

She eyed her clothes, then Hawke, her heart skipping a beat when he turned suddenly and gazed down at her with a look that she had grown to recognize — a look of love.

"Why did you leave the bed?" she finally found the courage to ask. "Did . . . did . . . I say or do something wrong? This is so new to me." She hung her head. "I have never been so . . . so . . ."

Hawke went to her quickly and placed his arms around her waist, drawing her up to stand before him.

Clinging to the blanket so that it would not slide from her shoulders, Scarlett looked slowly up at Hawke. "I'm so confused," she said, searching his eyes. "Please tell me what I've done wrong that made you leave the bed and turn your back to me."

"My woman, you have done nothing wrong," Hawke said. He reached a hand to her face and gently shoved some of the fallen locks of hair back from her cheeks. "It is I who could be accused of that."

"Why would you say that?" she asked, oh, so aware of his nakedness only a heart-beat away.

She could smell the manliness of his skin.

She remembered how wonderful it had been when their bodies had touched, if even for a moment.

She loved him so much, she had not felt any shame in what she was sharing with him.

She was afraid, though, that he felt guilty for having disrobed her.

"You are an untouched woman, a virgin," Hawke said slowly. "Perhaps we should wait until later?"

"Will it not be the same later as now?" Scarlett murmured, fighting these feelings of longing that made her want to reach out and touch his body, to familiarize herself with every inch of his copper skin.

"You do not feel that it is too soon?" he asked, peering intently into her eyes. "Would you rather —"

She placed soft fingers to his lips. "I

know that perhaps my behavior is wanton, for Mother taught me what is right and wrong," she murmured. "I have always believed in all that she taught me, yet today I feel things that I have never felt before. I . . . feel . . . such a need for a man . . . for *you.* I do not think I could bear waiting. My father will not easily give his permission for us to be together. It's not because he is a man of prejudice. It is because he had a vision of what my life would be once I met the man I loved. He wanted me to live close to him in my own house with all of the lovely things I am used to, not in an Indian village married to an Indian and living in what he would say was a crude setting."

"Do you see my life and my way of living as crude?" Hawke asked, gently taking her hand from his mouth. He kissed its palm, then continued to hold it.

"I see nothing about you or your way of life as crude," Scarlett murmured. "I spoke only of my father and his feelings. My love, I would live without even a roof over my head if it meant I could share the rest of my life with the man I love."

"You do love me?" Hawke asked thickly. "You love me as I love you? *Nei-com-mar-pe-ein.*"

"Yes, oh, yes," she said, suddenly flinging herself into his arms, causing the blanket to fall away from her shoulders.

She trembled with passion as she felt his hard body against hers, even that part of him that she knew should embarrass her since she had never seen a man . . . there . . . before in her life.

Being with him seemed only natural . . . only right. She had to convince him that she lived her life the way she wanted to live it, not the way her father would wish it to be.

She gazed up at him. "Please make love with me," she said softly. "Being with you in that way is right in my eyes, for I do love you so much. I want you more than I've wanted anything in my life."

"As I want you," Hawke said, sweeping her up and into his arms, then bending low and placing her on the bed again, on her back.

He stood there for a moment just looking at her, savoring every sweet inch of her. He saw her eyes move slowly over him; in her expression he read appreciation, love and need.

He was filled with the same needs. His heart was racing so hard that he felt dizzied by the building passion.

Scarlett reached her arms out for him. “Please come to me,” she said with a huskiness in her voice that was new to her. But wasn’t everything she was doing today new to her?

She was eager to learn, especially how to make love with a man she adored.

There were strange, beautiful sensations within her that he had awakened.

She anticipated the heightening of those sensations when she gave herself to him.

His eyes dark with need, his pulse racing, his manhood tight and ready, Hawke bent lower over her. He sucked in a quivering breath of pleasure as their bodies strained together while he placed his heat against the tight curls at the juncture of her thighs.

He knew he must be gentle and slow, for he did not want to frighten her when she felt the pain that came with making love for the first time.

It was the first time for them, but it would be far from the last. This was the beginning of the rest of their lives of making love, for he would marry her soon, even if he had to fight her father for that right!

Realizing just how tight Scarlett’s body had become, Hawke brushed soft kisses across her lips as he slid one of his hands slowly down her body until he reached that place of a woman's paradise.

He leaned slightly away from her so that he could caress her there with his fingers. He heard her soft cry of passion, proving to him that she was discovering how it felt to have a man slowly awaken her to a pleasure that would soon astound her.

As feelings ignited within her, Scarlett's eyes widened. She gazed up into Hawke's face while he caressed her where she had never been touched before. Pleasure was spreading outward from that spot, causing her heart to beat rapidly within her chest.

When the feelings mounted, along with a wondrous feeling of rapture, Scarlett closed her eyes, realizing that the soft moans she was hearing were her own!

She gasped when Hawke's lips came to hers with a meltingly hot kiss as his fingers slid away from the core of her passion. They were replaced by something even hotter and harder.

"I will kiss away the pain," Hawke whispered against her lips, then again kissed her passionately while he slowly pressed himself inside her. Slowly, her tightness gave way to the first entry by a man.

When he reached that barrier that until

now had protected this woman from intrusion — the barrier that proved she was, indeed, untouched by a man — he paused.

Feeling that he should wait a few seconds longer before pushing his way fully into her, he slid his lips downward. As his hand cupped one of her breasts, his mouth covered its nipple, drawing gasps of pleasure from Scarlett.

Slowly he flicked his tongue over and around the nipple, and then moved to the other breast and did the same.

"I never knew such feelings could exist," Scarlett whispered, her cheeks hot with awakened passion. She gazed into Hawke's eyes as he slowly pressed himself farther inside her.

He saw a look of wonder enter her eyes as he broke through the barrier that gave him full access to her. Now he could awaken her fully to how it felt to be a woman.

"It is done," he said huskily as he paused long enough to allow her to get her bearings.

He again moved within her with gentle thrusts. "You are now a true woman," he whispered against her lips.

She twined her arms around his neck, her heart pounding inside her as she gazed deeply into his eyes. "It hurt for only a moment," she murmured. "And now, as you slowly move within me, I am feeling oh, so much more than pain."

She swallowed hard, momentarily closed her eyes as she concentrated on the pleasure that she was beginning to feel. Then she gazed up at him again, smiling.

"How does it feel to you?" she asked softly. "Are . . . are . . . you experiencing something close to the euphoria that I am feeling?"

"More than that," he said huskily. "My woman, my woman."

Loving how he called her "my woman," and now overwhelmed by the desire swelling within her, she drew his lips to hers and gave him a kiss that was all-consuming. Her body moved with his, as though she had done this before.

She clung to him as he thrust into her deeply. Then he withdrew and fully entered her again, with faster, quicker, surer movements, bringing sharp gasps of pleasure from deep within her.

Hawke cradled her close as he was overcome with feverish heat. He was glad that she opened herself wider, her hips responding in a rhythmic movement all their own as she clung and rocked with him.

He had never felt so alive. There was a stirring fire within him that was growing.

And then there was a lethargic feeling of floating as he pressed endlessly within her.

His whole body quivered as the passion spread, leading him almost to the crest of rapture.

Breathing hard, he paused; then his mouth closed hard upon hers as he gave her a kiss that stole her breath away, while he again moved within her.

Her hands clung to his sinewed shoulders; finally she gasped out her pleasure as her body shook and quaked against his, while his did the same, his arms tightly holding her.

After they came down from that plateau of ecstasy, they lay together, clinging and breathing hard.

He leaned away from her and gazed into her eyes. "You are everything to me," he said, his voice soft with loving. *"Nei-commar-pe-ein."*

"As you are to me," Scarlett said, reaching her hands to his cheeks, which were slick with perspiration. "How could it happen so quickly between us? I knew that I loved you immediately. It was as I have heard it said — love at first sight. I just never believed it could happen."

"But it has, and we are now intertwined for an eternity," he said huskily.

They heard a soft knock on the front door, followed by a tiny voice they both recognized.

"Scottie!" Scarlett gasped, rushing from the bed.

She trembled as she pulled on her clothes, while Hawke hurried into his own.

"My face. Is it red?" Scarlett asked as she tried to smooth out wrinkles in the skirt of her dress, then ran her fingers through her hair. "My hair. Is it mussed so much that everyone will be able to tell what we have done?"

"Your face is no longer flushed, nor are your clothes in such disarray that someone will know what we just shared together on my bed," Hawke said, now fully dressed. He went to her and ran his fingers through her long tresses until her hair lay smoothly on her back. "Your hair is also presentable."

She moved into his arms and gazed up at him. She gazed into his eyes. "I feel different," she murmured. "Will people see that difference? Will . . . my . . . father?"

"You do have a glow, but most of what you are feeling is inside you, so, no, no one will know that we have shared lovemaking," he said. "Come. We must go and open the door for Scottie."

"Then I must hurry home with him," Scarlett said, lifting the hem of her dress as she walked briskly beside Hawke.

She stopped and turned to him before he opened the door. "I shall never forget what we shared this night," she murmured. She lowered her lashes bashfully, then gazed up at him again. "Never in a million years would I have thought that I could share such wonderful moments with a man. But I must remind myself that you are not just any man; you are the one I love."

He pulled her against him, gave her a fierce kiss, then turned to the door and unlocked and opened it.

Scottie raced inside, his face flushed. He turned to them. "I learned so much from Eagle Thunder," he said in a rush of words. "I want to be a shaman when I grow up. I want to be just like Eagle Thunder."

Both Scarlett and Hawke were taken aback by what Scottie said, yet both saw his eagerness, and realized that he was quite serious.

"Truly?" Scarlett said, falling to her knees before Scottie and taking his hands. "You truly want to be a shaman?"

"Yes," Scottie said, his eyes beaming. "I want to be able to make people feel better with my words, and I want to heal people like Eagle Thunder knows how to heal. Can I? Can I learn from him how to be just like him?"

Captivated by this young white boy's interest in something intrinsically Indian, and seeing that the child was, indeed, serious about it, Hawke went and knelt beside Scarlett. He gazed into Scottie's eyes.

"It is quite a responsibility to be a shaman," he said. "Many depend on a shaman's knowledge and spirituality. Can you say that you can truly live that sort of life?"

"I know I can," Scottie replied, then looked into Scarlett's eyes. "But only if I am allowed to." He swallowed hard. "Scarlett, I don't want to be with my mother anymore," he said, his voice breaking. "I don't want to go with her when your father orders her away. Please, oh, please let me stay on your ranch so that I can come and be with Eagle Thunder and learn from him. I . . . I . . . feel truly alive for the first time in my life."

He flung himself into her arms and sobbed. "I feel truly happy for the first time," he said. He clung to her. "Please ask your father to allow me to stay and live with you, not go with my mother. She . . . she . . . only knows evil, not good. I . . . I . . . want to be good. If I go with her, I will surely learn only the evil ways of life as I grow older. I want more than that. Please?"

As she clung to him, tears fell from Scarlett's eyes. She looked over at Hawke, whose own eyes were damp with tears.

Then she held Scottie away from her. "I promise you that you won't have to go with your mother," she said, realizing that she had just made a promise she might not be able to keep.

But she must! This child's whole life depended on it.

Scarlett was determined to do what she could to assure this young man's future, so that he would have his own identity, and one that he could be proud of.

"Thank you," Scottie sobbed, still clinging.

Then he moved away from Scarlett and gave Hawke a fierce hug. "And thank you," he cried.

Hawke patted his back, then held the boy away from him. "You want something beautiful out of life, so I will do all I can to make that possible," he promised.

"Me, too," Scarlett said. "But for now

we must go back home."

She placed a gentle hand on Scottie's head. "Come on, sweetie," she murmured. "I don't want to worry Father."

Scottie moved away from Hawke. He smiled up at the Caddo chief. "Please tell Eagle Thunder how I feel?" he asked, his eyes eager.

"I will tell him," Hawke said, nodding. "And he will be so pleased."

Scottie sighed deeply, took Scarlett by the hand and walked outside with her and Hawke.

Hawke walked them to the horse and buggy. He hugged them both before they climbed aboard, then stood back and watched as they rode away.

He was awed that this woman had come into his life so quickly, and with her this boy whose heart was so sweet and pure.

"Child, I will make all things possible for you," he whispered, then gazed after Scarlett. "And you as well, my woman. And you as well."

He watched until he could not see them any longer, then turned and smiled at Eagle Thunder, who had just stepped to the door of his lodge. Eagle Thunder returned the smile, as though he knew what would soon be revealed to him about the child.

He came to Hawke and placed a hand on his shoulder. "The child is special," he said solemnly. "As is the woman."

Hawke nodded. His whole universe had been changed by this woman, for now he could envision a son in his image, and even a daughter!

"You will marry her soon?" Eagle Thunder said matter-of-factly, as though he had read Hawke's mind.

"Soon," Hawke agreed. "Very, very soon."

"That is good," Eagle Thunder said. "That is right."

"Even though she is white?" Hawke asked.

"I see not the color of her skin," Eagle Thunder murmured. "She is a woman of heart . . . of compassion . . . of goodness."

Hawke smiled.

Chapter Twenty-one

Scarlett lay somewhere between sleep and wakefulness, having been woken earlier when she had heard her father leave on his horse for work. She had found it hard to wake up at that time because she had been dreaming about yesterday and her wonderful moments with Hawke. In her mind, heart and dreams, she had been with him again, being loved by him, experiencing feelings she had never known possible.

Even now she lay there wanting to hold these precious feelings for just a while longer before beginning the new day.

But a noise outside in the corridor finally made her open her eyes. It sounded like someone tripping over something.

She sat up quickly, the patchwork quilt falling down away from her. The strap of her lacy, sleeveless gown slipped from her shoulder.

She listened carefully and recognized that the footsteps were not Malvina's. Hers were heavy and very discernible since she was such a large woman.

This was someone walking very lightly, almost furtively. Surely it was not Scottie.

That left only one person who could be sneaking around so early in the morning.

"Mary Jane," Scarlett whispered, scrambling quickly from the bed.

Her heart pounded as she threw her nightgown off and slid into the nearest thing, a freshly washed and ironed riding skirt and blouse that Malvina had placed across the back of the chair for Scarlett the night before. Scarlett had told her that she would be horseback riding this morning after she had a quick bite to eat.

Her plans this morning were to follow Mary Jane and see where she went every day. The woman hadn't been in the Coral Creek area for very long, so how could she know anyone to drink with?

"Unless she knew someone here before she arrived as a mail-order bride for my father," Scarlett whispered to herself as she hurried into the last of her clothes, and then sat down and yanked on her boots.

Just as she stood up, she caught a glimpse through the window of Mary Jane running toward the stable.

Scarlett knew that Jason, the stable hand, didn't come to work until later. That would give Mary Jane the freedom to pick any horse she pleased, and to leave without telling anyone her destination.

"I've got to hurry," Scarlett whispered, sliding the drawer of the bedside table open and grabbing a pistol, a replacement for the one she had lost during her scuffle with Blue Raven. Her father had given her this second one and told her to be more vigilant, or she might not be as lucky a second time someone decided to abduct her.

"I will, Papa," she whispered as she slid the tiny firearm into the front pocket of her skirt. "But I must do this today to finally get to the bottom of this thing with Mary Jane."

Just as Scarlett opened her bedroom door, the aroma of coffee brewing in the kitchen told her that Malvina was stirring downstairs, ready to begin her morning chores.

Surely Mary Jane had left the house without Malvina being aware of it.

Hearing a horse ride away outside, Scarlett knew that she might have taken too much time already.

She ran down the corridor, then down the stairs, and without stopping to tell Malvina where she was going, hurried outside to the stable.

She quickly saddled Lightning, then rode from the stable at a breakneck speed, glad that she could see Mary Jane in the distance. The woman was just making a sharp turn right, away from the outskirts of Coral Creek.

As Scarlett's red hair blew in the breeze behind her, she watched Mary Jane's golden hair fly out as she took off.

She was surprised to see that Mary Jane rode very well. Perhaps sometime in her past she had lived a normal life, with a father who loved her as much as Scarlett's loved her. Perhaps he had taken the time to teach his pretty blond-headed daughter how to ride.

"I wonder when and where it went wrong for her," Scarlett whispered to herself. "And why."

But she made herself forget that and focus on now. She was riding far enough behind Mary Jane that the woman would not be aware of being followed. She seemed determined to get somewhere, and fast.

Scarlett hated to think of what awaited the woman . . . another day of drinking and carousing?

"But with whom?" Scarlett wondered again to herself. It had not taken long for

Mary Jane to begin her shenanigans after arriving at the ranch.

"It has to be a man who is drawing Mary Jane to him, like a moth is drawn to a flame," Scarlett said aloud. "But how on earth did they manage to make these arrangements before Mary Jane came to Coral Creek?"

Perhaps they had known one another sometime in Mary Jane's past, and had accidentally met again when she arrived in Coral Creek.

"That has to be it," Scarlett whispered.

Yet Mary Jane had slipped away almost the instant she arrived, so she had to have known ahead of time about this place, or person, that lured her from her son.

Scarlett's thoughts returned to last night, and what had happened when she had arrived home. When her father had met her and Scottie at the door, Scarlett had worried that he might see a difference in her and know that her life had been altered forever by a handsome Caddo chief. Could a man who had been in love recognize the signs in his own daughter?

But she had seen immediately that he treated her no differently, nor looked at her in any questioning way. Instead he had given her a fierce hug, then had lifted

Scottie into his arms as though the child were his, and loved by him as a father would love a son.

She would never forget how Scottie had given him a big hug, then rattled off quickly how much fun he had had at the Caddo village. He had even blurted out that he wanted to be a doctor when he grew up.

Scarlett had been so relieved that Scottie had forgotten the Indian word shaman and had instead called Eagle Thunder a doctor.

Had her father heard the child say he wanted to be a shaman, she had no idea how he might have reacted. She doubted it would have been in an approving fashion. Although he was not a prejudiced man, and he didn't have any true control over anything Scottie did, she doubted that he would want Scottie to live among Indians.

She had smiled when her father had laughed and joked with Scottie, then had grown more serious as he told the child that he was proud of him. He promised even to send him to school to become a doctor.

When Scarlett had seen a questioning look in Scottie's eyes, she could guess what he was about to say . . . that surely Indian doctors didn't go to white schools. Scarlett had quickly intervened, telling her father that Scottie had had a long day and should be taken to his bed.

Malvina had come in at that moment and carried Scottie away to his room. Scarlett had hugged her father and told him what a good man he was for caring so much about the child.

Then he had questioned her about her day, and what had transpired at the celebration. She had told him everything, except about her private moments with Hawke, of course.

That was locked away inside her heart, to keep safe until she found the right moment to share her feelings for Hawke with her father.

At about that moment Mary Jane had come into the house, stumbling and shaking. Scarlett had heard her falling against the wall out in the corridor, then laughing to herself and trying to walk onward.

Scarlett would never forget her father's rage. He had gone out and told Mary Jane that if she didn't stop these outings, he would tie her to a chair until the next stagecoach arrived in Coral Creek. He wouldn't hesitate to put her on it!

Mary Jane had laughed in his face, then stumbled on into her room.

Moments later, Scarlett had heard Scottie crying, and knew that he was surely cowering away from his own mother. Her blood might run through his veins, but her heart was cold and uncaring toward him.

"I've got to discover where she's going and who she is doing these things with, then report back to Father," Scarlett whispered as she squinted her eyes in order to see Mary Jane up ahead. Just then, Mary Jane made another sharp turn right and disappeared into a thick stand of trees.

Scarlett hoped that tomorrow Mary Jane would finally be put aboard a stagecoach and that would be the last she, her father and Scottie would ever see of her, for Scottie would not be leaving with her.

Her father had declared that last night. He had been adamant about his decision.

Scarlett sent her horse into a gallop, then slowed down when she came to the stretch of forest where Mary Jane had disappeared. She caught sight of Mary Jane leading her horse by its reins into the trees.

Scarlett also dismounted, but she didn't take her horse with her any farther. She tied its reins to a low tree limb and hurried on, alone. She was puzzled that Mary Jane seemed to know the area so well. How could she, when she was so new to Coral Creek?

Scarlett continued to follow Mary Jane, then stopped abruptly when the woman disappeared into what looked like the entrance of a hidden cave. She led the horse inside with her.

What was this hidden place unknown by the folk of Coral Creek and their sheriff? Scarlett was sure that if her father had known about it, he would have talked of it. He would have investigated it.

Again, Scarlett was stunned that Mary Jane knew more about the area than even those who lived in Coral Creek. She must have known about this place even before she came to the Coral Creek area. This hidden cave must be the reason why she had come — it certainly had nothing to do with Scarlett's father. The woman had used him in the worst way possible.

Feeling a mixture of excitement, confusion and fear, Scarlett hurried onward, then cautiously stepped past the bushes that hid the opening to the cave. It seemed to be a passage of sorts that led underground.

Having stepped into darkness, Scarlett wasn't sure she should continue onward, alone. But she could still hear the horse that Mary Jane had stolen for her outing today. Its hoofbeats rang hollowly as they made contact with the rocky ground.

Scarlett continued onward, and found that the passage sloped downward, the footing worse with each step she took.

She wasn't sure where the walls were on either side of her. She just tried to walk in a straight line, glad that the ground beneath her had finally leveled out.

Suddenly her eyes spotted something up ahead. There were actually remains of buildings, on two sides of what looked like a street, where candles glowing from pole lights illuminated the scene.

"The underground city!" Scarlett whispered to herself, her heart racing at her discovery. She had heard her father mention the underground city, and how he had searched for it but never found it.

"It's real," Scarlett whispered, stopping to peer more closely at what she had discovered. Some of the false-fronted buildings were still intact, looming upward to where the roof of the underground city disappeared in the darkness. It was truly a remarkable thing to see — this town that had been built beneath the ground.

"I can't believe my eyes," she said, inhaling a shaky breath. "But here it is."

Yes, this underground city was real enough, with its old, dilapidated buildings. It was a dark place, and surely dangerous. If she was caught there, what would happen to her?

But she would let nothing dissuade her from pursuing Mary Jane. In her astonishment at what she had discovered, Scarlett had momentarily lost sight of the other woman.

Now she looked ahead, where lamplight was flickering from the windows of a building that seemed somewhat sturdier than the others.

"Mary Jane," she gasped as she saw the woman tie the reins of her horse among others at a hitching rail, then hurry inside the building.

Her heart pounding, Scarlett continued walking onward, her hand now inside her pocket, her fingers clasped around the tiny firearm. She was feeling anxious and terribly alone.

But she could not give up what she had started.

She wanted more than ever to discover the dark, hidden side of this woman.

Keeping watch on all sides of her, Scarlett slipped silently through the shadows until she came close to the building Mary Jane had entered.

Breathing hard, her pulse racing from fear of getting caught, Scarlett hurried to the side of the building. There was just enough space for her to squeeze between it and the building beside it. She crept up to a window and peered inside.

She was stunned to see a number of gamblers sitting around tables. Even more shocking were the many Chinese coolies sitting together along one wall, their queues wound round their heads and their long, embroidered shawls wrapped around their shoulders, their feet encased in satin shoes.

Scarlett was reminded of those she had seen in San Francisco. She couldn't believe that there were coolies here in this underground city.

She stared at the opium pipes they were sucking on. She was familiar with such pipes. While her father was sheriff in San Francisco, many coolies had been jailed for smoking opium. Her father had confiscated their pipes.

Sighing, wondering what her father would say when he discovered that he had not left such things behind after all, Scarlett looked slowly down the line of people who sat along the wall. There were others besides the coolies there.

She saw both white men and women, and then her eyes fell on Mary Jane. The woman was surrounded by smoke coming from the pipe between her lips.

Now Scarlett knew where Mary Jane went each day and why she always came home so disoriented and drunk. She was addicted to opium.

No doubt the woman had frequented the opium dens in San Francisco and had known of Scarlett's father and his plea for a mail-order bride.

It had all been planned, how she would dupe her father into marrying her, while all along she was only interested in traveling to Coral Creek to smoke opium with those who had fled San Francisco for this underground city.

A loud, angry voice at the table of gamblers drew Scarlett's attention. Her heart skipped a beat when she saw someone else she recognized.

"Hawke's brother!" she whispered to herself, watching as he threw his cards on the table, his eyes narrowed angrily as a man dressed in a red vest and cowboy hat dragged all of the coins in the center of the table toward himself.

She recalled that night when Hawke and his brother had brought her stolen horse back to her, and how this man had cowered beside his chieftain brother.

She recalled how Hawke had later spoken of the brother he hardly knew any longer because of the way he behaved.

And here he is, in a place Hawke would despise, she thought.

She was uncertain about what to do. Go and tell her father that she had found Mary Jane? Or run to Hawke and relate where she had seen his brother?

The first, most important thing was to get out of here before someone caught her.

She hurried from the underground city and to her horse.

As she rode through the forest, she debated the two courses of action. Should she reveal the location of the opium den to her father so that he could arrest its denizens, including Mary Jane?

Or should she give Hawke a chance to get his brother before all hell broke loose when her father and his deputies arrived in the underground city to arrest everyone?

Her jaw firm, she chose to go to Hawke first, hoping that when her father learned of this, he would understand.

She wheeled her horse in the direction of the Caddo village and rode at a hard gallop as soon as she was free of the trees. Her hair flew in the wind. Her heart beat rapidly within her chest.

Oh, Lord, she hoped she had made the right choice!

Chapter Twenty-two

It seemed only natural that Scarlett would be beside Hawke now as they rode toward the underground city. There was a bond between them that would never be broken. It was as though they had always known one another, and loved. She didn't see how she had endured life before she'd met him, for in truth, a part of her body, heart and soul had been missing.

As they continued onward in the mid-morning sunshine, the air soft and sweet against Scarlett's face, she glanced over at Hawke, riding tall and straight in his saddle. It wasn't hard to read his thoughts. When she had told him about finding his brother in the underground city, she had seen a mixture of emotions on his face — sadness, anger and disappointment. Finally, he had looked up and told her that this was the last time his brother would embarrass him. He was going to banish him from the tribe.

"I gave my brother many chances," Hawke suddenly said, looking over at

Scarlett as though he had just read her thoughts. "I told him I would give him one last chance. Why did he not listen? I am his older brother. A younger brother is supposed to listen to an older brother's advice, and learn from it. But Fast Deer had too many demons inside him to listen to anyone but his cravings for all the wrong things in life."

"I'm so sorry," Scarlett murmured. "I wish I hadn't had to tell you what I saw, but I knew you would want to know. That place is dangerous. Tempers could quickly flare and someone could be killed. It could be your brother."

"He is already dead," Hawke said, his eyes sad. "But I am glad you came for me. And now, what of the woman — Scottie's mother? You saw her there, too."

"I plan to try to talk sense to her and take her from that place, but when Father hears this latest news about what she has been up to, he won't hesitate any longer to send her away," Scarlett said.

Then her jaw tightened. "I will not allow Scottie to go with her," she said. "No matter what she says or does, that child will never be with her again. He has a second chance at life now. I shall see that he doesn't lose that chance."

"You said you are going to tell your father about the underground city," Hawke said. "Why did he not know about it already?"

"When you see how well hidden it is, you will understand," Scarlett said. "It's amazing. I don't see how it was ever established. It had to have taken years to dig deep enough to build a city. I wonder why it was built here in the first place."

"A place hidden beneath the ground like that must have been established for hidden purposes," Hawke said tightly. "I wish my brother had never found it. I might have eventually been able to turn him onto the right road of life. Instead, his body and soul have been poisoned forever. As I see it, he is no longer my brother. He . . . is . . . a stranger."

"Again, I'm so sorry," Scarlett said, her voice breaking. "I'm sorry that you had to know your brother has become involved with such people. How could two men be so different? You are so pure and noble. Your brother is —"

"Do not say the words that eat away at my heart," Hawke broke in. "Let us just go and do what must be done. I will take my brother to our council house, where he will stand before our people as he is given the order of banishment. You take the woman to your father so that he can pronounce her fate. As I said before, both my brother and the woman are lost souls. They are beyond help."

Seeing the familiar thick forest up ahead, Scarlett led Hawke through it, her thoughts on her father now, and what his reaction to this news would be. She had chosen twice to go to Hawke's village before she went to her father, and she felt a little guilty.

She now hoped that she could get Mary Jane to go with her without a fight, for Scarlett was determined to take her to her father, no matter what the woman said or did.

"There is the entrance, beyond that thick brush," Scarlett said, halting Lightning. "I left my horse outside when I was here before so no one would hear me approaching."

"I will leave mine outside, too," Hawke said.

"The men who are there won't like it that they have been discovered, especially the Chinese coolies," Scarlett said, tying her reins to a low tree limb beside Hawke's. She watched him take a rifle from the gun boot at the side of his horse.

Scarlett reached inside her pocket to rest

a hand on her pistol. With her free hand she held some brush aside to show Hawke the entrance.

"I have heard tales of an underground city, but thought that was all they were — stories told around night fires," Hawke said. "I chose to ignore the existence of this place as did my father before me. Now that I know it is true, I marvel at its reality."

He paused before entering the passageway. He turned to Scarlett. "Perhaps you should not go inside with me," he said. "There will be trouble."

"I know," she said softly. "But I have faced danger head on before."

"I will center my anger on my brother, so perhaps the others there will not interfere," Hawke said tightly. "And you?"

"I don't plan to take no for an answer when I confront Mary Jane," Scarlett said. "As far as I'm concerned, this is Mary Jane's last day in Coral Creek. She will be on the next stagecoach, no matter its destination. My father will gladly pay her passage just to be rid of her."

"Those in the underground city will not be happy that others know about it, especially a Caddo chief," Hawke said, walking inside with Scarlett. He kept her close with an arm around her waist.

"I know," Scarlett said, a chill riding her spine at the prospect of what those men might do. She now had second thoughts about her decision. Surely she should have told her father first so that he could come with his deputies and a posse and clean out this hornets' nest.

"The fact that I am chief may work in our favor," Hawke said, keeping his voice low so that no one else could hear them. "I know of no man who wants trouble from a chief and his warriors."

"I hope none of them know that I am the daughter of Coral Creek's sheriff," Scarlett said. "But there wouldn't be any way they could know. It has always been my father's practice to keep his home life separate from work, so as not to bring danger into my life, or Mother's."

She hung her head as remembrances of her mother swept through her mind. "My mother," she said, her voice breaking. "She died so needlessly."

"I am sorry you have suffered such a loss," Hawke said, then went quiet as he saw light up ahead.

"We're almost there," Scarlett whispered to Hawke. "I . . . I . . . am suddenly afraid."

"I will keep you from all harm," Hawke

said, sweeping her around so that their lips were close. He brushed soft kisses across hers lips, then leaned away and peered into her eyes now that the candles' glow allowed him to see her. "Stay close by my side. I will convince the men that all I am interested in is my brother, and all that you want is the woman. I believe they will gladly sacrifice those two, to prevent my warriors from attacking this place and wreaking havoc."

"I hope you are right," Scarlett said, gulping hard. "But what if the men are so lost to opium they can't see reason?"

"They will have no choice," Hawke said, walking now beside Scarlett, his hands on his rifle, while Scarlett held her own pistol before her.

She said a silent prayer that this would soon be over and they would be away from the underground city, safe.

Once they were close to the building, Hawke stopped and gazed down at Scarlett. "I think it would be best if you stayed outside," he said, placing a gentle hand on her cheek.

"You don't know Mary Jane, so I must go with you to identify her," Scarlett said, her voice shaky with apprehension.

"I will step inside first," Hawke said. "I

will make certain it is safe before you enter."

Scarlett's eyes were wide as she nodded. "Okay," she agreed, again gulping with fear. "But I won't be far behind you."

He nodded, then stepped away from her and quickly entered the building. Those inside were taken off guard, looking up from the poker tables and from their places along the walls where they were smoking opium.

"I want no one but my brother," Hawke quickly stated as he held his rifle steady before him. He felt rather than saw Scarlett come in and stand beside him.

"I want no one but Mary Jane," Scarlett said tightly, holding her pistol steady before her.

A keen disappointment swept through her when she looked around the room and didn't see Mary Jane.

She had already left!

No one said anything. They sat there stiffly as they looked slowly from Hawke, to Scarlett, and then back at Hawke.

Hawke's eyes were on his brother, who had just risen shakily, his eyes filled with humiliation and regret.

"How did you know?" Fast Deer gulped out.

"This is not the time to talk," Hawke said angrily. His eyes narrowed as he saw how unsteadily his brother stood. Obviously, he had shared an opium pipe before sitting down to play poker with the unruly-looking men at the large table.

Hawke motioned with the rifle toward his brother. "Just come on, Fast Deer," he commanded. "It is time for you to go home and face your people."

Fast Deer cowered, lowering his eyes, then looked slowly up at Hawke again. "Does this mean banishment for your brother?" he asked, tears shining in his eyes. "You will not forgive me just one last time?"

"Forgiveness means nothing to you," Hawke said, his jaw tight. "You listen to nothing but your basest needs. You have embarrassed this brother for the last time. *Huh,* in council you will be given the order of banishment for what you did."

Fast Deer staggered toward Hawke, hardly able to stand, much less walk. But Hawke held him up with one arm, holding his rifle with his free hand.

"Do not follow us," he said over his shoulder to those who were watching. "As I said, all I want is my brother."

Scarlett wasn't sure how to feel about

Mary Jane's absence. She had wanted this proof of wrongdoing to get Mary Jane out of her life. But she didn't truly need proof. Her father would believe her.

Her knees trembling, she walked beside Hawke while he held his brother steady.

Just as she stepped forward to shove the swinging door open, so that she and Hawke and his brother could leave, she heard a sudden grunt of pain behind her. She spun around, horrified when she saw that someone had thrown a knife at Fast Deer and it was lodged in his back.

Hawke gazed helplessly into his brother's eyes as he took his last breath of life.

Hawke was scarcely aware of the commotion behind him. Everyone in the building was fleeing out the back door.

Scarlett noticed that the last to leave was a group of coolies. They were shouting something in Chinese as they disappeared.

"Fast Deer," Hawke said, tears filling his eyes as he held his limp brother in his arms. "Is this how it must end between us? How did you go so wrong? How?"

"I'm so sorry," Scarlett murmured as she placed a gentle hand on Hawke's arm. "So very, very sorry."

"His banishment is final and complete now," Hawke said thickly. "He is no more."

Scarlett leaned down and picked up his rifle, looking around for any signs of the coolies. She was glad to see that they had all fled.

She doubted they would stay away for long, though. Their opium was still there, as well as stacks of coins on the gamblers' tables.

There wasn't a sound of movement outside on the streets of the underground city as Scarlett and Hawke hurried toward the entrance.

She was vastly relieved when they were safely out in the open again. She watched as Hawke carefully placed his brother's body over the back of his horse, securing it with a rope from his saddlebag.

Then he turned to Scarlett. "I will escort you safely to your home, and then I must go to my people and prepare my brother for burial," he said sadly. "It is a dark time for me and my people."

Scarlett placed a hand on his copper cheek. "My love, you go on with your brother. I don't need to be escorted anywhere."

"You truly will be alright?" he asked, searching her eyes.

She slid his rifle in his gun boot, placed her own pistol in her pocket, then flung herself into his arms. "I love you so much," she said, her voice breaking. "Go. Do what you must. I will be alright. I learned long ago how to take care of myself."

Hawke framed her face between his hands. "Will you come to my village tomorrow?" he asked thickly. "I want you to be with me as I mourn."

"Yes, I will be there," she murmured, glad that he had asked.

He leaned low and kissed her, then took her hands for a moment and held them. At last, he went to his horse and swung himself into the saddle.

He waited for her to mount her own steed, then rode with her for a while until they came to a place in the road where she had to go one way, he another.

She watched him ride away, and continued watching until he was out of sight. Then she went her own way, but not toward the ranch. She knew her father would be at his office.

Oh, Lord, she wondered, what would he say when he heard what she had been up to today?

She continued on until she was riding down the main street of Coral Creek, her heart pounding in her chest as she stopped before her father's office and dismounted.

As she wrapped her reins around the hitching rail, she couldn't take her eyes off the door to her father's office. Finding the courage to get this over with, Scarlett went inside the office.

She found her father alone behind a large oak desk that was cluttered with papers, and an ashtray half filled with cigar butts.

He smoked only at the office, never at home. He always bathed as soon as he entered the house, for he did not want to spread the smell to her clothes or skin.

"Daughter?" Patrick said, his eyes widening when he found her standing there. "What brings you into town? You didn't tell me you had shopping to do."

"I don't," Scarlett said, smiling sheepishly at him.

She sat down in a chair opposite the desk from him and told him everything that had happened that day. She watched his expression change from horror, to surprise, to horror again, until she was through with the whole story.

"Mary Jane wasn't there when I returned," she said. "I hate to think of where she might be. I'm sure it isn't back home being a good mother to Scottie."

Patrick ran his fingers through his thick

black hair as he tried to absorb all that she had told him.

Then he glared at her. "I can't believe you did this," he said tightly. "You actually went to that underground city without first telling me? You . . . went . . . there twice?"

She nodded.

"I don't know what to think," he went on. "Daughter, do you want to die an early death? Don't you know those lowlifes who frequent the underground city will be out for your blood now, as well as Hawke's?"

"I believe they will be too afraid of stirring up the wrath of the Caddo nation to cause me or Hawke any trouble," Scarlett said, trying to convince herself that what she said was true.

"I have to work fast on this," her father said, rising. He went to the wall and took his holstered pistols from a peg and secured them around his waist, then went to his gun rack and yanked a shotgun from it, which he quickly loaded.

He slapped his hat on his head. "Go home, Scarlett. I don't want you involved in any more of this."

"You're going to round up a posse?" she asked, as she walked outside with him.

"Yep, and quick," he said, going with her to the hitching rail. "Draw me a map in the dust, Scarlett. Show me how to get to the underground city."

She did this; then they both mounted.

"And as for Mary Jane, we'll see to her when we get home. She'll show up there sooner or later," Patrick said. "Daughter, would you like an escort home, since you've gotten yourself involved in this mess?"

"Papa, you know better than that," Scarlett said, sighing. "Go on. Get done what must be done, and . . . and . . . be careful."

"Thanks for the information," Patrick said, tipping his hat to her. "But, damn it all, Scarlett, don't do anything like this again."

"Even if it gets you the gratitude of all the townsfolk after you clean up that mess in the underground city?" she asked, smiling almost wickedly at him.

"Go on home, Scarlett," Patrick said, his eyes now twinkling. "I can't imagine you ever playing a violin. You've too much spunk for that."

"That's why I didn't want to play it in the first place," she said, grinning at him.

He nodded, gazed at her for a moment longer, then rode off to gather his posse.

Scarlett watched him go, then swung her

horse around and headed toward home. She hadn't told him everything . . . that she would be going to share Hawke's grieving tomorrow as he mourned the loss of his brother.

She shivered at the memory of seeing Fast Deer with the knife in his back, knowing it could have been Hawke's back . . . or her own!

She did realize now how reckless her actions had been today.

She hoped that her father would come out of the underground city as unharmed as she and Hawke had.

Chapter Twenty-three

Scarlett continued to worry about her father as she rode back toward the ranch.

A cold shiver raced up and down her spine at the thought of the viciousness of the men in the underground city, especially the man who had thrown the knife into Fast Deer's back.

I hope Father finds not only that man, but all the others, too, Scarlett thought.

She could still smell the opium, as the smoke penetrated not only her hair, but also her clothes. She couldn't see how anyone could enjoy smoking it. The stench was enough to make one want to vomit.

The ranch house now came into view, looking serene and pretty. Yellow daisies grew all across the front, thanks to Malvina, who not only loved to cook, but also to garden.

Back home in San Francisco, Malvina had always planted a garden. Along with flowers, she had planted an assortment of vegetables, among them green beans, Scarlett's favorite.

Even now, as Scarlett drew closer to the house, she could smell green beans cooking on the stove. The smell reminded Scarlett that she had not eaten today. She had rushed out of the house without breakfast.

Her stomach growled as she grew closer to the house and recognized the aroma of chicken roasting in the oven for the evening meal.

Scarlett was eager to take a bath, eat, then rest in her room while reading a novel before she retired for the night. She needed the diversion of reading tonight to help her forget all that had happened today. She had seen someone murdered in cold blood. The more she thought about it, the more she wondered if she would have any appetite, after all.

Sighing, she rode to the stable and dismounted, smiling a quiet thank you to Jason as he took Lightning's reins and walked the horse to his stall.

"Be sure to rub him down good, Jason, and give him an extra helping of oats. He deserves it today," Scarlett said over her shoulder as she walked from the stable.

"Yes, ma'am," Jason replied, already removing the saddle from Lightning. The horse whinnied and nuzzled the young man's hand as Jason grabbed a handful of oats from the bucket that he had readied for the animal's return.

Unable to banish everything that had happened from her mind, and wondering if she would ever be able to forget this day, Scarlett walked toward the front door. She stopped abruptly when she saw something lying in the garden, far back where the forsythia and lilac bushes grew.

"Lord, is . . . that . . . a hand?" Scarlett gasped.

She closed her eyes and shook her head, before taking another look. Surely her mind was playing tricks on her.

"No, it can't be," she tried to reassure herself, yet she was afraid to open her eyes and take a second look. How could anyone imagine seeing a hand?

Her heart pounding, and feeling suddenly cold all over, Scarlett opened her eyes as she slowly walked toward the bushes.

She felt sick to her stomach when she realized that it wasn't her imagination working overtime. It was most definitely a hand, and where there was a hand, there would be a body.

She stopped before reaching the bushes, thinking that she shouldn't go on alone.

She glanced over her shoulder at the stable, and then at the hand again.

No. She wouldn't go for Jason. He was just a teenager.

She sucked in a deep breath, reached inside her pocket for her pistol, then walked slowly onward. She looked from side to side, watching for someone to leap out at her, or for someone who might be lurking amid the trees.

The hand hadn't moved an inch since Scarlett had first seen it.

Gathering her courage Scarlett went onward. She stopped in amazement when she finally saw the body that the hand belonged to.

"Mary Jane!" she said in a harsh whisper, her eyes moving quickly over Mary Jane. She lay on her stomach in the bushes, a knife exactly like the one that had killed Fast Deer protruding from her back.

"The person that killed Fast Deer must have followed Mary Jane here and killed her, too," Scarlett whispered to herself. "But why?"

The dead woman's eyes were open and locked in a death's stare. Scarlett reached down and touched her hand. It was still warm.

"Mary Jane, Mary Jane," Scarlett said, kneeling beside her. "What led you to this terrible end? Or should I say who? Surely you were done wrong sometime in your past. Was that what sent you on the downward spiral of evil that led to your death today? I can't help pitying you now. You poor, unloved thing. I hope you are finally at peace."

Scarlett slowly rose. "Your son will be taken care of," she said, her voice breaking. "He will be given a good life. I promise you that."

With listless steps, Scarlett went back to the stable. Jason looked up in surprise as he slowly brushed Lightning's coat.

"What is it, ma'am?" the teenager asked. "You look as though you've seen a ghost."

"Well, in a sense I have," Scarlett said, sinking down on a packed bale of straw. She sighed and shook her head, then looked up at Jason again.

When she explained about having found Mary Jane, the color drained from his face.

"Murdered?" he gasped. "So close to where we are?"

"Yes. Her body is not yet cold," Scarlett said, visibly shuddering. "Whoever did this had to have done it only a short while ago, yet I didn't see anyone on my way here."

She looked toward the thick trees surrounding the ranch. They were part of a wood called The Thicket because of the density of the trees. Wild things roamed there at night.

"I guess whoever did this came and went by way of The Thicket," she murmured. "If the killer isn't familiar with the lay of the land, he may never come out alive."

"I've heard tell of cougars living in there," Jason said uneasily. "I wouldn't think you'd want your house this close."

"We're safe enough from wild animals here on the edge of The Thicket," Scarlett said, rising to her feet. "Jason, I hate to leave Mary Jane's body just lying there until Father gets home. Will you help me bring her body here to the stable where we can lay her out until the undertaker comes?"

Jason dropped the brush and took an unsteady step away from her. "You want me to do that?"

"You and Malvina are the only ones here, and I don't think Malvina has the strength to do it," Scarlett murmured. "So, Jason. Seems you are the only one who can help me."

"Touch . . . a . . . dead body?" Jason said, his face taking on a twisted shape. "I —"

"You can do it, Jason," Scarlett said, placing a comforting arm around his thin shoulders. "Come on. I need a man to help me. You're the only one I see."

"Me? A man?" Jason said, taken aback by what she'd said. Then he smiled. "Yep. I'm a man. I sure can help you, Scarlett. Let's go and do it."

She smiled at him, then grew serious again when they reached Mary Jane's body.

When Scarlett helped lift her up, she felt nauseous again, but fought the feeling off as she and Jason struggled the body into the stable and covered it with a wool blanket.

"Now the worst thing of all lies ahead of me," Scarlett told Jason as he walked with her to the door of the stable. "I've got to tell the boy that his mother is dead."

She went straight to Scottie's room. After she told him, he didn't cry, but instead clung to Scarlett.

"Scottie, you are going to be alright," Scarlett murmured. "I will take care of you. I would love to take you in as my own son."

"Until I become a shaman?" Scottie murmured.

"Yes, until you become a shaman," Scarlett replied. "Until you are grown up enough to be called a shaman, you will be my little medicine man."

"I'd like that," Scottie said, suddenly beaming.

The arrival of a horse outside alerted Scarlett that her father had returned home.

She ran to the window and watched as he tied his horse's reins to the hitching rail, then lumbered into the house.

Relieved that her father was safe, she ran from the room and flung herself into his arms just as he stepped into the front foyer.

"Papa, I was so worried," Scarlett said, clinging to him. "If anything should happen to you, I —"

"Sshh, daughter," Patrick reassured as he gently stroked her back. "I'm fine. I took care of the mess. No one will ever have an opportunity to go to that underground city again for any reason."

Scarlett stepped away from him. She searched his eyes. "What do you mean?" she asked softly.

"When my posse and I arrived, only a few coolies and women were there," he said. "Apparently, the gamblers had been frightened off by what had happened to Fast Deer."

"What did you do?" Scarlett asked, awaiting the right moment to tell him about Mary Jane.

"We rounded up the coolies and the women, and as they watched, we set fire to the buildings that were still standing in the hidden city," Patrick explained. "You should have heard the coolies. They shouted over and over again to us in Chinese. They cried as they watched their opium go up in smoke."

"Where are they now?" Scarlett asked, her eyes wide.

"They're behind bars," Patrick said, sighing. When Scottie came into the room, he lifted him up and held him. "I don't think I'm going to bother with prosecuting them, myself. I'm shipping them off to San Francisco, where arrest warrants await most of them . . . except the women, of course. I think I'll keep them in the hoosegow a few days, then set them free on the condition they leave town right away. All that's important is that they leave us in peace. I'll make certain none of the folks in my fine town ever sees the whites of their eyes again. The men that helped me today are still at the underground city, doing all they can to seal up the entrance so no one can ever find it again."

"Mommy is dead," Scottie blurted out, drawing Patrick's eyes quickly to him.

"What . . . did . . . you say?" Patrick asked, obviously stunned by the news.

"Mommy is dead," Scottie repeated matter-of-factly. "Scarlett told me."

Patrick set Scottie on his feet and turned to Scarlett. "What happened?" he asked.

Scarlett explained how she had found Mary Jane.

"And so her miserable life is over, huh?" Patrick said, turning his eyes to Scottie again. "Son, are you alright?"

"He's fine," Scarlett said just as Scottie nodded his head. "I'm going to see that he gets all of the opportunities she has denied him."

"We'll do it together," Patrick said, going to Scottie and lifting him into his arms again.

Scarlett knew this wasn't the time to tell her father of her feelings for Hawke, or that she hoped to marry him soon. When she did, she wanted to take Scottie with her to the Caddo village and raise him as her own and Hawke's.

No, this wasn't the time; nor was it the moment to tell him that tomorrow she planned to join Hawke as he mourned his brother.

For now, it was enough that she and her father were home safe, and that Scottie had accepted the death of his mother.

"Where is she?" Patrick asked, looking toward the door.

"In the stable," Scarlett murmured.

"Has he seen her?" Patrick asked, looking quickly at Scottie.

"No, and I don't think he should," Scarlett murmured, giving Scottie a hug.

"I'll go for the undertaker," Patrick said. "She'll be buried in Boot Hill."

Scarlett nodded.

Patrick put Scottie down; then, hand in hand, Scarlett and the boy walked her father to the porch. They watched him ride away, then went back inside where Malvina stood with a platter of freshly baked cookies.

"I heard it all," she said. "I think these cookies might make Scottie feel better, don't you, Scarlett?"

"I do believe so," Scarlett said, watching Scottie take a cookie and quickly eat it, then reach for another.

Scarlett smiled a thank you to Malvina.

Malvina returned the smile.

Then Scarlett turned and gazed in the direction of Hawke's village. It would be wonderful to be with him again, even under sad circumstances.

And once Hawke's grieving was behind him, they could begin the rest of their lives together.

Chapter Twenty-four

It was a serene, windless day, with a cloudless sky and gentle temperatures. Dressed in the same black dress she had worn to her mother's funeral, Scarlett stood behind Hawke, who knelt beside his brother's grave. Fast Deer's wrapped body lay on thick bulrush mats in the freshly dug grave a small distance from the village.

She knew Hawke's sorrow, could even feel it. It wasn't all that long ago that she had mourned someone in her own family. Her mother. She would never forget the day of the funeral, how so many people came to their home on Nob Hill, to pay their last respects while her mother's body lay on view in the parlor.

Scarlett would never forget the sickening sweet aroma of flowers that almost filled the room. Her mother had been loved by everyone who knew her.

And then came the long, horrible moments of the actual funeral. Because her mother had been so beloved, many took the time to speak about her, sharing their feelings with those in attendance.

Her father had asked Scarlett to say something about her mother, too, but she was suffering the loss too much to share it with anyone.

Sometimes she regretted not having done this for her father, for she now knew that it would have helped him in his time of grief.

But if she was given the opportunity all over again, she knew she would still not be able to do it.

But today the responsibility for Fast Deer's burial lay in Hawke's hands, for he was the sole survivor of their family, and he was their people's chief. He spoke at each burial rite, but this time it was obviously harder for him.

Scarlett could tell that by the drawn look on his usually calm copper face. She could tell by the sorrow in his eyes.

He wore only a breechclout today, and was barefoot for the ceremony, while others wore clothes devoid of any ornament.

There was no music or singing. It was quiet, except for an occasional birdsong that came from overhead in the willows. Beneath those weeping trees lay the grave of a fallen brave who had never been given the honor of being called a warrior, for he had not done anything to deserve the title.

She watched Hawke now, with such sadness for what he was experiencing. He still knelt beside his brother's grave with his head bowed, praying to *Ayo-caddi-ay-may,* while others stood back behind him, waiting for the moment they could go to the grave to leave their gifts for the departed.

Those gifts would take the place of the possessions Fast Deer had gambled away. They would go to his grave with him.

Earlier this morning, before the gathering at Fast Deer's grave site, Hawke had told Scarlett that he wouldn't be taking the usual length of time to mourn his brother. Fast Deer had turned his back on the true traditions and meaning of being a Caddo long ago.

Embarrassed by his brother, Hawke had decided to get the burial over with as quickly as possible, then move on with his life.

Before Fast Deer had been murdered, a fishing trip had been planned by the entire village, men, women and children alike. The trip had been delayed for only the time taken to prepare Fast Deer for burial. After the burial rites, the people would proceed with their plans.

Hawke had asked Scarlett to spend those

two or three days of fishing with him and his people, and then join them for a feast of fish.

Knowing that the trip would take her away from home for so long, she had hesitated to tell her father. He had seen her growing closer and closer to Hawke, but, surprisingly, he hadn't objected to the trip.

So after only a brief hesitation, she had agreed to go on the trip. She only hoped that her father wouldn't suddenly change his mind and refuse to let her go.

Ever since Hawke had saved her life, her father's attitude toward him had changed dramatically. And going on a trip with a whole village of Indians was vastly different from going with one Indian alone.

She wanted to include Scottie on the trip, but wasn't sure if he was yet strong enough for such an outing. He still took many naps during the day. He was growing stronger every day, but not strong enough to be away from his own bed, and regular meals.

She would promise him that he could go on the next fishing outing with her and Hawke.

Her thoughts were interrupted when Hawke came back and stood with her as people started filing past Fast Deer's grave to pay their respects.

Some of the men lay four, six or more arrows in the grave with Fast Deer, while one gave him a bow. The women gave him beautiful deerskins wrapped in mats, while one small child walked up to the grave and gave Fast Deer the doll her mother had made from corn husks.

Others came with offerings of food and drink, feathers, and even a flute so that he would have entertainment on his journey west.

When the Caddo people seemed to have brought all that they would bring, Thunder Eagle made his appearance. Until then he had remained back from the others, praying.

He knelt beside the grave, waved his fan of eagle feathers over it, spoke softly to the deceased, sprinkled herbs from a small bag over everything, then laid his fan among the other gifts.

He stood and stepped back to rejoin the others, his head bowed, his lips moving in a constant silent prayer.

Scarlett stepped up to the grave with her own gift. She bent to her knees and laid down a small buckskin bag of beautiful coral rocks that she had collected from the banks of the Coral River. It was Hawke's suggestion that she present this particular gift, for Fast Deer had been mesmerized by those rocks from the moment he had first seen them.

Hawke had said that these rocks would make his brother's journey to the hereafter more pleasant, for some would be carried, while others would be walked upon to make his path west a lovelier one.

Scarlett turned to stand with the others as Hawke stepped forth again to proceed with the ceremony.

Hawke raised his head and his outstretched arms heavenward. "*Ayo-caddi-ay-may,* oh, God of my people, I speak to you today as chief of the Cougar Clan and as a humble man who has lost a brother. Oh, God of my people, forgive my brother for what he has done on earth. He is now but a child again, innocent and pure," he cried out. "My brother's soul has left his body and travels now toward the west. From there his soul will rise into the air and join those beloved ones who have departed before him. I pray that you will allow him rest and forgive any wrong that his body did while he was of this earth. Many gifts have been given to our loved one to bring him comfort while his soul is on its way to the west. There he will seek direction to the house of pleasure. I pray you will show him the way, so that he will have in heaven what he did not have on earth."

He paused, bowed his head, then looked heavenward again. "*Ayo-caddi-ay-may,* please give my brother's soul a peaceful heart, which he did not have while of this earth," he cried. "I humbly ask that you answer my prayers."

He unfastened a small buckskin pouch that he had tied to his breechclout. He opened it and took from it a handful of corn, which he threw to the four winds. Then he stepped back from the grave, beside Scarlett, as several warriors approached to lay thick mats over the body and gifts, making way in turn for others who smoothed dirt over everything.

Then several warriors placed rocks over the grave until all of the fresh dirt was covered, ensuring that no animals could defile the remains of the dead.

Thunder Eagle stepped forth and prayed over the grave, then gave Hawke a big hug. Finally he turned and walked with the others back toward the village, while Hawke and Scarlett remained a while longer at the grave.

"It was such a useless life that my

brother led," Hawke said, his jaw tight. "Where did I go wrong? Where did Father and Mother go wrong? Fast Deer seemed filled with something evil from the day he was old enough to make decisions on his own. None were for the right reasons. My father and mother tried so hard to get inside his mind and heart, but he would not allow it. It was as though he wanted to die an early death, for everything he did led him there."

"I know you must be feeling terrible pain to have lost a brother in such a way," Scarlett murmured. "I have never known such pain, for I never had a brother or sister. But I understand the pain of loss, for I felt it when I lost both sets of grandparents at a young age, and then my mother and Aunt Emma not so long ago. It is a pain unlike anything else to lose someone you love so much."

"I did love my brother, but I feel that that love was not returned. If it was, why did he not listen to reason when I tried to make him see the wrong in all he did?" Hawke said, swallowing hard.

"Come away from the grave," Scarlett softly urged, gently taking him by the hand. "It is done. There is nothing more you can do. Think of it in this way, Hawke.

He is finally at peace, perhaps for the first time in his life."

Hawke nodded as he twined his fingers through hers. "Finally at peace," he said, slowly walking away from the grave with her. "*Huh,* I will think of him in that way."

"Let's talk of something else, unless that is not respectful so soon after your brother's burial," Scarlett said, gazing up at Hawke and seeing the despair in his eyes. "Tell me more about the fishing trip. I'm excited about it. Did I tell you I know how to fish? Father taught me when I was old enough to hold a fishing pole, for I was the son he never had."

She laughed softly. "Hawke, the first time he put a worm in my hand, I was mortified," she murmured. "To think that I had to put the worm on that sharp object sickened me."

"Did you do it anyway?" he asked, his eyes beginning to take on the look of peace they usually held in her presence. "Were you brave enough?"

"I knew it was important to my father that I enjoy fishing with him, so, yes, I finally baited the hook. Do you know, I caught a fish on that hook my first try."

"A big one?" Hawke asked, his eyes devouring her. She was so good for him at this time. He could hardly bear the truth that he had not won this battle to save his brother. But he would be glad to see Scarlett out of those black clothes. They reminded him too painfully of death.

"The fish was so tiny, I wanted to keep it for a pet in a fishbowl," Scarlett said, giggling like a schoolgirl at the memory of that day.

"A . . . fishbowl?" Hawke said, raising an eyebrow.

She realized he had never seen such a thing and explained.

"Did he allow you to keep it in a fishbowl?" he asked, remembering how he and his brother had run after fireflies when they were just old enough to stand, to catch the flashing lanterns in the palms of their hands before they went to bed for the night.

That remembrance was good, and he realized that there were some times with his brother that were unforgettable — but only when they were small and innocent.

"Yes, and then we caught another so that it wouldn't be all alone," Scarlett said. "One day when I looked in the bowl I saw a lot of tiny round eggs. My mother told me I would soon have baby fish, and I did. A whole bowlful of them."

"And what did you do with so many?" Hawke asked softly.

"We put them in another larger bowl, and when they had grown enough so they wouldn't be gobbled up by the bigger fish in the pond, we turned them loose," Scarlett said.

"Are you ready to catch fish again?" he asked, a sudden twinkle in his eyes. "But this time to keep and eat? There will be a big feast after the fish are brought in, and some of the fish will be prepared to eat later."

"I can hardly wait," Scarlett said, smiling at him. "I'll go home now, then return tomorrow. What time should I get here?"

"We leave for our favorite fishing grounds at dawn," he answered. "If you would stay the night with me, you would not have to get up so early."

"If only I could," Scarlett said. She looked to her left, where far ahead of her his people were returning to the village.

She turned to him and wrapped her arms around his neck. "But I can't," she murmured. "I'm surprised that my father didn't cause a fuss when I asked to go fishing with you, especially after I told him I would be away overnight. But when he saw my determination, and how badly I wanted to go, and knowing your entire village would be there, too, he gave in."

She laughed softly. "I have always had a way with my father, you know," she said. "I guess that is only normal when a father has an only child, especially a daughter."

"He also is a man who holds trust for this Caddo chief inside his heart," Hawke said. "He is the sort who would check carefully on a man who shows interest in his daughter, is he not?"

"Yes," Scarlett said, laughing softly. "And he could not find one thing about you that was bad."

"Except for having a brother he obviously despised," Hawke said sadly, his eyes lowering to the ground. "But now he is gone. Forever he is gone."

"Let's concentrate on tomorrow and the fish I challenge you to catch," Scarlett said, bringing his eyes back to her. In them was a renewed soft gleam.

"Yes, I will think only on tomorrow," he said, pulling her fully into his arms and giving her a passionate kiss, which erased everything else from both their minds.

Afraid someone would see them, and not wanting to give his people any reason to disapprove of her, Scarlett eased from his arms.

They walked on to the village, where she mounted Lightning. "Tomorrow?" she murmured.

"*Huh,* tomorrow," he said, taking her hand, holding it for a moment, then releasing it.

He watched her ride away, her hair even more brilliantly red against the black dress she wore today.

"You will be my wife," he whispered to himself.

Yes, he would ask her soon. He had no doubt what her answer would be.

That knowledge made his grief much easier to bear. He went inside his home and sat down beside the fire, tears filling his eyes again at the thought of the uselessness of his brother's life.

"Had you only known a woman like Scarlett," he whispered, "my brother, your life would have been changed forever, and only for the good!"

Chapter Twenty-five

The ship's white sails fluttered in the soft sea breeze. The flag with its skull and bones proudly waved above Blue Raven as he stood on the top deck, his brass telescope at his eyes as he slowly swept the land that had just come into sight.

His heart was pounding to be back in waters where he might catch a glimpse of the scarlet-haired wench he had planned to take with him to his island.

"Until she was stolen from right beneath me nose," he grumbled to himself. "But I'll get 'er back, I will. I'll hunt for 'er til me dyin' day if that's how long it takes to find 'er again. There ain't none other like 'er, that's fer sure."

"It isn't wise to be this close to land again where we stole the lady," Fat Jaws said as he came to stand beside Blue Raven, his own eyes gazing ahead at the land that grew closer and closer. "She's poison to us pirates, she is."

He turned his scowling eyes to Blue Raven. "Mate, let it be," he growled.

"We've done perfectly well without 'er. If we need ladies for entertainment, we know the places to go get 'em without bringin' trouble into our lives. Many are a'willin' to join up with us pirates because they like the special gifts they get for their time."

"I've me one very special gift to give the scarlet-headed wench," Blue Raven said. He lowered the telescope from his eyes and looked over at Fat Jaws. "Me, my friend. Me."

"Ye don't remember how she spat at yer feet, do ye?" Fat Jaws growled, his red cambric shirt opened to his waist. "What makes ye think it'd be any different this time, even if ye do succeed at findin' 'er and bringin' 'er on board the *Eclipse*?"

"If?" Blue Raven said, his eyes widening. "What kind o' talk is that? Ye know I'll find 'er." He chuckled low. "And the time she's spent away from me has given 'er time to think on me commanding figure and the riches she can 'ave as me special prize."

He lifted his telescope to his eyes again, and slowly scanned the horizon as the land grew even closer.

He then lowered it and turned to the men on deck. "Lower that pirate flag," he shouted. "Me mistake before was allowin' the skull and bones to show for too long. If no one had seen it, they'd never knowed we was pirates."

"I have never seen ye when ye didn't want to show yer flag to everyone," Fat Jaws said, lifting an eyebrow.

"That's because I hadn't found me a lady I wanted for keepin'," Blue Raven said, snickering. He gazed down at the clothes he was wearing, his best ones. He had on an elegant brocaded waistcoat, bright red breeches and wide-topped high boots that shone from polishing. Loops of gold earrings hung from each of his earlobes.

"Aye, I'm ready for 'er when we find 'er," he said as he again lifted the telescope to his eyes. Again he slowly scanned the approaching shore. "I'll promise 'er many trinkets. This time she won't refuse."

"One thing in our favor, if ye're determined to do this, is that ye now know not to drop anchor where we did before," Fat Jaws said, taking out his own spyglass and peering through it. "It's good that we're mooring the ship farther down the coast than where we last dropped anchor."

"But close enough to where we took the lady hostage," Blue Raven said, nodding.

Blue Raven dropped his telescope to his side again. "Once we are on land, we're going to steal horses and ride toward Coral

Creek," he said. "Surely me lady lives somewhere near there."

"We're going to steal horses dressed like this?" Fat Jaws said. He threw his head back in a fit of laughter, but the sound was strangled off when tight hands suddenly circled his throat.

He gazed into Blue Raven's angry eyes. "Stop that," he gasped. "Ye want to kill me?"

"If I hear any more talk like that, aye, ye will be feed for the sharks, that's fer certain," Blue Raven growled out. "Don't ye think I've thought o' that? We'll dress in clothes very different from what we wear today on me ship. I've some in a trunk I stole the other day when we dropped anchor near that house that sat isolated away from all the others. I made certain I took some of the man's clothes, for I knew even then what me plans were."

"Ye knew all along that ye'd return for 'er, didn't ye?" Fat Jaws said, rubbing his sore throat when Blue Raven dropped his hands away from it. "Ye want 'er so badly, ye'd chance losin' all we've worked for in our partnership of twenty or so years?"

"Me gut aches for 'er," Blue Raven said thickly. "Nary a night goes past when she doesn't visit me in me dreams. I was foolish not to take 'er to me bed that night she was on me ship before she was stole away from me. Had she known me skills of lovin' 'er, she'd have chosen me over the one who took 'er away."

"She was stolen too easily from us," Fat Jaws grumbled. "I feel foolish to 'ave been duped that easily."

"We'll be ready this time if anyone tries to get 'er once we have 'er aboard again," Blue Raven bragged. "Let 'em come and try. We've many a stick o' dynamite to throw at 'em this time, and we've our cannon. We'll be able to fight off anyone who tries to get aboard me ship."

"We have to make certain our crew stays awake to protect us with that dynamite," Fat Jaws grumbled. "We should've got rid of 'em and took on a brand new crew."

"There ain't many a man who is brave enough to ride the high seas in a pirate ship," Blue Raven said, chuckling. "It takes a different sort o' man to be a pirate. Those we 'ave are true men; they just weren't prepared for attack that night."

He circled a hand into a tight fist at his side. "Now they will be."

"None of this talk of dynamite or anything else means aught if we don't have the lady, and I, for one, thinks she ain't worth it," Fat Jaws said. "I still say, let's turn around and take the *Eclipse* back to the high seas. Why risk all that we've got just for one scarlet-headed lady?"

"Because there ain't no other lady like 'er, that's why, and because she got away," Blue Raven grumbled. "So let me hear no more talk from ye about forgettin' 'bout 'er. She's the same as mine, but she just don't know it."

He threw his head back in a fit of laughter as Fat Jaws once again gazed shoreward with his telescope.

Something deep within him knew that this was the beginning of the end for himself and Blue Raven, and for all those who rode with them. No amount of dynamite would keep them safe, he feared.

He began making plans of his own — plans that would take Blue Raven totally out of the picture.

"Aye, we'll steal horses and search for 'er until we find 'er," Blue Raven said, looking through his telescope. "I will find 'er, that's for sure. I will take 'er aboard me ship, and pity anyone who gets in me way. They will die at the hands of the pirate Blue Raven!"

Fat Jaws dropped his telescope to his side and gave Blue Raven a silent glare.

Shaking his head, he walked to his own cabin.

He sat down and dropped his head in his hands. "It is all over unless I do something," he whispered. "And for what does he risk our lives? Someone Blue Raven will tire of in one day!"

Aye, he knew that the main thing driving his friend was the loss of his special prize. Blue Raven could not stand to be bested by anyone.

Well, Fat Jaws had his own ideas on the subject. He'd play his own hand soon, and to hell with Blue Raven!

Chapter Twenty-six

The second day of fishing had just ended and night was beginning to fall. Scarlett had bathed with the other women in one of the hidden lagoons that had not been used for fishing.

She had discovered that there were many lagoons only a few miles from the Caddo village. There was an abundance of fish in them, both bull and rainbow trout.

Scarlett now sat with Hawke beside the large outdoor fire that had been built their first day there, a fire that had not been allowed to go out since. Many fish had been cooked over that fire. Some of the women were constantly preparing the fish that were caught. Part of the catch would be cooked immediately, the rest smoked and dried.

A good quantity of fish would be taken back to the village and divided equally among all the families.

Scarlett had learned the Caddo word for fish, *dorado*. She had also learned that the net the Caddo used was called a trat line.

As dusk fell, the Caddo laughed and talked as they sat beside the huge outdoor fire, contentment in their eyes.

Even Hawke had been able to momentarily forget the sadness that had come into his life upon the death of his only brother. Although Fast Deer had never found the right road, Hawke never loved him any less.

He felt guilty that he had not been able to help his brother live a decent, useful life. Scarlett knew that that guilt would lessen in time, and she was there to help him.

"My people are amazed at your skill in catching fish," Hawke said, moving closer to Scarlett. They were sharing a comfortable red mat, upon which had been spread a blanket.

"I'm amazed that I caught anything; I'm not used to your people's way of fishing with nets," Scarlett murmured. She set aside her empty dish. She had eaten so much delicious fish, she thought she might pop.

She was still surprised at how the Caddo cooked and prepared the fish. With bear grease.

When she said something about this to Hawke, he said that was the best way to cook fish. He told her he would take her on a bear hunt soon, for one was already planned.

"Do you truly hunt and kill bears?" she blurted out.

"It is a natural part of the Caddo warrior's life," Hawke said, reaching a hand to her hair and stroking it. It was still damp from her bath in the lagoon. And she smelled like the lilies that grew in the water in a variety of colors.

"You asked me to go with you," Scarlett said, so happy that he openly showed his love for her in the presence of his people.

She was also happy that the Caddo people had so readily accepted her, for as he ran his fingers through her hair, and then placed an arm around her waist and drew her next to him, some watched and smiled, then continued with what they were doing, either talking or eating.

"*Huh,* and that is because you have said you wish to be taught all about my people and their habits," Hawke said, nodding a thank you to a young brave when he brought a wooden tray of sliced fruits to him to share with Scarlett. "One of our main hunts is the bear hunt."

"I read somewhere that Indians say it is taboo for women to join the hunt with their warriors, that women bring them bad luck," Scarlett said, smiling when he placed a wild strawberry to her lips. The fruit was sweet on her tongue as she chewed, then swallowed it.

"You are a woman, that is true," Hawke said, giving her a look that melted her insides, "but you bring this chief only good luck."

Some children ran from the crowd and began playing tag, laughing and giggling.

Scarlett watched, suddenly reminded of Scottie. She knew how badly he had wanted to come on the fishing trip.

Watching the children at play reminded Scarlett of how Scottie had bonded so quickly with them earlier. She knew that the bond would grow, for she would be bringing him back to the Caddo village often.

"You are watching the children at play," Hawke said, his eyes following the path of hers. "Do you want many children when you become a wife?"

She turned quickly toward him. She found his eyes watching her intently. Her heart pounded hard in her chest, for it seemed that he might be ready to ask her to marry him. She wanted nothing more than that in her life. She could never love anyone as much and as dearly as she loved Hawke.

"I was an only child, so, yes, I want several children," Scarlett murmured.

She thought again of Scottie and how he had been raised alone without the companionship of a brother or sister. She had seen the loneliness in his eyes and never wanted a child of her own to have the same lost look.

"I, too, want many," Hawke said, nodding. "A son. I want a son to walk in my footsteps as chief."

She wanted to confess to him that she wished to bear him that son, but it was not her place to suggest such a thing, not when they had not yet spoken of marriage.

"A son born in your image will be a handsome young man," Scarlett murmured. She laughed softly. "A son you can teach how to fish."

She looked toward the lagoon, where fishing nets were stretched out in the water for the early morning catch. It would be their last, for they planned to return home after hauling in those fish for cooking.

"I was surprised to see just how your people catch their fish," Scarlett said, recalling the way the Caddo warriors drew their huge nets from the lagoon filled with fish of all sizes.

Fishing lines were fastened along the entire length of the nets, about a foot apart. At the end of each line was a fish hook upon which the people put little pieces of hominy dough, and sometimes little pieces of meat.

The ends of the lines were tied to dugout canoes and were drawn in two or three times a day.

But today she had learned about something more than fishing. Hawke had taken her to a little stream, from the banks of which he had taken a good quantity of dried salt, called *naouidiche*. He had taken a bag of this salt back to the camp and it had been used to season the fish.

She remembered something else special that had happened today. As she and Hawke had left the others, to be alone for a few moments, they had come upon a sight so mystical and beautiful it had almost taken her breath away. They had seen a couple of great herons standing knee deep at the edge of the water. The birds had stood motionless in the water, and when they had moved, they hadn't created a ripple.

Their gray-blue plumage and thin profiles were so lovely. They stood three or four feet tall on stilt-like legs, and at the end of a long neck and small head was a dagger-like bill.

Scarlett had been fascinated by the way the great blues caught their fish. They speared it, and then came up with it and swallowed it, all in one continuous motion.

Hawke's voice brought her back to the moment. She looked over at him as he spoke.

"*Huh,* our way of fishing is much different from the way you described catching your first fish," Hawke said, placing a hand on her cheek. "My woman, it has been a long day. Shall we go to our blankets?"

He gazed heavenward, his eyes searching the sky, which had become totally dark. He saw flashes of lightning some distance away, and then heard the ensuing rumbles of thunder.

"The spirit horses are uneasy in the heavens tonight," he said. "Hear the thunder of their hoofbeats?"

"I hope it doesn't storm," Scarlett said, rising with Hawke as he pushed himself to his feet. "If so, will the wickiup you prepared for our privacy be enough to keep the rain out?"

"It is shelter enough," Hawke said, nodding.

He turned to his people and bade them good night, then walked away from the fire with Scarlett toward the wickiup. He had built the small private dwelling even before his people had left the village for the fishing trip. It sat a good distance from the spot where the large outdoor fire had been built. His people would sleep near the fire, so he and his woman could have their privacy, yet they would not be so far that they were totally isolated.

The first night, they had only slept in each other's arms, for both were exhausted from the day's activities.

But today he had made certain neither of them would be so tired, for he wanted this night with her for more than sleeping.

After they reached their small private campsite, Scarlett helped him place logs on their little fire, which had burned down to glowing embers. She had seen him go more than once today to tend the fire, so that it would be ready for them when they returned tonight.

It was not so much for warmth as for safety. As long as the fire burned, they would be free of unwanted four-legged visitors.

Even so, last night they had been awakened by a coyote's cry, which did not seem all that far away.

They had gone outside and added wood to the fire, then snuggled back down in their blankets and were soon fast asleep again.

"I found more coral rocks today when you were out in the canoe with the others," Scarlett said, reaching inside her pocket and gathering them into her hand. She took them out and showed them to Hawke. The light of the fire reflected off the pinkish rocks. "They are so beautiful, aren't they?"

"You are the beautiful one," Hawke said, framing her face between his hands. "*Nei-com-mar-pe-ein,* I love you."

As he drew her lips to his, Scarlett opened her fingers and allowed the rocks to roll free.

She twined her arms around his neck and returned the kiss, her whole body throbbing with need of him.

Soon they were inside the dwelling, their clothes tossed aside.

As Hawke stretched out atop Scarlett, his body hard and defined against hers, her skin quivered with acute awareness of that part of him that would soon send her to paradise.

His fingers reached up and entwined in her hair as he kissed her, his mouth urging her lips open as his kiss grew more and more passionate.

Desire such as she had never known before meeting Hawke shot through Scarlett as she felt his heat being pressed inside her, where she throbbed with need of him.

His mouth bore down even harder on

hers, exploding with raw passion, causing bright threads of excitement to weave through Scarlett's heart.

His mouth was hot, sensuous and demanding as he began his steady, rhythmic thrusts within her.

Scarlett clung to him and she trembled as her body responded to every nuance of his lovemaking.

A sudden curl of heat tightened inside her belly. She was shocked at the intensity of her feelings as his hand moved down to mold one of her breasts.

Hawke found it almost too hard to breathe, his passion was so intense. He kissed Scarlett and held her and stroked her, quietly groaning against her lips as he felt the passion building and spreading.

Everything within him was alive for only one reason — to give pleasure to his woman, and to take what she returned to him.

It was agony and bliss, how he felt about her, as he finally gave himself over to the wild ecstasy of the moment. Their bodies jolted and quivered as he pressed endlessly deeper, until he seemed to reach the center of her being.

They clung.

They moaned.

They kissed.

They rocked and quivered, and then it was over, that breathless rapture that only two people truly in love could share.

Hawke still lay over Scarlett, molding his body perfectly to the curved hollow of her hips, and once again he felt the heat rushing into his manhood and knew that he was ready to go a second time to the heavens and back with her.

Her gasps became long, soft whimpers as she threw her legs up and around him.

He thrust his tongue into her mouth and flicked it in and out, moving it along her lips, as he rhythmically moved within her.

Again, there was a great shuddering in his loins. He could feel Scarlett straining her hips up at him, crying out at her second fulfillment of the night while he welcomed his own.

"I love you so," Scarlett whispered against his lips, breathing hard, her whole body weak from the passion they had just shared a second time.

"I have never loved as I love you," he whispered back to her. "And I wish that we could stay here, alone, forever. Would it not be a perfect world?"

"Yes, a perfect world," she murmured, reveling in being in his arms, and so loved by him.

He held her for a moment longer and then sat up.

"But no world is perfect. We must dress. It is different out here, from being home where all things are normal through the night. I am chief and must be ready if beckoned, even if it is in the middle of the night," he said.

He took his clothes out beside the fire and dressed in them, as Scarlett came out and dressed in her skirt and blouse. She left off her boots. Her poor toes needed rest.

"I didn't realize how tired I was," Scarlett said, yawning as she raised and stretched her arms over her head. "I doubt that I shall hear a coyote tonight, even if one howls."

Hawke gazed heavenward. "There is still lightning and thunder," he said. "But so far, it is distant. The storm might pass farther out to sea."

He took Scarlett by the hand and led her back inside the small dwelling, stretching out on a blanket with her. Soft mats had been piled beneath the blanket for their comfort.

She cuddled up next to him and was soon asleep.

Hawke stayed awake awhile longer, just

to watch her sleep. He bent over her and brushed soft kisses across her brow, then snuggled against her and went to sleep smiling.

Chapter Twenty-seven

"The lady and the Indian should be asleep soon and then we will abduct not only her, but him too," Blue Raven said as he gazed at the spot where he had seen Scarlett and Hawke disappear inside the wickiup.

"Why would you abduct the man when it is only the lady ye want?" Fat Jaws asked, sliding closer to Blue Raven who lay on his belly behind some thick bushes.

"Indians are always alert, especially the warriors," Blue Raven said, still watching the wickiup through the parted limbs of the bushes. "How could ye possibly think we could abduct the lady while the warrior is in the lodge with her? One movement in that lodge and he will be awake. Aye, I could silence him with a knife, but I 'ave other plans for him."

"What plans?" Fat Jaws asked, glancing at Blue Raven.

Fat Jaws wished he hadn't been the one to suggest traveling in this direction; otherwise the lady never would have been found and Blue Raven would eventually have given up and returned to the ship.

As it was, Fat Jaws was afraid all hell would soon break loose!

If the other group of Indians awakened and discovered what was going on, their lives would be forfeit.

"And why?" Fat Jaws continued. "All ye've talked about is the lady. Why not grab 'er, kill the Injun and be on our way? Anything else is too risky. I say sink a knife into his throat, then take the lady."

"Did ye not see the affection they 'ave for one another?" Blue Raven said, chuckling. "Would it not be somethin' to see that Injun imprisoned on the *Eclipse*, forced to watch as the lady he loves is taken by some other man, namely me? If we kill him, we'd miss out on seein' the torture in his eyes as he realizes that he has not only lost his lady, but will soon lose his life."

"You seem to have something against Injuns, a vendetta of sorts," Fat Jaws said, still watching the wickiup for any signs of movement.

He then looked at the larger outdoor fire, and saw that everyone there had also retired for the night.

He was still worried about abducting the lady. If one sound was made, those others would be awakened and would attack.

He recalled the pirates' earlier attempt to find a corral of horses so that they could steal mounts for all their men.

They hadn't met with good fortune. They found no houses, or horses, but they *had* seen a glimmer of fire through the trees and followed it until they came upon this campsite of Indians, among them the very lady Blue Raven was seeking.

They had crawled up close, hidden in the bushes and watched as the lady ate with the Indians. Then she had accompanied one of them to a small lodge a short distance from the others.

They had watched Scarlett and the lone Indian add wood to the outdoor fire, then go inside the small lodge where surely they had made love, for when they came out again, they were unclothed.

Fat Jaws had looked over at Blue Raven as the old pirate gazed hungrily at Scarlett, her nude body fueling the fires inside him. Fat Jaws had glanced over his shoulder at the other men and seen the same hunger. They had all been without a lady for too long.

He saw danger in their lust, for once the lady was aboard the ship, might not fights ensue over the wench?

Even now, as Fat Jaws went over all that

had transpired this evening, he wished that the lady had stayed safe in her home, and that they hadn't been able to find her. That was what should have happened, for all they knew about her home was that it ought to be near the spot where they had last moored the *Eclipse*.

The idiocy of Blue Raven's plan made Fat Jaws cringe even now. His partner was ready to risk everything to find her, even though Fat Jaws was dead set against it.

It was now that Fat Jaws saw just how little Blue Raven thought of him. Blue Raven not only put capturing this lady above Fat Jaw's welfare, but he had also claimed their ship as his alone.

Fat Jaws was filled with resentment for his friend. Aye, he'd help Blue Raven get the lady and her Injun lover aboard the ship, but it would be Fat Jaws who'd see to their release as well.

Somehow, aye, somehow he would see that those two were freed and put off the ship. They could be long gone by the time everyone woke up the next morning.

There was one thing, though. Somehow he'd find a way to make it look as if Injuns had done the deed.

"Fat Jaws?"

Hearing Blue Raven say his name made

Fat Jaws aware that he had been so lost in thought that he had forgotten the importance of accomplishing the abduction without being caught. One wrong move, one sound, could bring the entire campsite of Indians down on them.

"Fat Jaws, where's yer mind wandered to?" Blue Raven whispered, flinching when a great growl of thunder reminded him that the threat of a storm out at sea might delay their escape once they had the fair maiden on the *Eclipse*. "I was tellin' ye why I have such hatred for Injuns. Seems ye wasn't interested in it after all."

"Me mind wandered, that's all," Fat Jaws said, frowning at Blue Raven. "So tell me again. What's in yer past that makes ye resent Injuns so much?"

"Me mother was abducted by a band of renegade Injuns, raped and thrown away like she was no more than a piece of meat," Blue Raven growled. "I was a mere lad of five when it 'appened. They murdered me pa and took me and me ma hostage. After they raped and killed me mother, they all took turns spittin' on me, then turned me loose out into the wilds alone."

"How did ye survive?" Fat Jaws asked, his eyes wide.

"On me own, that's 'ow," Blue Raven

said, sighing. "I had heard me pa talk of Bluebeard, me distant cousin, so I took on the name of Blue Raven and knew then and there I'd one day have me own ship and would ride the high seas. I've always steered clear of Injuns until now. It's fate that now I've found a lady I want as me own, she's shacked up with a redskin."

"I'd think ye'd want to kill him instead of abduct him," Fat Jaws said, his eyes back on the wickiup.

"It will be torture for the Injun to know his lady belongs to another man, especially a pirate," Blue Raven said, chuckling. "I plan to chain 'er to the wall one full night next to the Injun, to give them one last night together, so to speak, and then tomorrow morning I will have me way with 'er as the Injun is forced to watch."

Blue Raven laughed throatily. "And then I'll kill the Injun and toss him overboard to the sharks when we get far out at sea."

A lurid flash of lightning lit up the dark heavens, and Fat Jaws looked quickly upward. "It appears to me that we'll be spendin' at least this one night close to shore," he said tightly. "Ye'd better say a little prayer that we can leave before the Injuns awake in the morning and find the lady and the warrior gone."

"Aye, we don't dare risk takin' the *Eclipse* out to sea if there is a severe storm." Blue Raven growled out. "Luck might not be with us, yet that's the chance we 'ave to take." He laughed again. "Not knowing whether or not we can take the ship out to sea as soon as we 'ave the lady and Injun aboard just makes this more excitin' for me."

Fat Jaws frowned at Blue Raven and didn't respond to another idiot thing the man had to say. He was losing all sense of reality.

"I say it's time to go and do the deed," Blue Raven said, standing. He turned to the men who awaited his command, then yanked his cutlass from its belt and waved it in the air. "Come with me, but be silent as ye walk. All we want is the lady and the one Injun, not the whole slew of 'em, do ye hear?"

They all nodded, then with their own cutlasses drawn, most proceeded down a slight hill toward the small campfire, while a few others stood guard around the main campsite.

They had been told to attack if anyone awakened and kill all the Indians.

Another flash of lightning lit the heavens, followed by the loud rumble of thunder. Blue Raven stopped and glanced toward the larger campsite. He waited to see if anyone stirred, but when he saw that they still seemed to be sleeping soundly, he and Fat Jaws proceeded onward until they came to the wickiup. They stopped just outside the door.

"Ye know what to do," Blue Raven said, nodding toward Fat Jaws. "Silence the Injun with the gag, while I tie his wrists. Should the lady show any signs of screamin', ye have me permission to knock 'er out with a blow to 'er head. But don't hit 'er so hard she'll be mindless, do ye hear?"

Fat Jaws nodded, then slipped inside the small wickiup beside Blue Raven. Before Hawke could do anything to protect his woman, he was quietly gagged and tied. He watched helplessly as Scarlett was trussed up and similarly silenced before she was awake enough to realize what was happening.

"We must now hurry back to the ship," Blue Raven said, yanking Scarlett up, as Fat Jaws grabbed Hawke by an arm and half dragged him from the wickiup.

Blue Raven stepped closer to the fire, so that the reflection of the flames would be caught in the blade of his cutlass. He waved it over his head for his men to see. When they began running in his direction, Blue Raven yanked Scarlett along beside him while Fat Jaws forced Hawke onward.

By the time they reached the cove where the ship was moored, the waves were crashing against the longboats, threatening to capsize them. It was definitely too dangerous to take the ship out to the open sea where the waves would be even fiercer.

"Hurry!" Blue Raven said, almost throwing Scarlett into one of the longboats, while Fat Jaws shoved Hawke into another.

They fought the waves as they rowed the longboats toward the ship, but finally they made it, and ropes were handed down to them so that the longboats could be hoisted on deck.

Finally safely aboard ship, Blue Raven shoved Scarlett down the narrow staircase to the brig. Hawke was secured there by her side with chains.

After their gags were removed, Scarlett was the first to speak. "You are crazy to do this," she cried. "When Hawke's men find us gone, you will wish you had never seen my face."

"They won't have any idea what happened to ye," Blue Raven said, stepping up to Scarlett and running a hand down her cheek. She drew back and shivered with disgust, then spat in his face.

"Ye are no less a wildcat now than when I had ye in me clutches before," Blue Raven growled out as he wiped the spit from his face with a red handkerchief. He walked over and stood before Hawke. "Ye will get yers, too, before this is all over with. Ye may think yer warriors will find ye, but we left no evidence behind. They'll have no idea at all where ye've gone, or who took ye."

Blue Raven looked at Fat Jaws. "We're at the mercy of the damn weather again," he growled. "We need calm waters in order to get safely away from this shore. The ship isn't strong enough to withstand these waves and blustery winds."

Hawke glared back at Blue Raven, but he was worried when he heard another clap of thunder. If it rained, all traces of their trail would be erased. Otherwise, his warriors were accomplished trackers, and would find the ship in a heartbeat.

Yet if the storm did blow over, he now realized that this crazed bunch of men would take the ship out to sea. In that case, Hawke knew he would never see any of his people again. He expected to be toyed with for a while, then killed, for it was evident that this pirate was obsessed with possessing Scarlett.

Fat Jaws smiled crookedly at Scarlett, and then at Hawke, for he still planned to carry out his plan to remove them from the ship while Blue Raven and the others slept.

Aye, he'd have the satisfaction of knowing he had finally bested Blue Raven. Why should his partner get everything even though Fat Jaws had worked just as hard?

He could hardly wait to see the look on Blue Raven's face when he found the woman gone again!

Chapter Twenty-eight

The moon had dipped low in the sky. Dawn had not yet appeared along the horizon. The warrior assigned to awaken Hawke before daybreak, so that they could go and haul in the nets one last time, walked toward the wickiup.

The first thing he noticed was that the campfire had been neglected and was now nothing but gray, cold ashes amid the circle of stones. He knew his chief would never have allowed such neglect. All knew the importance of keeping a fire burning during the night.

Then something else drew Two Wings' attention. By the light of the torch he carried, he saw that a blanket lay askew just outside the wickiup entryway.

Two Wings' heart began to race as he hurried to the wickiup and knelt down before it. He almost knew without looking that his chief and the woman were no longer there, so he did not call Hawke's name.

Instead he lowered the torch so that its

light was directed fully into the small dwelling. He went cold inside when he realized that what he had surmised was true. Two Wings stared down where his chief and the woman had slept. The blankets were in disarray, which seemed to point to a scuffle.

"They were surely forced from the lodge," Two Wings whispered to himself. His gut feeling told him that his chief was in mortal danger, as was his woman.

His pulse racing, Two Wings rushed from the wickiup and held the torch low to the ground, searching for tracks in the soft sand.

A rumble of thunder sent his eyes heavenward. The storm had raged out at sea all night without touching land. It seemed to be lessening now, for the thunder was only a low sort of growl.

He fell to his knees and held the torch even closer to the sand. His insides tightened when he saw the marks of many feet. And they had been made by white men's shoes, not moccasins.

He knew then that his chief and the woman had been abducted.

Anxious to see where the prints led, he followed them around to the back of the wickiup and on to the grass, where he could still follow them since it was heavy with dew and the blades had been crushed.

Realizing that time was wasting and he would need all of the warriors in order to find and rescue Hawke and Scarlett, Two Wings bolted. He ran toward the campsite, shouting as he ran.

"Our chief is gone!" Two Wings called. "So is the woman."

"How? Who? Where?" voices demanded as the villagers rose to their feet and quickly gathered around Two Wings.

"I followed the prints for a short distance, then came for help," Two Wings said. "Come, warriors. We must save our chief and his woman."

They all armed themselves with knives and rifles, some even with bows and arrows, and after they slipped into their moccasins, were soon away from the campsite and the women and following Two Wings' lead as he found the prints again. His torch was the only one being used, for to use many more might alert those who had abducted Hawke and Scarlett.

When a drop of rain came from the heavens, Two Wings cringed. If the rain began in earnest, his torch would be extinguished and the footprints washed away.

But as he had thought earlier, the storm

was too far out to sea now to be a true threat. The drops did not continue.

Two Wings and the others continued following the footprints, realizing that the abductors were staying close to the ocean.

"A ship! Do you see it?" one of the warriors said, coming up to Two Wings. "Put out the torch! Those aboard the ship will see it. The prints lead to the sea now, where there were surely smaller boats awaiting those who captured our chief and his woman."

"It is the same ship that was here before," Two Wings observed. "It is the same ship where my chief's woman was held prisoner before. I have been aboard it. I know its layout."

Two Wings hurried to the water and thrust the flames of the torch into it, extinguishing it.

Then he and the others studied the ship. They saw no movement, or light. It was apparent that those aboard were either waiting out the storm before taking their vessel to sea, or perhaps preferred daylight to travel. It seemed they were all now foolishly asleep.

"They made a mistake in hesitating to travel from the land of the Caddo," Two Wings growled out. He looked from man to man. “All we need are our knives. Leave your other weapons on land, then follow me. I am familiar with how to get aboard this vessel.”

They all followed his lead, walking into the water until it became deep enough to dive in. They would swim toward the anchor and use the chain as a way to get aboard this devil ship. They would save their chief and his woman, and then let Chief Hawke decide the fate of both the ship and its crew.

Chapter Twenty-nine

Fat Jaws crept through the dark passageway toward the brig, where he planned to release Chief Hawke and the lady. He smiled as he thought of the confused look that would appear on Blue Raven's face when he came to get the lady to have his fun with while her Injun lover watched.

"We will be far out at sea by the time that Injun gets back to his people," Fat Jaws whispered to himself. "There will be no way he can avenge himself on us."

And never would Fat Jaws and Blue Raven enter these waters again. Fat Jaws would not allow it. After tonight, Fat Jaws would take his rightful place among those who rode the *Eclipse* with him. He would no longer be second in command.

Aye, once it was seen by all the crew how the Injun made a fool of Blue Raven by so easily escaping, the captain would lose their respect.

Aye, no one but Fat Jaws would know the truth, that it was he who'd set the Injun and the woman free.

"Aye, I will gain the ground that Blue Raven loses," Fat Jaws said, chuckling to himself.

He stopped and listened to hear if anyone on deck was stirring. Morning was near and everyone had been told that the ship must leave before daybreak.

But he heard nothing except his own rapid breathing; he could not help being apprehensive over this task. One sailor discovering Fat Jaws at his game would be all that was needed for Blue Raven to realize that he had almost been duped by his closest friend. Fat Jaws would die that quickly!

"I must not make a sound," he whispered. Knowing that time was running out, he hurried his steps and finally came to the brig, where a torch burned low on one wall.

He went to where the ring of keys hung next to the barred doors of the cell. As he took the keys from the peg, the noise awoke both Hawke and Scarlett.

Nervous sweat broke out on Fat Jaws' brow, yet he felt fortunate that Blue Raven had not ordered one of their crew to stand guard. It had seemed an unnecessary precaution because the chains holding the two prisoners were secure, as were the barred doors.

"Say nothing, just follow me," Fat Jaws said as he rushed into the cell. "I 'ave come to release ye. No one is awake. Once ye are set free, go from the ship quickly. Ye know the way topside. I do not want to be seen with ye if anyone awakes, or me head will be separated from me shoulders."

"Why are you doing this?" Scarlett asked, sighing with relief when the chains fell free of her wrists.

Hawke didn't ask anything. With much suspicion in his dark eyes, he watched the pirate set him free. He didn't trust this man or what he was doing. He feared that he and Scarlett were being sent into a trap that would end in their deaths.

But no matter what had prompted the pirate's actions, Hawke knew that if he didn't act now, while his hands were free, he might not get a second chance.

"Go!" Fat Jaws said, motioning toward the open door that led out to the dark passageway and the steps that led topside.

Scarlett turned to Hawke. She could see that he was wary of the pirate, as was she.

She looked at Fat Jaws as he stepped away from them, then at Hawke just as Hawke lunged toward the man and grabbed his cutlass from its sheath.

Fat Jaws felt the color drain from his

face when he realized what had happened. He turned to find Hawke holding his cutlass, his dark eyes filled with vengeance.

"No . . . please . . ." Fat Jaws begged. When he saw Hawke hesitate, he reached for his pistol.

Before he could get it, Hawke brought the heavy handle of the huge knife down hard on Fat Jaws' head, quickly rendering him unconscious.

Scarlett gasped. "You didn't kill him," she whispered, looking up at Hawke.

"No one should ever kill needlessly," Hawke said, grabbing her by the arm and quickly ushering her from the cell. "He will not awaken for a while. That will give us time to escape."

"But what if he does wake up before we get away?" Scarlett whispered, looking up at him as she ran breathlessly down the small, dark passageway with Hawke.

She almost fainted when she collided with someone. She was so afraid, she couldn't even scream.

There was enough light, though, from a torch further down the passage, for Hawke to get a good look at who was there.

"Two Wings?" he said, his eyes wide as he saw other warriors appear in the passage behind him.

"We came for you," Two Wings said in a low, cautious voice. He gazed at Hawke in surprise. "How is it that you are free of your bonds?"

"I will tell you later," Hawke said, then looked past his men into the darkness ahead. "We must hurry. The men on this ship will awaken at sunrise to sail the ship far out to sea. I know because I heard the order given to those who were down by the cell before they left for their sleeping quarters."

"I saw no one stirring yet," Two Wings said as he and the other men followed their chief up the small ladder that led to top deck.

When they were all there, they looked slowly around them. No one had awakened yet.

Then Hawke gathered his men quickly around him. "My warriors, when it is discovered that the white men no longer have their captives, they will come again to search for your chief and his woman," he said. "Their determination will bring them to land again. This will place all of our people in danger, not only your chief and his woman. We must do all we can to keep this from happening."

He glanced at Scarlett, remembering that only moments ago he had told her it was not good to kill needlessly. Yet he must take steps to protect his people.

"I understand anything that you feel you must do," Scarlett said, as though she had read his thoughts.

Hawke gave her a tender gaze, then turned toward his warriors again. "We will put a stop to this madness tonight," he said. "I heard some mention of dynamite being on board. Let us make good use of it, but we must hurry. See the sky? It won't be long before the sun appears over the horizon."

Hawke stepped closer to his men. "We must find the dynamite quickly." He looked at one of his warriors. "But to ignite it we must have fire. Go for the torch in the brig. Bring it to me, but be quiet about it."

The warrior nodded and rushed back below decks, while Hawke, Scarlett and the other warriors searched for the dynamite. They found it just a stone's throw from Blue Raven's private cabin.

Hawke hurried to it, opened the boxes and began handing out the dynamite. "Place it in strategic positions, but hurry," he said flatly. "We will set fire to the ship far enough away from the dynamite so that we can escape the ship before it goes up in smoke."

The warriors hurried around, placing the dynamite here and there, and then took the torch and set fire to the furled sails and the flag with the white skull and bones.

Everyone scurried down the anchor chain and swam quickly toward shore, reaching it just as the first stick of dynamite exploded, erasing the name *Eclipse* from the side of the ship.

More explosions ensued, sending great sparks of fire into the sky, until the boat was consumed by flames.

Scarlett covered her ears so that she could not hear the screams coming from the burning ship. She shivered at the sights and sounds of death, glad when Hawke placed a comforting arm around her waist.

"It is done," he said solemnly. "You have nothing to fear ever again from Blue Raven or his crew."

"But that one man who set us free," Scarlett said, shivering again. "I pity him."

"Do not pity any of those lost souls," Hawke said tightly. "If he was a good man, he would never have allowed the abduction in the first place."

"Yes, I'm sure that's true," Scarlett said, snuggling closer. "Hold me. Just hold me."

Hawke swept her against him and embraced her, then held her away from him and gazed at her as the flames of the burning ship were reflected in her eyes. "We must go and find my people and return home," he said. "I will then take you to your home and explain to your father what has happened."

"I love you," she murmured. "Thank you for saving my life tonight. If you had not grabbed that man's cutlass, who is to say where we might be even now?"

"I want to protect you for the rest of your life," Hawke said, searching her eyes. "I want you to be my wife. Will you marry me soon so that we shall never have to part again?"

"Marry you?" she murmured, her heart pounding with the joy of the moment. "Oh, yes, yes, yes, I will marry you. I don't want to live without you."

He kissed her sweetly, then swept her up into his arms and carried her away from this place of death. In his heart he felt only hope for their future.

Although Scarlett had answered an unhesitating yes to his question, she knew that she had one obstacle to overcome before she could speak her vows with the man she loved. Her father.

And then there was Scottie. She wanted

to raise the little boy as her own. Would Hawke want this child in his life?

He must! she thought to herself. For she wanted to be the one to shape Scottie's tomorrows.

But first things first. When she arrived home, she would talk with her father.

She would ask Hawke about Scottie next. She did not fear his answer, though, for did he not love the child as much as she?

Chapter Thirty

Feeling drained after everything that had happened, Scarlett rode beside Hawke toward home.

Hawke had asked his people to gather the nets without him so that he could escort her home right away. Concerned about how she was faring after the ordeal she had just come through, he gazed at her now. Scarlett wore a doeskin dress instead of her own, which had been drenched when she swam to shore.

He saw how beautiful she was as she sat straight in her saddle. The fringes at the hem of the dress and at the sleeves blew softly in the breeze, the beads sewn on the bodice picked up the soft rays of the early morning sun.

He could envision her wearing nothing ever again but doeskin and buckskin. They would become man and wife as soon as she got her father's approval.

He gazed at her face, at her rosy cheeks and perfectly shaped lips, the soft curve of her jaw. She gazed straight ahead, unaware that he was studying her and loving her even more by the minute. He had witnessed her courage more than once since he had met her, and each time he felt he loved her more deeply.

His attention was drawn away from Scarlett by the thunderous sound of hooves approaching.

Scarlett had also heard. She drew rein and gazed questioningly at Hawke, who wore only a breechclout and moccasins today, his long hair loosely hanging down his muscled back.

She saw concern in his eyes as he gazed back at her.

"Who could it be?" she asked.

A moment later, her father came around a bend in the trail. There were many men with him, all on horseback.

Her heart thudded when she realized that he had already seen her and the way she was dressed. He had to know that things weren't right, that she had become entangled in something dangerous.

He drew rein beside her and the others stopped a short distance away.

"Daughter, I was so worried about you," he said, hardly even noticing what she wore. His full attention was centered on her face.

"How did you know I was in trouble?" Scarlett asked, searching his eyes and regretting that she had caused him distress.

She had never seen him with such concern in his eyes.

"I didn't," Patrick said, taken aback by what she had just said. "I mean . . . I wasn't certain . . ."

"Then why have you formed a posse?" Scarlett asked, seeing her father's eyes move to Hawke and rake over him. He frowned that Hawke should be so scantily clad in the company of his daughter.

He looked quickly back at Scarlett. "An explosion rocked me in my bed, awakening me," Patrick explained. "And then I saw the distant glow of fire outside my bedroom window. I got this god-awful sick feeling in the pit of my stomach when I realized which direction it came from. I was afraid you might have fallen into some sort of danger, for I knew that whatever had blown up had to be somewhere close to where you were fishing with Hawke and his people."

"You knew . . . where . . . we were?" Scarlett asked, feeling a little sick. If he knew where the Caddo were fishing, he must have actually come and investigated. Had he seen the wickiup where she and

Hawke had slept separate from the others?

"I could not rest until I knew where you were, and how you were," Patrick said tightly. "I searched and found where the nets were being brought in with a heavy load of fish." He smiled. "I saw you helping."

He leaned closer to her and reached a hand to her face. "Daughter, I saw such contentment in your eyes that I knew I had nothing to worry about," he said. "I returned home happy to know that you were enjoying your outing so much."

He drew his hand away and gazed over at Hawke. "I saw you, too, and how you were looking out for her welfare. I knew that my daughter was safe with you," he said, his eyes then narrowing angrily. "Was I wrong to trust so much?"

He glanced back at Scarlett, studying her attire. Then he looked at Hawke's breechclout; if the wind blew just right, it might reveal that part of a man's anatomy no unmarried woman should see.

"What happened, Hawke?" he demanded. "What caused the explosion and fire? Why is my daughter dressed in Indian attire?"

"After two successful days of fishing, everyone was asleep for the night when someone came in the dark, and by knifepoint abducted both your daughter and me," Hawke said, his voice drawn. He was embarrassed that he had allowed such a thing to happen while Scarlett was entrusted to his care.

"It happened quickly," he continued. "I did not have time to draw a weapon."

Scarlett felt a flash of heat rush to her cheeks, for she knew that if her father thought over what Hawke had just said, he would have to realize that she and Hawke were alone at the time of the abduction, or it would have never happened. There were so many warriors in the camp, they could not all be overcome.

Patrick's jaw tightened as he noticed the blush on Scarlett's cheeks. She and Hawke had not been sleeping with the others, he concluded.

He started to lash out at her, to shame her, but stopped before speaking a word. He remembered just how old she was, and how passionate she was about everything she had ever done in her life. When it came to a man, would she be any less passionate?

And he felt a strange peacefulness in his heart to know that although they had been abducted, they had come out of it alright.

His daughter was alive.

She was safe!

Yes, that was all that mattered, at least for now. He would have a serious father-to-daughter talk when they were home, and alone.

"The explosion?" Patrick pressed. "Surely that had something to do with you and my daughter being abducted. How is it that you escaped unharmed, especially since the explosion that I heard was so fierce?"

"Scarlett and I were taken aboard a ship," Hawke explained.

"A ship?" Patrick gasped, interrupting Hawke's explanation. "What . . . ship?"

Then he felt the color drain from his face. "Not *that* ship," he quickly interjected. "Lord, don't tell me it was the same ship —"

"Yes, the same one. We were abducted by that same man I told you about earlier, the one who claimed to be a pirate," Scarlett quickly said. "He's the one who boasted of being kin to the famed pirate Bluebeard, but I believe he is . . . or was . . . just a crazy man."

"Lord . . ." Patrick said, visibly shuddering as he again looked at Hawke. "Finish the story. Tell me how it is that you got free, and . . . what caused the explosion."

"My warriors came to rescue us," Hawke

said, then told Patrick the rest of the tale.

"I came to this land thinking it was safer than San Francisco, yet I have found nothing but trouble," Patrick said. He kneaded his brow as he looked from Scarlett to Hawke, and then back at Scarlett. "First there was Mary Jane and the unrest she brought into my home, and then there was the underground city, the opium, and the coolies who were hidden away there. And now this? A pirate? Someone who wanted my daughter so much he risked everything to have her, not just once, but twice?"

He sighed heavily. "I think it's time to move on, Scarlett," he said. "I promised your mother the day you were born that I would always look out for you and keep you safe. Seems I've gone back on that promise more than once since she died."

"Papa, you shouldn't blame yourself for any of this, especially what's happened to me," Scarlett said, moving her horse so that she was alongside her father's. "And, Papa, you shouldn't worry so much about me. I'm a grown woman. Papa, please let me be responsible for what happens to me."

"Like being abducted and taken to ships?" Patrick said, reaching over and taking one of her hands. "Like letting you go and stay overnight with Indians?" He slid his gaze to Hawke. "Overnight, alone, with . . . their chief?"

Scarlett's face became hot with another blush.

She looked over her shoulder at Hawke, who had sat quietly by, listening, but who was riding toward her now. He took up a position on her other side.

He suddenly whisked her from her horse and placed her on his lap. Patrick's color went from ashen gray to bright red as he gaped openly at Hawke. Then he turned to Scarlett, who was not protesting what Hawke had just done.

"What do you think you're doing?" Patrick gasped out, suddenly aware of all the men behind him. They were witnessing all of this, how his daughter openly showed her feelings for this Indian chief, sitting on his lap as though she belonged there.

"I am openly showing you my feelings for your daughter, and hers for me," Hawke said, proudly lifting his chin as his eyes met and held Patrick's in silent battle. "I want her for my wife. I want to marry her soon. She wants to marry me. But she wants . . . needs . . . your approval. Does she have it?"

"Scarlett?" Patrick said as he shifted his eyes to her. "What do you have to say about all this? Scarlett, must I remind you that this man was only a short time ago a stranger to you? And . . . Scarlett . . . he is an Indian."

"Yes, we met only recently, but I knew the moment I saw him that I had found the man I wished to marry someday," Scarlett murmured. "Papa, that day has come. I do want to marry him, and soon. And as for Hawke being an Indian, when I look at him, I don't see the color of his skin. I see the man I love, the man I want to grow old with."

"Grow old . . . ?" Patrick gasped. "Also . . . have . . . children with? I would have half-breed grandchildren?"

"Would it matter if a child of mine had copper skin?" Scarlett murmured. "Papa, can you truthfully say you would love that child less, knowing that it was mine?"

"Scarlett, oh, Scarlett, when you were a child, you learned to walk long before any other children I have known; your love for horses came almost the instant you took your first step. How could I think that you would be any less passionate about the first man you fell in love with, be his skin white or copper?" he said, reaching out and taking her hand.

"Papa, are you saying . . . ?" Scarlett asked, afraid to continue, for if he gave the wrong answer, she would be forced to turn her back on her father for the first time in her life.

"I am saying that, yes, you have my blessing," Patrick said, sighing heavily as he glanced at Hawke. "And you also have it. But you had best take better care of Scarlett than you did last night. The next time, you . . . we . . . might not be as fortunate. We might lose this lovely, special woman."

"Papa, you heard Hawke tell you that it was he who rescued me from that madman, not only once, but Lord, twice. How can you condemn him for something that no one, not even you, could have stopped?" Scarlett said, her voice breaking. "He saved me, Papa. Saved me! You should thank, not chide, him."

"I apologize," Patrick said, reaching a hand out toward Hawke. "Shake on it?"

Hawke smiled and accepted the handshake.

"The child, Scarlett," Patrick went on. "Without you at the house, what about Scottie? He looks to you as a mother. If you leave —"

"I shall take him with me, for I want to

raise him as my own," Scarlett said, interrupting him. She looked over her shoulder at Hawke. "That is, Hawke, if you will accept Scottie as part of our new family. He has been so badly mistreated all of his life. I would like to see that he is never mistreated again."

"I know the child well enough to know that I would welcome him in our lives as a son to us," Hawke said gently. He smiled at Scarlett. "Did I not tell you that I wished for a son? Scottie will be that first son, and then we will give him a brother."

Tears filled Scarlett's eyes. She turned and flung her arms around Hawke's neck. "You never cease to amaze me," she said, her voice breaking. "Thank you, my love. Oh, thank you."

"Seems you are always feeling as though you must thank me for everything I do," Hawke said, holding her near and dear to his heart. "My woman, you do not have to thank me again for anything. Know that what I do for you is from my heart. My actions need no acknowledgment."

"Tha . . . I mean, oh, Hawke, I love you so much, how can I not feel thankful over and over again for all that you do for me, and now Scottie?" she said, looking up at him.

Then she turned her eyes to her father. "Now do you see why I love him so much?" she murmured.

Patrick's eyes beamed. "Yes, I see," he said, nodding. "I do see."

"The wedding will be soon, very, very soon," Hawke announced. "As my wife, your daughter's needs will all be filled, as will the small brave's. I will see that his life has a purpose."

"Scarlett, will you come home with me today so that we can have more time together before you leave to join Hawke in marriage?" Patrick asked. "Please? I just want a little bit more time with my daughter. When you become a wife, your time will be centered around your husband and the child . . . not your father. So will you?"

She gazed up at Hawke, smiled, then smiled at her father as Hawke placed her back on her horse.

"Yes, I'll come home with you, Papa," she murmured. "I will have the rest of my tomorrows with Hawke, but I will also share them with you if you will come often to visit us."

"You know I will," Patrick said, tears shining in his eyes.

"Hawke, thank you for understanding

this time that I need with my father," Scarlett said, reaching over to place a hand on his cheek. "I shall see you soon, my love."

He took her hand and kissed its palm, then released it.

"Hawke, are we truly going to be married?" she asked, her eyes wide as she gazed into his.

"*Huh,* and soon," he said, giving her a soft smile. Then he wheeled his horse around and headed back in the direction of his village, looking over his shoulder and giving Scarlett a nod as if to promise that their lives would soon become one.

Chapter Thirty-one

It was a day that seemed just made for a wedding. Scarlett sat with Hawke where everyone had just congregated, awaiting the moment their chief would take a wife. The sky was clear blue overhead, without a cloud in sight. The wind was soft and sweet, not stirring the crown of wildflowers that the women of the village had made for her.

She sat on a special seat made of two saddles that had been tied together, to unite the bride and groom.

A house had been built especially for the newlyweds at the far side of the village, where this forest would provide privacy. It was a circular structure with walls made of branches. The roof was covered with grass in the shape of a round dome.

She had not been inside it yet, for she had been told that no one entered it except those who had prepared it for the newlyweds' arrival. And only once their vows were shared could Hawke and Scarlett enter.

A huge outdoor fire had been built in front of the newlywed hut. All of the Cougar Clan, as well as some members of other clans whose villages were not far away, sat now around the fire. The men and women, old and young, sat together, while the children sat among themselves far back from the grownups.

Scarlett gazed into the crowd and found her father sitting amid the men. In his eyes was a gentle contentment, even pride, making Scarlett happy to know that he had accepted Hawke completely.

She smiled at her father, then looked farther and found Scottie with the children. Once again they were all listening as he talked with them.

She felt proud that he fit in so easily. She had such love for this child who was blossoming right before her eyes.

She watched as he took from his pocket a handful of coral rocks that he had gathered, sorting through them and handing one and another to these newfound friends. She remembered when she was the same age, and how the boys traded pretty-colored marbles back and forth. She had had her own bag of marbles which she had traded with them. The other girls had giggled and poked fun at her for being more boy than girl, but their mocking hadn't stopped her.

Today she felt anything but boyish in her beautiful doeskin dress with all its tiny shell and bead ornaments and fringe that had been dyed pink to match the pink beads sewn on the bodice.

She glanced at Hawke. He wore his favorite scarlet coat along with a white linen shirt. Otherwise he was dressed in Indian magnificence with feathers tied into his long, flowing hair, and fringed buckskin breeches that matched his new buckskin moccasins.

Her gaze was drawn to the far right side of the gathering, where Eagle Thunder sat alone on a bench covered with plush hides. He was dressed in deerskins fringed and bordered with beads of various colors. His hair was tied at the neck with a red rabbit skin which had been dyed with a special herb for the wedding services.

He sat with his legs crossed beneath his long robe, his arms folded across his chest. He looked at nothing in particular, but there was a peacefulness about him that made Scarlett happy, for if this powerful shaman didn't approve of his chief marrying a white woman, things could be very different today. Scarlett and Hawke would be marrying with a heavy weight on their shoulders.

But as it was, they both sat as peacefully and as happily as the village shaman.

Scarlett's attention was drawn back to the moment. One by one the people were coming toward Hawke and her, each carrying a special gift appropriate for a man and woman who would soon set up housekeeping together.

Her presents were given to her first, among them blankets, trinkets, young corn, muskmelons and tamales. Others brought necklaces made from little white shells that were shaped like beads.

There were many, many gifts, which were laid aside on the ground beside Scarlett as she thanked and smiled until her jaws began to ache.

Then once all of her gifts were given, the men filed past, giving Hawke an assortment of gifts which included arrows, new bows, a quiver made from the pelt of a rare white panther, and many knives and pelts.

All of these were shown appreciation by Hawke, and set down on his side of the seats. Then one other warrior came forth and spread out a beautifully painted deerskin at Hawke's feet. The warrior took powdered tobacco from a pouch made of the skin of a skunk and sprinkled it across the deerskin, while another man came carrying a new pipe made of stone, and adorned with white feathers.

Hawke thanked these two warriors and watched as one of them gently folded the deerskin all around the pipe and tobacco, then placed these with the other gifts at Hawke's left side.

As the sun shifted to begin its slow descent in the sky, dancers appeared in a wide circle around the fire. Some were decked out in bright feathers of various colors. Others were dressed in skins decorated with multicolored beads, while still others wore dresses with tiny bells sewn onto them.

The main dancers wore snake rattles and deer hoofs fastened to their leather garments which made a great deal of noise as they danced to the beat of drums.

It was all merriment and fun, as the children joined the dancers, mimicking the older ones. They kept time to the music, stamping their feet and nodding their heads, while others sang in tune with the music.

Scarlett was stunned when she saw Scottie among the children, following their lead as he danced and swayed and sang.

His expression was one of total contentment as he glanced occasionally at Eagle Thunder, to see if he was watching, and then at Scarlett and Hawke. Each of them nodded to show that they were observing him joining in with the Caddo children of his age.

It made Scarlett so very proud and happy to see such a change in this young boy whose life, up until now, had been one of misery and loneliness.

He did not look as though he had ever been ill, for he was strong, his cheeks were rosy, and he was finally putting flesh on his bones thanks to Malvina's fine cooking. She loved the child so much that while Scottie had lived at the ranch, nary a day had passed when Malvina hadn't made Scottie a new batch of some type of cookie.

Malvina even sent cookies now and then to the village, making sure there were enough for all the children.

The dancing and music ceased. Everyone became quiet and attentive as Eagle Thunder stepped down from his platform. In one hand he held a new fan of eagle feathers that he had made for himself, in the other, a small pouch. He came and stood before Scarlett and Hawke. There was a gentle, prideful happiness in his eyes as he looked from one to the other.

"Let us first pray to *Ayo-caddie-ay-may,*" he said, closing his eyes and lowering his head. He spoke the prayer so softly, no one could understand what he was saying, but all bowed their heads and waited until he was finished.

And when he was, he patted Scarlett gently on the head with his fan, and then Hawke. He spoke to them of love and happiness, and what was expected of them both as husband and wife.

"In this bag I carry herbs which will assure your happiness always," Eagle Thunder said in conclusion, laying his fan aside long enough to open the small bag.

He reached inside and took a handful of the herbs, then sprinkled some in Hawke's hair, and then Scarlett's.

Then he laid this aside as well, and reached for one of Scarlett's hands, and then Hawke's. He brought their hands together so they touched, with Hawke's above Scarlett's. "From this day forth you are as one, in heart and in soul, for you are now man and wife," he said slowly.

Without the need of rings, or signing any special papers, or anything that was required in the white world when a man and a woman got married, Scarlett finally found herself married, and not to just any man, but to the most wonderful man in the world.

Smiling from one to the other, Eagle Thunder lifted his hand from theirs and picked up his fan and small bag. "The games will now begin," he said joyfully.

The warriors behind him were already up on their feet, anxious for the foot races and wrestling, which the Caddo were so fond of.

Hawke had no interest in any games. He had eyes only for his wife. He smiled as the women and children scattered along with the warriors, all hurrying away from the private love nest that had been prepared for their chief and his wife.

Even her father had left with the men, as Scottie ran off with the children.

Scarlett was glad her father had truly accepted that she no longer belonged solely to him, but instead to another man.

She hoped he might find a woman some day to fill the void in his life, yet knew that after the travesty with Mary Jane, he might be hesitant to try again.

"Do we join them?" Scarlett asked as she watched the excitement building among the men and the children. Some of the women had separated from the others to tend to the food cooking over another fire far from the newlywed house.

She had been told that some women had spent the morning brewing tea from laurel leaves for the celebration.

"Do you want to?" Hawke asked, gazing intently into her eyes. "This is your day to do as you wish."

She placed a hand on his cheek. "No, my love, this is *our* day," she murmured.

"My wife," he said, covering her hand with his. "It sounds good coming across my lips, does it not?"

"I feel so good," she said, laughing softly. "I feel wonderful inside. Is that what comes with marrying such a handsome, caring man as you?"

"It comes with happiness," he said, standing and reaching out to lift her fully into his arms.

He first carried her to where they could gaze across the river. A lush array of blue spruce, with frosty needles and dangling cones, stood against a robin's-egg sky.

Western tanagers with brilliant yellow bodies, black wings and white wing bases, flitted here and there, singing their beautiful songs.

"Imagine the landscape around you

being your place of worship," Hawke said. "Your gods live nearby and walk the earth, and are guided by the moon. They leave footprints when they dance. My wife, look closely and you may think you recognize an acquaintance behind the guise of eagle feathers or rabbit skin or the feathers of a songbird. My wife, all this I give to you, to have, to hold, and marvel over."

"I could never want for more than that, and now, I have you as well," she murmured.

"Let us go inside. The women took much time preparing this newlywed house for us. Let us make good use of it."

"Yes, let's," Scarlett said, giggling like a schoolgirl. Yet today she knew that she was anything but that small child of long ago. She was a woman. A wife!

She twined an arm around his neck as he carried her around the seats, then bent low to take her into the tiny dwelling.

Scarlett's eyes widened when she looked around her and saw the loveliness inside. Candles burned everywhere, throwing a soft glow onto the curved walls. Thick, luscious pelts were spread across the earthen floor, and there were tiny coral rocks reflecting the candles' glow around the edges of the grass floor, alongside the pelts.

"It's all so beautiful," she murmured.

As Hawke laid her on the thick pelts, she ran her hands across them. “I have never felt such softness,” she said.

“For so long I have sought the white deer for its pelt, which I have been told is the softest of all, but not for myself,” he said, gently lifting the crown of flowers from her hair. “It is for my father that I seek this elusive deer.”

“Why?” she murmured as she removed the feathers from his hair, laying them aside with her crown of flowers. “Why is this one deer so important, when you do not even want it for yourself?”

“My father sought this deer for many moons and went to his grave without it,” Hawke said, gently pulling her dress up and over her head, revealing her luscious body to his feasting eyes. “If I ever find it, I shall take its pelt to my father and cover his grave with it. Finally my father will have it. He will look down from his home in the sky and smile. I will feel his thank you deep inside my heart.”

“That is so beautiful,” she murmured, shivering with ecstasy when he bent low and flicked his tongue over one of her nipples, and then the other. Then he brought his lips to hers and gave her a deep, passionate kiss.

“You are beautiful,” he whispered

against her lips. "I never get enough of looking at you, or touching you."

"I feel beautiful," she whispered back to him, then eagerly waited for him to remove his own clothes. When he was naked and the candles were casting their golden glow on his copper skin, she reached out and ran her hands over his powerfully muscled chest and arms, then down across his flat belly as he knelt over her. He sucked in a wild breath of rapture when she touched his manhood. Reverently she gripped it and slowly moved her hand on him.

He closed his eyes and his jaw tightened as the pleasure wove its way into his heart. Her hands were like magic against his flesh, his skin quivering with awareness as she continued caressing him.

He felt too close to the brink of total rapture, so he gently took her hand and removed it from his heat.

He then swept his arms around her and imprisoned her against him. His mouth forced her lips open so their tongues could touch.

His mouth was demanding, hot and sensuous, and she sighed from the pleasure of this frantic passion they were sharing as man and wife.

Completely overwhelmed with these

pleasurable, soaring sensations, feverish with desire, Scarlett felt her head begin to reel. She trembled as her blood surged in a wild thrill, her entire being throbbing with quickening desire.

"My love, my wife," Hawke whispered against her lips.

He paused long enough to get his breath.

He was stunned by the intensity of the feelings that were being awakened again between them today.

He leaned a little away from her and ran his hands along her soft, creamy flesh. His hand moved down to curve over one of her breasts.

"My husband," Scarlett murmured, running a gentle hand over the slope of his hard jaw and through his thick, black hair, and then down again to touch him where he had slightly withdrawn from her as he paused before taking her to that final leap of passionate wonder.

She could see the fire burning in his eyes, the hunger that she, herself, felt.

But as he continued to gaze at her, she saw his eyes soften and grow smoky.

"Touch me again," he said huskily as he withdrew from inside her. "Your hands are so soft, so sweet . . ."

He said nothing more, only closed his eyes and moaned in ecstasy as she stroked his silky stiffness. He quietly groaned, then reached for her hand and drew it away, to again thrust himself deep within her.

His loins aflame with need, he kissed her again, darting his tongue moistly into her mouth, and then he lowered his mouth from hers, his lips brushing the smooth, glossy skin of her breasts. He kissed the nipple, sucking it.

She drew in her breath sharply and gave a little cry, just as she felt that familiar wondrous bliss that he had brought into her life the first time they had made love. She felt it spreading, spreading, spreading, until she was aglow with the exquisite bliss of the moment. Their bodies quivered and quaked against each other, soon falling away into exhaustion as they both lay on their backs on the thick pelts, their fingers still entwined.

"This is what we have to share forever and ever," Hawke said huskily. "Until the day our hair turns gray and we are too old to enjoy anything but dreaming of these moments we shared in our youth."

"And, ah, what memories we are making," Scarlett said, slowly running a hand down across his belly. Then she turned on her side and pressed her body against his. "Tonight is ours, all ours. We are husband and wife!"

"Yes, husband and wife," Hawke said huskily, his eyes moving slowly over her. Then he gazed into her eyes. "Tomorrow is the bear hunt. Will you be too exhausted to join me?"

"Why would I be?" she asked, raising an eyebrow.

"I plan to make love with you over and over again tonight, that is why," Hawke said, chuckling. His eyes twinkled and gleamed as he gazed into hers. "Do you wish to make love all night?"

She laughed softly. "I wish never to stop," she said, challenging him with her own gleaming eyes.

He laughed throatily.

He then swept her up on top of him, and kissed her as he thrust his thickened manhood up and into her again. He took her breath away with rapture.

"This is a new way to make love," she whispered against his lips.

"I shall teach you all ways," he whispered, not missing a stroke.

"*Nei-com-mar-pe-ein,* I love you," she murmured, her head spinning anew with the pleasure that came with his kisses, his touch, his love making. . . .

Chapter Thirty-two

The hunt had been successful. Several bears had been killed and were already quartered and wrapped in hay, ready to take home, where they would provide the Caddo with a good supply of bear grease for the whole year.

The fat and grease that came from the bear were used not only for frying their food, but also for seasoning the greens they prepared for their meals. Bear grease and fat accompanied all of the Caddo's meals.

And Scarlett had discovered the purpose of the Caddo's Jubine dogs. They were raised expressly for the bear chase. With their long, pointed snoots, they were as cunning as their masters. She had watched as the dogs treed more than one bear today, barking continuously until the warriors came and killed the bears.

"It was a good hunt," Hawke said, interrupting Scarlett's thoughts. "There will be enough grease and bear meat to last the Caddo families a full winter."

"There were so many bears today,"

Scarlett said, brushing a lock of fallen hair back from her brow as the breeze turned into a brisker wind.

"That is because the crop of nuts and acorns up north was not as plentiful as usual because of the unusual amount of ice and snow last winter," Hawke said. "This sent the bears south to get what they could not find elsewhere."

"You wouldn't think that ice and snow would affect us this far south," Scarlett said, stiffening when she heard a strange grunting sound in the brush at her left side.

She gasped when a wild boar came into view not far from the trail the Caddo were using on their way home. It was rooting around the ground for food.

"A boar," Hawke said, reaching for his rifle in its gun boot but stopping when the animal ran away and was soon lost to sight.

"It looked like the hogs my grandparents used to have in their backyard. I loved to visit their home when Mema and Papa were alive," Scarlett said.

"These are the same type of animal, except the one you saw today runs wild," Hawke said, taking his hand away from his rifle. "Had we not had such a successful bear hunt, I would have made chase and taken boar meat home instead. As it is, it is best to leave the animal alone so that it will multiply and make a better hunt when we decide that we want boar meat instead of deer or bear."

Now they rode onward beside a beautiful body of water. "It's not too difficult to believe in a guiding spirit when you see that pond and the flowers that grow in it," Scarlett murmured, noting how the stillness of the water created a crystal-clear mirror to double her pleasure in the flawless blooming waterlilies.

She looked elsewhere and saw mosquitoes swarming in columns of sunlight, shifting and wavering in the breeze. Warblers and vireos swept in and out of those shimmering columns, feasting.

These birds' plumage was the same color as a summer forest, green and gold, and they veered and swerved like the tracings of some invisible conductor's baton.

Suddenly a southern leopard frog leaped onto one of the leaves, finding a warm place to soak up the late afternoon sun.

Scarlett was so at peace with herself and the world. Her husband felt proud of the successful hunt, and had promised her more than one plush bear pelt for their bed this coming winter.

Glancing over at Hawke, who seemed lost in his thoughts, Scarlett again felt so blessed to have found him. Of all the men in the world, Hawke had been placed there for her to have as her own, as she had been born so that he could take her as his wife.

She smiled when she thought of Scottie. He had so badly wanted to come on the bear hunt with her and Hawke, but when he saw that no other children were allowed such a privilege, he had accepted that he must stay home, too.

She wondered what activity he would choose today to pass the time.

Would he go to Eagle Thunder for more guidance and teaching about how to be a shaman?

Or would he be playing with the children, enjoying the companionship he had been denied for so long?

She imagined he would find a way to do both.

Hawke gazed over his shoulder at his warriors. "Go on home. My wife and I will soon follow," he said, drawing Scarlett's eyes quickly to him. "This will be the last time she will be on the hunt with us. I want her to see things she will not get the opportunity to see again."

"What things?" Scarlett asked as she

followed his lead and guided Lightning to the left. They moved deeper into the forest, where the sun was blocked by the thick foliage.

He gave her a devilish grin. "There is nothing to see, only to do," he said, sidling his horse over closer to hers.

"Oh, I see," she murmured. "You can't wait until tonight, can you? You want me in your arms now."

"As soon as I find a place where we can be comfortable, yes, I want you — *all* of you," he said huskily.

"What if a bear comes upon us, or that ugly wild hog?" she teased. "You might have to fight to have me."

"All bears that my warriors and I did not take today are long gone from here by now," Hawke said, spying another pond up ahead, around which lay soft moss. "And as for that boar? It seemed too hungry to want a confrontation with us."

"*I* am not ever gone for long," a voice said from the thick cover of bushes at their left side. "Ye were a fool to separate yerselves from the others. I've been following, hoping to find ye alone. Since ye're lovebirds, I figured if I waited long enough, I'd have me chance at the two of ye, to kill ye dead so that you will be made to pay for what ye did to me, me crew and me ship. I am the only survivor."

Scarlett grew pale when she recognized the voice as that of Blue Raven.

"How can it be?" she gasped.

He stepped into view, leveling a rifle at Hawke. "I survived the fire," he said thickly. "I would 'ave preferred dying." He raised a hand to his face. "This face is not something anyone likes to look at."

"The scars," Scarlett said, shuddering with disgust as she peered into a face that was so scarred, she wouldn't have known him except for his voice.

"And so you have come seeking revenge?" Hawke said, stiff in the saddle, his rifle close, yet too far away to reach before Blue Raven would fire.

But his knife. It was close at hand in its sheath, and, as he recalled, he had not closed the sheath the last time he had used the knife. If Blue Raven looked away at Scarlett again, his eyes lingering on her, then Hawke could yank his knife free of the sheath and hurl it into the man's chest before he had a chance to pull the trigger.

"I have come for the lady," Blue Raven said, looking quickly at Hawke. "She belongs to me, not ye. I will take 'er far away. No one will find 'er, especially ye, Chief

Hawke, for yer life ends here today."

He nodded angrily toward Hawke. "Dismount," he said, his voice tight with hatred. He nodded toward Scarlett. "Ye dismount, too, but step away from the chief. I don't want his blood spatterin' on ye. We've a piece to go before reachin' my planned destination."

"You'll never get away with this," Scarlett said, slowly stepping away from Hawke, who now stood beside his horse, his eyes two dark coals of anger.

"No one'll come for ye any time soon, for they figure their chief is having a tryst with his lady, knowing that was why ye separated from the others," Blue Raven said. "Wench, come and take me cutlass from its sheath. Hand it to me. I can't kill the chief with this rifle. It would draw attention and bring his whole clan down on me. I want to get far away before they find him dead."

"And you think I'll do as you ask?" Scarlett said. "If I ever get the chance to grab your cutlass, I'll use it on you, you crazy man."

Seeing frustration building in Blue Raven's eyes, Hawke smiled slowly. "You did not plan this well enough, did you?" he said, his eyes gleaming. "If you shoot the rifle, my warriors will come. Yes, I will be dead, but you will soon follow. So what does this get any of us? Lower the rifle, Blue Raven. Place it on the ground and I will have mercy on you. I won't kill you. I'll take you to the white authorities and let them decide your punishment."

"Ye're daft if ye think I'll do anything ye say," Blue Raven said. He glanced quickly at Scarlett. "Ye know that I don't value me life too much now, so if I get killed, it don't matter, but I would like to have the chance to be with ye for one night before I die," he muttered. "Come and take me cutlass, but know I will shoot the Injun if ye try anything."

She gave Hawke a questioning look.

He nodded at her, but she wasn't sure what that nod meant. What did he want her to do?

Then she became aware of something else. She heard a grunting sound, then saw the wild boar make a quick dash from the brush, startling Blue Raven so that he looked away from Scarlett. The boar was running toward him, its huge, curved tusks gleaming.

Scarlett realized this was not the same boar that she and Hawke had seen earlier. This one was larger and deadlier with sharp, long tusks, and it was definitely not afraid of humans.

Blue Raven seemed frozen to the spot as he watched the boar running toward him. Taking advantage of his distraction, Hawke yanked his knife from its sheath and pitched it into Blue Raven's chest, causing him to lose his grip on his rifle.

Just as Blue Raven clutched at the knife in his chest, the rifle fired, its bullet catching the boar directly in the middle of its head as it began to lunge for the pirate.

Man and boar fell to the ground at the same time, dead.

Scarlett was trembling so much, her knees could hardly hold her up. She stumbled to the ground and rested her back against a tree. Then she held her face in her hands and cried.

"Finally," she sobbed. "Finally the nightmare is truly over. He . . . he's dead."

Hawke hurried to her and fell to his knees before her. He reached gentle hands to her face and lifted it so that their eyes met and held.

"It *is* over," he said thickly, just as several of his warriors rode up at breakneck speed on their horses, their rifles drawn.

He took Scarlett in his arms as his warriors gaped openly at the dead man and boar, then looked over at their chief.

"The man," Two Wings said. "He is so scarred, yet I can guess who he is."

"*Huh,* it was the same man whose ship we set fire to," Hawke said, gazing at the pitiful sight of Blue Raven again. "It seems he survived the fire for only one reason."

"Your wife?" Two Wings said.

"My wife," Hawke confirmed.

"What should we do with him?" White Horse asked as he came up and drew rein beside Two Wings.

"Leave him," Hawke said, leading Scarlett to her horse and helping her onto the saddle. "I am taking my woman home."

He mounted his own steed, then rode off with Scarlett close at his right side, his dutiful warriors following closely behind.

"The day was so beautiful until —" Scarlett said, but Hawke interrupted her before she finished.

"The day still is beautiful even more so now, since that man who brought ugliness into our lives has finally been silenced," Hawke said, seeing that his wife was still affected by what had happened.

"My wife, it will be alright," he said soothingly. "You will be able to put this behind you soon. There is too much good in our lives for this one incident to mar it."

"I know," Scarlett murmured. "It is forgotten. I will think of it no longer."

He gave her a sweet smile, and then they rode onward toward their home, truly at peace because the only person who had ever threatened their happiness was finally gone.

Chapter Thirty-three

Filled with contentment, the months had passed quickly by and Scarlett now lay in the birthing hut, in labor with the first child born of hers and Hawke's special love.

The birthing hut had been built on the outer fringes of the village, and birdsong filled the air in the forest behind it.

The door faced east so that the sun, as it rose to shine upon another day, blessed those in the tiny lodge.

Several days ago a bright fire had been kindled outside of Scarlett and Hawke's home. It would be kept burning for ten days and nights after the birth of the child, to keep away evil. It was said that there was a great animal with wings who ate human beings, especially babies, but that the animal never came near the powerful light of the fire.

It was also said that there was a greater monster than this, called "Cannibal Person." In every tribe there were some of these wicked people. They looked like anyone else, but at night, when it was dark, they set forth and stole human children to eat. Like the animal who ate human beings, these "Cannibal Persons," too, could not go near the fire that was built to frighten them away.

Then too, fire was related to the sun, because the sun gave light and heat, and so it gave a special blessing to the newborn child.

But today not all attention was on the birthing hut where the Caddo chief's wife lay in labor. All but those few who sat with Scarlett in the birthing hut were congregated beside the river that ran close to the village, where a different sort of birthing was taking place.

Scarlett's father was there because he looked upon Scottie now as his grandson.

Even Hawke was at the outdoor ceremony, since no man was allowed in the hut where his wife would give birth to their child, not even if the man was a powerful Caddo chief!

He stood beside Patrick and watched as Scottie went through a ceremony that would bring him closer to his dream of becoming a shaman one day.

Scottie had been attentive in the lessons taught him by Eagle Thunder. Today he took one more step in his initiation. Scottie was dressed in a soft doeskin robe, his golden hair now grown long. He stood with Eagle Thunder, ankle-deep in water.

Eagle Thunder rested a gentle hand on Scottie's shoulder as the boy lifted his face heavenward and said a prayer to *Ayo-caddi-ay-may.*

"*Ayo-caddi-ay-may,* make me strong to endure all things, so that heat and cold, rain and snow, may be as nothing to my body."

Solemnly, meditatively, Eagle Thunder and Scottie stepped from the water, the crowd following them to Scottie's newly constructed house. He would now live separately from his adoptive parents, so that he would have a place where eventually he could practice his shaman's skills.

A fire burned just outside the entranceway. Scottie did now as he had been taught to do as part of the ceremony. He picked up a stick and carried it to the fire, as Hawke watched, glancing anxiously now and then at the birthing hut.

Holding the special stick, Scottie stepped nearer to the fire, with Eagle Thunder close beside him.

Again Scottie lifted his eyes skyward. "*Ayo-caddi-ay-may,*" he said as everyone quietly watched. "Help me to live and become a good man, and to help others to live. *Ayo-caddi-ay-may,* protect me, keep me from danger and give me a long life of success as a shaman, so that I can help others, as our Caddo people's Eagle Thunder helped me when I was someone I now no longer know. I am a new person, reborn in every way."

"With this rebirth comes a new name," Eagle Thunder said as he took the stick from Scottie and laid it on the ground.

He then held Scottie at arm's length. "From this day forth you will be called Winter Owl," he said, then drew Scottie into his arms. "You make me proud to call myself shaman, for I am proud of you."

"Thank you for everything," Scottie murmured, clinging to him. "I love my new name. I shall cherish it always."

He stepped away from Eagle Thunder when he heard the sudden gasps that rippled through the crowd. As he looked up, he saw that all eyes had turned away from him and Eagle Thunder.

It was the white deer!

It seemed to have appeared like a ghost from nowhere!

Hawke stared disbelievingly as the white deer calmly approached the crowd of Caddo and trustingly, walked up to Hawke.

Hawke, whose heart pounded like thunder in his chest, held a hand out for the noble white creature as though the deer were willing him to do so. The beautiful animal stepped even closer and lovingly nuzzled his hand.

Then as Hawke's and the deer's eyes met, the warriors who knew of Hawke's desire to have the deer's pelt scrambled to get their weapons, which had been left in their lodges for the special ceremony.

When some returned with arrows notched to their bows, Hawke was brought out of his reverie. He spoke quietly, yet firmly, so as not to frighten the animal away. "Do not harm the animal," he said. "Warriors, do you not see that what is happening is magical? Never has a deer come this close while so many are gathered. Never has one so trustingly come and shown love in such a way!"

The deer lingered for a moment longer, stepped back from Hawke, lifted its dark round eyes to look into Hawke's again, then turned and sprang away.

"We can go for him!" a warrior shouted. "This time he won't get away!"

"No!" Hawke said firmly. "Do not do this. This deer has brought a message of love . . . of celebration. Let it return to its home untouched. Never shall we hunt it again!"

Suddenly the cry of a child wafted through the air from the birthing hut.

Hawke's eyes widened and his heart skipped a beat when he knew whose baby was crying.

His!

The deer had come to bless two special occasions — Scottie's growth as a shaman, and the birth of Hawke and Scarlett's child!

Pride in his eyes and anxiousness in his heart, he broke through the crowd, running toward the hut. As he entered the small dwelling, Scarlett was holding her arms out for the newborn, who had just been washed and wrapped in a soft blanket.

"We have another son," Scarlett murmured, her face flushed, her eyes revealing how worn out she was from having labored so long with the child.

Dressed in a fresh, clean gown, a quilt, covering her up to her waist, she held the bundle of joy up for Hawke as he fell to his knees beside a fresh pallet of furs and blankets. Those which Scarlett had lain upon during her fourteen hours of labor had already been taken from the hut.

"My son," Hawke said, taking the tiny bundle in his arms. He gently pulled a corner of the blanket back so that he could see the face, pride filling his very soul when he saw his child's copper face. It was topped by a shock of red hair, so that all who looked upon him would see a part of both his mother and his father.

"He is quite handsome," Hawke said, laughing softly as he gazed at Scarlett. "Our son, Scarlett. A brother for Scottie."

"I am no longer called Scottie," Scottie said as he came into the lodge alongside Eagle Thunder. "I am now called Winter Owl. It is my new given name. Eagle Thunder gave it to me."

"Your new name," Scarlett murmured, marveling at all the changes in the boy.

"Huh," Winter Owl said, then beamed when Hawke handed the baby to him. He was so proud to know that he was trusted enough to hold the tiny infant.

"Your brother," Hawke said, his voice thick with emotion.

Almost afraid to hold the child, Winter Owl gazed down at the tiny face that was a replica of his father's. He giggled when he looked at the red hair, then smiled at Scarlett. "He is certainly yours," he said, his eyes dancing. "Mother, I love having a brother."

"I am happy to oblige," Scarlett said, laughing softly. "And, my little medicine man, besides being given a new name, how did things go?"

"Very well, and before long you will no longer call me your little medicine man, but instead a shaman," Winter Owl said proudly.

He looked at Eagle Thunder and saw the eagerness in his eyes. Without asking permission, he placed the baby in the shaman's arms. He watched Eagle Thunder's eyes as they swelled with tears, as though the child were his own, and in a way, he was. All Caddo children were his, to love, to cherish.

Winter Owl then looked down at Scarlett. "I felt *Ayo-caddi-ay-may's* blessing during the ceremony," he said. "I almost feel the shaman in me already."

"You are close," Eagle Thunder said, smiling at him. "Stay on the right road of life, my son, and all that you wish for will be yours."

"We are so proud of you, Winter Owl," Scarlett said, just as Hawke drew the boy into his arms and hugged him.

"The name for the newborn child," Eagle Thunder said, drawing all eyes and attention to him. "You have chosen?"

"Little Hawke," Scarlett quickly answered, knowing the customs of the Caddo when names were decided upon. It was proper to give a name that was a diminutive of one of the parents' names.

"It is agreed upon by both the mother and father?" Eagle Thunder asked, looking from Scarlett to Hawke and then back again at Scarlett.

"It is the name chosen by both of us," Hawke said, drawing Eagle Thunder's eyes to him.

"Then it is the name given to the child today," Eagle Thunder said, brushing a kiss across the child's brow to bless him and his given name. "And so you are called Little Hawke."

Eagle Thunder handed Little Hawke over to Hawke. "It is time for your people to be introduced to your son," he said, rising and standing beside Hawke. "I shall go with you. I shall stand at your side as you make the announcement."

"Can I go, too?" Winter Owl asked, eyes wide, and his voice sounding more like the child he was than the adult shaman he strived to become.

"*Huh,* you can go," Hawke said, then gazed quickly at Scarlett as she began getting up from her bed. "Wife, no —"

"I am strong enough," Scarlett murmured, ignoring the pain that came with standing as she made it to her feet. She held her abdomen as she walked outside beside her husband, with Winter Owl and Eagle Thunder on Hawke's other side.

Hawke held his son over his head. "My people, I present to you our son!" he shouted. "Our son Little Hawke!"

There was deafening applause and chanting, while Scarlett's eyes filled with joyful tears, tears that came with a contentment she never knew existed until she met the man who became her husband.

When her father made his way through the crowd, his own tears of joy streaming from his eyes, Eagle Thunder gently placed the baby in his arms.

"My grandson," Patrick whispered, pride in his voice.

"You now have two grandsons," Winter Owl quickly interjected, drawing Patrick's eyes to him.

"Yes, two grandsons," he said, giving Winter Owl a smile that warmed his heart.

Scarlett was glad when Hawke swept an arm around her waist, for her knees were near to buckling from the weakness that came with not only giving birth, but from being in labor for so long. But in the end, all the grueling hours were worth it.

She thought back to the time when she had not known Hawke. She could never have envisioned such a day as this, yet here she was, a part of a wondrous savage vision!

"The white deer came just before our Little Hawke's birth," Hawke said, drawing Scarlett's eyes to him as he helped her back into the hut. "It came and nuzzled my hand so trustingly."

"It came?" Scarlett gasped, marveling over this news. "And . . . you . . . ?"

"I let it return safely to the forest and vowed never to hunt it again, nor will my warriors," Hawke said quietly. "It deserves to live."

"It seems to have been elusive until today for a reason," Scarlett said softly as Hawke turned her so that they were eye to eye.

"*Huh,* it brought a message of peace and love just as Scottie was given his new name and just moments before our son Little Hawke sent forth his first cries of life," Hawke said, placing gentle hands on her waist.

"But your father always wanted the pelt," Scarlett said, searching his eyes.

"Do you not see?" Hawke said. "That deer . . . he . . . *was* my father. He came in spirit today to bless everything and everyone."

Awed by his words, Scarlett believed them implicitly. Her husband was, above all, a man of truth and understanding.

"It's a beautiful thing," she murmured, sighing with love as Hawke drew her into his arms and embraced her.

"*Huh,* a beautiful thing," Hawke said.

Letter to the Reader

Dear Reader:

I hope you enjoyed reading *Savage Vision*. The next book in my Savage Series is *Savage Arrow*, about the proud Sioux. The book is filled with much romance, authentic history about the Sioux, and a few surprises!

Those of you who are collecting my Indian romance novels and want to hear more about the series and my entire backlist of Indian books can send for my latest newsletter, autographed bookmark, and fan club information by writing to:

Cassie Edwards
6709 North Country Club Road
Mattoon, Illinois 61938

To be assured of a response, please include a stamped, self-addressed, legal-size envelope with your letter.

You can visit my website at: www.cassieedwards.com.

Thank you for your support of my

Indian series. I love researching and writing about our nation's beloved Native Americans, our country's true, first people.

Always,
Cassie Edwards

About the Author

CASSIE EDWARDS: Having always loved history, Cassie became immediately hooked on reading the historical romances her friend lent her, which one day led her to write her own.

Cassie, whose grandmother was a fullblood Cheyenne, soon found her true passion: writing Indian romances. They are her tribute to the first people of our land who have suffered so much injustice. Her Indian romances have appeared on bestseller lists all across the country, including *USA Today*'s list. She has also won the *Romantic Times* Lifetime Achievement Award and Reviewer's Choice Award for her Indian romances.

Cassie and her husband, Charlie, have two grown children and live in Mattoon, Illinois. She lives in her dream home, which is the perfect place for her to create her Indian novels.

Cassie plans to write many more Indian romances. In her *Savage* series, she endeavors to write about every major Indian tribe in America.

We hope you have enjoyed this Large Print book. Other Thorndike, Wheeler or Chivers Press Large Print books are available at your library or directly from the publishers.

For more information about current and upcoming titles, please call or write, without obligation, to:

Publisher
Thorndike Press
295 Kennedy Memorial Drive
Waterville, ME 04901
Tel. (800) 223-1244

Or visit our Web site at:
www.gale.com/thorndike
www.gale.com/wheeler

OR

Chivers Large Print
published by BBC Audiobooks Ltd
St James House, The Square
Lower Bristol Road
Bath BA2 3BH
England
Tel. +44(0) 800 136919
email: bbcaudiobooks@bbc.co.uk
www.bbcaudiobooks.co.uk

All our Large Print titles are designed for easy reading, and all our books are made to last.